*This one's for
MARY FORSTER*

*My medical colleague for twenty-five years,
my friend for forty and counting.*

*Both assignments were tough duty for her at times,
and I'm grateful past words.*

A Perilous Conception

Larry Karp

Poisoned Pen Press

Poisoned Pen Press
6962 E. First Ave., Ste. 103
Scottsdale, AZ 85251
www.poisonedpenpress.com
info@poisonedpenpress.com

Printed in the United States of America

Acknowledgments

I'm indebted to Dr. Mary Forster, former Director of the Reproductive Technologies Facility at Swedish Medical Center in Seattle, for extensive consultations regarding the scientific and clinical details of in vitro fertilization in its earliest days. Without her help, I could not have written this story. I wouldn't even have tried.

Mary also read and offered general comments on a late draft of the manuscript, as did my friend, children's author Peg Kehret, and my wife, Myra. All readers came up with points that needed my attention, many of which I'd not have noticed on my own.

The laboratory team that opened Swedish's Reproductive Technologies Facility in 1983 consisted of Dr. Mary Forster, Dr. Ronald Gellert, Carol Zeigler, Jean Emrich, Dianne Smith, and Penny Cerdena. The clinical physicians who worked with these scientists were Drs. Robert E. McIntosh, Barry Stewart, Donald Smith, Jane Uhlir, and Wayne Weissman. All were exemplars of competence and professionalism; it was my good luck to have had the opportunity to work with them. Thanks to their efforts, countless Pacific Northwest couples over the past quarter-century have been able to raise children who otherwise never would have been conceived.

Thanks to Dr. Roger Donahue, my fellowship supervisor, who, with good humor, taught the principles of chromosomal analysis and ovum/embryo culture to a trainee unable to bring himself to sacrifice experimental mice.

A bow to the redoubtable Morrie Robkin for critical information on firearms and their use.

Last, but not nearly least, thanks to the good people at Poisoned Pen Press. Barbara Peters, my editor, as patient as she is incisive and insightful, went far above and beyond to show me how to improve this book—as she has helped me improve all my books—by orders of magnitude. Publisher Rob Rosenwald and Associate Publisher Jessica Tribble have been unfailingly enthusiastic, encouraging, and helpful. When I've had questions, Nan Beams, Annette Rogers, Elizabeth Weld, and Marilyn Pizzo have been right there with answers. And I can't imagine a friendlier, more supportive group of authors than the Poisoned Pen Posse.

The author takes sole responsibility for any errors in *A Perilous Conception*.

"Great perils have this beauty, that they bring to light the fraternity of strangers."

—Victor Hugo

Chapter One

Thursday, April 28, 1977

Sanford

One last look in the hall mirror. I straightened my tie, brushed my hand over that unruly clump of hair above my right ear. Should I be suave and assured, or would I come off better as wide-eyed and enthusiastic, maybe even a little eccentric? As I glanced at the gray fabric-covered log book in my hand, I caught the reflection of my smile in the mirror. Perfect. Cool, self-possessed, yes. Suave was the way to go.

I didn't need to check my watch, but did anyway. Couple of minutes past one, almost an hour till the press conference. By five o'clock, I'd be on the local news, right at the top, and tomorrow morning, my face would be on every screen from San Francisco to Timbuktu. Well, my face and Giselle Hearn's, fair enough. I'd make sure to say I couldn't have done it without her, but there'd be no doubt who'd been the project leader, and who, the co-worker. I smiled again.

Good move, borrowing Giselle's lab log last night, then canceling my appointments and staying home this morning. My office staff would've been driving me nuts, wanting to know what all the fuss was about. Instead, I'd put in five solid hours, studying the log and my pile of reprints from *Nature, Lancet,* and *The American Journal of Obstetrics and Gynecology.* For more than a year, I'd been keeping up with that literature, but I wanted to be sure I had the material down cold, every detail. I couldn't afford a misstep.

I walked out into the corridor, took the elevator down to the lobby, clapped Albert, the doorman, on the arm. "Hey, Doc," Albert rumbled. "Them Seadogs gonna win today?"

The Emerald Seadogs, Major League Baseball's brand new representatives in the Pacific Northwest, were supposedly starting their existence under a lucky sign, double-sevens. But before the end of the first month of that auspicious 1977 season, the Seadogs were already hopelessly in the cellar, couldn't win for losing. "Don't know, Albert. I only bet on horses, but if I did bet baseball, I think I'd keep my money in my pocket on that one." The old doorman cackled.

With its long winters of short, gray, drizzly days, Emerald is the suicide capital of the country. This past season had been a prizewinner, barely a glimpse of sun between Christmas and Easter. But today, the sky was a glorious blue, not a cloud anywhere, and I threw back my head to take in the warmth of the midday sunlight. From this day on, that sun would shine on me, nonstop. Patients would clog my office. I'd see my photo in newspapers, magazines, on the tube. My name would be front and center in articles and popular histories; I'd get whole chapters in reproductive medicine textbooks. Rotary Club presidents and chairmen of university departments would book me for talks. It was not beyond reason to expect that one day I'd get a call to come give a speech in Stockholm. My parents would finally have to hand it to me. Their son was about to become a legend in medicine.

Most of my colleagues lived in big houses in one or another of the fancy Emerald suburbs, which entitled them to drive nearly an hour to and from work, sometimes in the middle of the night. Not for me. An easy seven-minute walk, and I was at my office in the Emerald Medical Tower, linked by skybridges to Puget Community Hospital on one side, and the new glass-

and-steel Washington Public University Medical Complex on the other.

I strode into the Tower Lobby, past patients, some in wheelchairs, or making their way slowly on canes. White-coated doctors talked to white-capped nurses. Techs pushed blood-draw carts and EKG machines. For all the attention they weren't giving me, I could've been walking along a sidewalk in midtown Manhattan, but that was about to change. Tomorrow, people on all sides would stop, point, whisper to their companions, "Hey, isn't that Dr. Colin Sanford? You know, the guy…"

As I walked into my waiting room, a buzz of talk went silent. Lettie and Sally, the receptionists, Kinsey and Ruth Ellen, the nurses, Megan, the nurse-practitioner, stood in a circle in front of the reception counter. One look at me, and they froze in place, a body with five chalky faces, five open mouths and ten saucer-eyes. Barbara Renfro, the office manager, stood off from the others, stone-faced, leaning against the end of the counter. Her Adam's apple bobbed up, down, up again.

The room reeked of trouble. Had one of my patients keeled over with a pulmonary embolism? Did the pediatricians find a serious birth defect in a baby? Nah, either way, a nurse would have called my beeper. I looked past the mob to Barbara. "Got something to tell me?"

She motioned me down the hall past reception, to my consulting office.

I followed her along the corridor, into the office, closed the door. She rested a hand on my arm. "Oh, Dr. Sanford. Dr. Hearn is…dead."

"Dead? No."

"She was shot. Murdered. In her lab, a little while ago. And…"

"What, Barbara?"

"Mr. Kennett did it."

"Mr. Kennett? Why on earth would he ever—"

"And after he killed Dr. Hearn, he shot himself. A Detective Baumgartner called here not five minutes ago, looking for you. He got your name off Mr. Kennett's newborn-nursery ID bracelet. I told him we expected you any time now, and he said he wants you to go over to the lab immediately to talk to him."

I pride myself on keeping a cool head in emergencies. "I'll get over there ASAP. Would you please cancel the press conference for me?"

"Of course." She took a step away. "Dr. Sanford…did the conference have something to do with the Kennetts?"

I nodded.

As she walked out of the office, I stared at the log book in my hand. Doubly fortunate now that it wasn't sitting in a desk drawer in Giselle's office, where the cops would find it. It was my ticket to the future, but it also contained seeds for disaster, which I'd stumbled onto the night before. No reporter at the press conference, rushing to get the story out, would have looked inside that log, but the scientists we'd beaten to the finish line would want to review it, and to say the least, some of the material could be embarrassing. I thought I knew what to do about it, and had figured to sit down with Giselle after the conference to get her on board. But that idea had been knocked into a cocked hat along with the conference. In any case, the log had to go someplace out of sight for the time being, absolutely-positively safe where no one would think of checking.

I scanned the room. Stash it in my desk? That'd be the first place anyone would look. Two walls of bookshelves, filled with medical textbooks, monographs, and leather-bound journals. Good camouflage, but not good enough. The faux-woodgrain metal file cabinet next to my desk? Negative. A file cabinet would be Number Two on any search, right after my desk…but wait, here's an idea. I stepped across the room, lowered a shoulder, tipped the cabinet. Below the bottom drawer was a nice little recess. Good. I tossed the log book into the cavity, gave a short silent thanks for all those after-work hours at the gym, then lowered the cabinet.

I hung my suit jacket on a hook behind the door, grabbed a white coat from an adjacent hook, shrugged it on, and rushed out, through the waiting room, into the hallway, down the corridor to the skybridge. I could deal with a little delay in my plans. First things first, and the first thing had to be a talk with Joyce Kennett. Going to the lab and talking to the cops would need to settle for second.

Chapter Two

Sanford

I'm a doctor, an OBGYN. I opened my office in Emerald in 1965, and by 1970, my practice was the biggest in town. Patients knew when they came to me, they'd get the best care possible, and they'd get it directly from me. No partners, no interns, no med students. I always did have an eye for the main chance—no point denying the obvious—and during the late sixties, I saw laparoscopy was the coming thing in my field. And why not? Would you want your surgery performed through the customary five-inch slash in the breadbasket if it could be neatly accomplished via a thin optical instrument slipped through a tiny puncture into the abdomen? So I took myself off to Philadelphia to learn the procedure from the guru, Guiseppe Allegri, and I've got to tell you, Allegri was impressed. He said he'd never seen anyone with such a knack for the procedure. When I got back home, I wangled an interview with the medical editor of *The Emerald Times,* to tell the city all about Band-Aid surgery, now available right in its own back yard. My office phones didn't stop ringing for days.

Then, in the midseventies, federal research grants began to dry up. The University faculty panicked. None of them had ever dreamed of dirtying their hands by laying them on patients, but necessity really is a mother, and the professors started promoting themselves as super-specialists, the ultimate experts. What they didn't say was that hands-on care at the U would in fact be provided by residents and med students, and the professors' role would consist of initialing trainees' chart notes. But you can sell people anything, and I started to notice a patient here, a patient there, leaving my care to go to "The Northwest's Preeminent Medical Center." Which pissed me off, royally.

You've got to keep an eye on your opposition, so I was a regular at the Wednesday morning University OBGYN Grand Rounds, where professors, fellows, and residents honed their one-upsmanship skills, pontificating on esoteric topics. At the first session after Christmas break, in January, 1976, the speaker was Dr. Giselle Hearn, a PhD embryologist. The room was packed. Dr. Hearn talked about her experiments on the behavior of chromosomes at fertilization in mice, which she hoped would shed light on factors that cause errors during that process, and produce conditions like Down Syndrome. Near the end of the hour, she said she was convinced there would be no real breakthroughs until studies being carried out in other research centers on human gametes started to yield up critical information.

I didn't realize she'd flung a gauntlet until Gerry Camnitz flew to his feet, no small accomplishment given the size and weight distribution of L. Gerald Camnitz, MD. The Professor and Chairman of OBGYN had the look of an angry, red-faced walrus in a sharply-tailored gray suit, pink shirt, and narrow blue tie. "Dr. Hearn, this is not a public forum for departmental policy. It is an educational session. Kindly stick to your subject."

Hearn's face and body language told everyone in that room they were about to get a preview of the Bicentennial fireworks display. She blinked at Camnitz like a cow, offended at having gotten a gratuitous poke in the udder from a stick in the hand of a nasty little boy. "I've not gone off my topic, Dr. Camnitz. I've merely stated a matter of fact. If it happens to conflict with your prejudices, you might do well to reconsider."

I'd had no idea what was obviously running deep below the calm surface waters of the University OBGYN Department. A couple of medical students snickered. Camnitz silenced them with a glare, then turned back to Hearn. "All right, Dr. Hearn. Since you insist on pursuing this, I will restate my policy. We are not going to start down the slippery slope of experimentation on human embryos, not in *my* department. The ethical, moral, and legal implications are too uncertain. Would you propose to flush human beings down a sink when they're no longer of use to you? Would you be concerned even the slightest bit that attempts at in vitro fertilization might produce monstrously abnormal children?"

"I never said anything about in vitro—" Hearn began, but Camnitz shouted her down with, "This conference is over. Thank you all for coming." I thought he might follow that with an order for Hearn to go to the Dean's office and serve detention, but instead, he stormed out of the auditorium. There was a brief silence, followed by a sound like the swarming of a million angry bees. Don Gardiner, a young assistant professor, poked an elbow into my ribs. "Welcome to the halls of ivy."

I muttered, "Yeah," but I was thinking about in vitro fertilization and embryo replacement.

Not a week later, I was talking to Joyce and James Kennett, one of my infertility couples. They had what's called idiopathic infertility, which is doctor-talk for "I don't have a goddamn clue." Joyce's temperature records showed she ovulated right on schedule, every twenty-nine days plus or minus one. X-ray contrast studies indicated no blockage of her fallopian tubes. Her uterus was perfectly normal, inside and out. James' sperm were lively and quick. The couple hit the mattress at a frequency that should already have borne them a football team. Artificial insemination with James' sperm had been no more efficacious than the natural process.

They were both up tight, squirming in the chairs opposite my desk. Not unusual for infertility patients. They'd been trying for a year before they first came to see me, and I'd been working with them for an equal length of time. Two years of having every menstrual period be a bitter cup of dashed hopes does things to people, and in any case, this couple was predisposed to emotional problems.

James had a history of borderline paranoid schizophrenia, had been doing well for years on psychotherapy and medication, but he'd gotten himself fired from several retail clerk jobs after customers complained about what they took as insults or smart-alecky comments. This translated into endless bouts of relapsing financial pins and needles.

Joyce, a biology teacher at Emerald Community College, had the anatomy, physiology, and biochemistry of conception down pat, which made the couple's failure—her word, not mine—all the more galling. She'd tried a bunch of dietary manipulations and folk remedies, none of which were any more effective than traditional approaches.

I brought up the possibility of adoption, but the two of them shot that down in a hurry. Joyce insisted she was going to have "my *own* baby," no ifs, ands, or buts. "And it's going to be *my* baby, too," James barked. "No way some other guy's sperm is going to get her pregnant, not if I have anything to say about it."

Joyce rested a hand on his arm, something I'd seen her do before when he looked like he might be about to lose it.

Once I saw his muscles relax, I reviewed the past eleven months of investigations and treatments, and was about to launch into an explanation of a journey through the terra incognita of infertility, when Joyce gave James a look that brought me up short. It asked, "Are you ready?"

He nodded.

Joyce turned back to me. "We've decided to go to the University."

Like a slap in the face. I was stunned. "Why?"

"We thought it would be a good idea to see one of the infertility specialists there."

I shook my head. "I guess you can do that, but they don't know anything I don't know. I read the same journals they do, and attend all kinds of conferences at the U and around the country."

James pulled at the back of his collar. Joyce sat a little straighter in her chair. "They work in this field all the time, but it's only a part of your practice," she said. "Maybe there's some new research that isn't even published yet."

They were going, no question. Infertility patients are like trains with disabled brakes. They wanted the benefit of new research. Were they thinking of in vitro fertilization? They weren't about to get that at the U, though, were they?

But they couldn't get it from me, either. I swallowed bile, got up, and extended my hand. "I wish you luck," I said. "Keep in touch. If they help you conceive, I'll certainly want to know the details."

James nearly fell over his feet, thanking me for trying to help. He pumped my hand as if he expected to see water gush out of my mouth. Joyce was cooler, but still cordial. "I'll definitely let you know," she said. "And if we're successful, I'd like to come back and have you take care of my pregnancy and delivery."

Knickknack, paddywhack, toss the dog a bone. "It would be my pleasure," I said.

◇◇◇

For the rest of the afternoon, I had to force myself to keep my mind on business at hand. After the office closed and I'd written up the charts for the day, I walked across the skybridge to the University Medical Complex, stopped by the cafeteria, grabbed some dinner, and picked at it. This was my personal Pearl Harbor, and I was not about to lie down and let those hypocritical University bastards wipe out my practice. I had an idea, which, I'll admit, made me more than a little nervous. If it didn't work out, things could get ugly.

But what if it did work out?

I left my tray with most of the food uneaten, no great loss, hustled out of the cafeteria, and down the hall to the Med Center Library.

The library closed at midnight, and that's when I left, stepping lively, carrying a fistful of copied journal articles from medical centers around the world. The papers described the scientific and clinical procedures which one day might produce babies through in vitro fertilization, and discussed the ethical and religious arguments that swirled around those procedures. Catholics were opposed, no surprise, but the secular ethicists were split into two camps. One group was as strongly opposed as the Catholics, claiming that since there was no way to tell in advance whether the procedure was safe and would produce normal children, it constituted unethical experimentation on the unborn, or even on the unconceived. The other group insisted the work was right and proper, because it might both alleviate the human misery of infertility, and give life to individuals who otherwise never would exist.

It was clear a race was on to be first to the finish line, and that the leaders were a team in England, consisting of Robert Edwards, a physiologist who'd spent some time doing research at Johns Hopkins, and Patrick Steptoe, a clinical gynecologist. Edwards seemed to have gotten a good handle on the protocol for fertilizing human eggs and culturing embryos. Steptoe's expertise? He was a leading laparoscopist who'd published a book, *"Laparoscopy in Gynaecology,"* which I'd read hot off the press in 1967. In the journal articles, he'd described his approach to recovering human eggs from ovaries just before ovulation, and I had no trouble seeing that with a little practice, it would be a piece of cake for me. The question was whether Giselle Hearn could pick up on Edwards' reports, and do the laboratory side of the work as well as I could do the clinical.

Once I set my mind to an idea, I never waste time. Next day, after I finished with my morning patients, I hustled across the skybridge to the Department of Obstetrics and Gynecology, then down the hallway to the research wing, and into Dr. Hearn's lab area. Hearn was standing in a corridor, talking to a young woman in a white coat, probably a tech. I waited until the girl smiled, nodded, and walked away; then, before her boss could move on to whatever she had in mind to do next, I walked up to her. "Dr. Hearn."

She had no idea who I was. "I'm Colin Sanford. I practice OBGYN at Puget Community."

Her face said, "Then why don't you go off and practice a little OBGYN?"

"I need to talk to you," I said.

"About what?"

"I have an idea I'm pretty sure will interest you." Then, I added, "I was at your conference last week." I looked around to make sure no one was close. "Gerry Camnitz is not only a pompous ass, he's a stupid man. You should be able to extend your work to humans, and I know how you can do it."

She didn't know what to make of me, and I couldn't blame her.

"We can't talk about it here," I said. "Let me take you to dinner tonight."

That earned me a world-class fish eye.

"Dr. Hearn, I'm not trying to mash on you, and I'm not playing games. I'm as serious as I've ever been. I don't think you'll want to walk away from my proposal. Meet me at Charley's Boathouse, seven o'clock, and I'll tell you about it."

She didn't say yes, she didn't say no. Just stood there, trying to sort me out.

"What can you lose?" I added. As it turned out, only her life, but how could I know?

Charley's is a posh seafood house in the Sunset Bluff neighborhood, out on a pier over the edge of Puget Sound. As I sat at a prime window table, waiting for Dr. Hearn, I could hear waves breaking against the shore. By ten past seven, I was beginning to wonder whether she was going to stand me up, but then the hostess brought her over. I stood to help her into the chair. "I'm sorry to be late," she said. "Parking was awful."

"They've got valet parking."

"Not to be offensive, Dr. Sanford, but PhDs don't have quite the discretionary cash MDs do. We tend to cut corners when we can."

I let the hostess move out of earshot, then said, "What I want to talk to you about will take care of that."

For the first time, she smiled, but it wasn't a smile of amusement. It was pure skepticism. I handed her a menu. "The halibut stuffed with crabmeat is terrific. Let's order. Then, I'll start filling you in."

When the waitress walked away, Dr. Hearn nodded in my direction. "All right. I've got to admit, I'm curious to hear what you have in mind."

"Let me ask you a question first," I said. "About Gerry Camnitz. Why is he so set against your doing any work on human gametes?"

She reached for her water glass, sipped, didn't take her eyes off me. "How do I know Gerry didn't put you up to this, and you're not going to go back and tell him what I say?"

"It's that bad, huh? Look, Dr. Hearn. I'm just a humble downtown doctor. Do I seem like someone Herr Professor Camnitz would send out on a spy mission?"

I'm good at using a preposterous little remark to loosen up a nervous patient, and the technique worked on Hearn. She laughed. "No, I've got to say, you don't," she said. "I guess if I'm wrong, fine. You can tell Gerry to shove my job up his ass. I don't really want to leave Emerald, but I've got to get out of his department. I've already sent feelers to a few places."

"When we get done with Camnitz, you won't have to move anywhere but into a bigger house," I said. "Tell me where he's coming from. What's his problem with having you do human research?"

She sighed. "That idiot. He's exactly what you said this afternoon, pompous and stupid. He's afraid of the heat he might get from religious and conservative groups, and worries that if the wrong people manage to get onto National Institutes of Health research committees and find he's been allowing work on human eggs or embryos, he might get blacklisted for federal grants."

"Is that likely?"

"I'd say no. But Gerry always wants to play the safe hand. And God forbid he should take any chances with his social standing. Do you know Horace Bancroft?"

"Big-time lawyer. Very Republican. Wasn't he chummy with Goldwater?"

"One of Barry's biggest contributors. He also keeps the Catholic church in Emerald in pocket change, and for good measure, he's on the University Medical Center's Board of Directors. Roe v. Wade damn near gave him a stroke. Let his son-in-law permit experimentation on human eggs and sperm, especially if there's any kind of public controversy, and Gerry'd be selling apples on a street corner."

I smiled. "That's an interesting image."

The waitress set salads in front of us. The smell of hot sourdough bread rose from a napkin-covered basket she set at the center of the table. Giselle's stomach gurgled; she went red. I laughed. "Good. You're hungry."

I broke off a piece of bread, slathered on butter. Then I used the bread as a pointer. "So you're going to be left at the gate, gnashing your teeth, when Edwards and Steptoe make their big announcement about the first in vitro fertilization baby."

Halfway to her mouth, Giselle reversed course, and set her forkful of lettuce back onto her plate.

"Right," I said. "You've been fertilizing mouse eggs and culturing the embryos. If you had permission, how soon could you be doing human work?"

"I could start tomorrow," she snapped. "Not that I'd expect to have much success right off the bat. I keep up with the literature, and I've got friends in a couple of labs I could talk to. But there are always intangibles. What works in one place may not work in another." She narrowed her eyes. "How is it you're so familiar with human embryo culture?"

"Since I'm a commonplace clinical doc?"

She didn't back down. "If you want to put it that way. I don't expect a clinician to know any more about embryo culture than I know about delivering babies."

"I know how to read journals," I said. "Not that I'd understand nearly the details you would, but I can get the gist well enough. Including that it takes two highly-skilled people to pull it off, a scientist with enough dedication and know-how to fertilize eggs and grow embryos, and a doctor with unusual laparoscopic skill who can get preovulatory oocytes in good condition to that lab worker. And those two people are sitting at this table."

She took a cautious mouthful of salad, not taking her eyes off me. "Why?"

"Because I know what's out there for the winners of this race. Names in history books. Magazine interviews, newspaper articles, TV shows. Lectureships. For me, a line of patients outside my office door and halfway down the block. For you, grant agencies lined up outside *your* office and halfway down the block, begging you to relieve them of their research funds. And the joy of being able to tell Gerry Camnitz where to get off. I'm betting if Hearn and Sanford go to work, they've got a damn good chance of beating out Edwards and Steptoe. But every day we wait lowers our odds. Wouldn't you like to jump right into a full professorship? And give your car to the valet at Charley's Boathouse?"

"A full professorship, huh?" Her eyes couldn't carry off the skepticism she tried to put into her voice. "I have about as much hope of that, being a PhD *and* a woman, as I have of waving my arms and flying."

"True right now," I said. "But as half of the first team to get an IVF baby, it'd be a whole new ball game for you."

The waitress took our salad plates and set the crabmeat-stuffed halibut before us. Giselle didn't even look at hers. "Nitty-gritty time," she said. "How is all this supposed to happen? Where do I get the equipment and supplies I'd need?"

"Whatever you can't free up from what's already in your lab, I'll subsidize. And then I'll get ova for you from my laparoscopy patients. I'll tell them it's for infertility investigations, true enough, and to compensate them for the inconvenience of needing hormone shots to time ovulation to their procedures, I'll write off any of my professional charges not covered by insurance."

She frowned. "Is that ethical?"

"What's wrong with it? Everyone comes out ahead. I'm not going to coerce anyone, just give them a choice. I'll get sperm from med students, the same as I do for artificial inseminations. Then, you'll do the fertilizations and cultures on the QT. When we've got it all down pat, we'll start doing it for real. If we're careful, Gerry Camnitz won't know a thing until we announce success, and at that point, with pictures of that beautiful little baby in every newspaper on earth, whatever complaint he'd make would be like pissing into the wind."

A smile spread across her face, then faded. "The schedule of ovum maturation, fertilization, and embryo development is pretty rigid and unforgiving. Working on my own, I'd have to put in some long and odd hours."

"You expect sympathy from me? With what *I* do for a living?"

She laughed. "Touché. But you'd better know how much money you'd be laying out. I'd need a sterile hood with a heat plate, a temperature-controlled CO_2 incubator, a centrifuge, a phase-contrast microscope, and a good dissecting microscope. All together, that's probably twenty to twenty-five thousand dollars."

"I'll put every cent where my mouth is," I said. "It'll be the best investment I've ever made. Give me the specs on the equipment, tell me where to get it, and I'll have it for you inside a week." I motioned toward her plate. "Eat up. Then we'll sort out details."

I was right. It came off like gangbusters. Giselle appropriated an alcove in her lab complex where she could work privately, and then, late one night, I came in and helped her set up the hood, microscope, centrifuge, and incubator, and move in supplies, everything from sterile gloves to petri dishes to pipets. The next day, I made my first arrangement with a patient: in exchange for her having a series of hormone injections prior to her upcoming laparoscopy twelve days later, I would waive my professional fee, no small consideration since the procedure was being done as part of an infertility workup, and medical insurance companies notoriously do not pay for infertility work.

For the first month or so, I did struggle a bit with the ovum recoveries, and Giselle had to fiddle with modifications of the standard Biggers, Whitten, and Whittenham culture medium, but by the time we'd done twenty retrieval and culture attempts, the work was going smoothly. Three of the patients ovulated before their scheduled procedures, and in another two, there were no eggs in the fluid I aspirated from their ovaries. But seventy-five percent recovery seemed pretty much in line with the rates I'd seen in journal articles, so I was satisfied.

For her part, Giselle got half of the eggs fertilized and developed to the stage of four- to eight-cell embryos, at which point it would have been time to introduce them into the uterus and hope they'd take root. She called me over there to see the first one, and it was something I'll never forget, peering through the microscope at that little clump of cells, shimmering in the culture medium. My heart actually skipped a couple of beats. It killed me to see Giselle pull the embryo out of culture and stain its cells to make sure its chromosomes were normal. But we had to be certain we weren't going to turn out malformed babies.

By the end of June, we'd had twenty-two successful retrievals, fertilizations, and cultures. Giselle was a little reluctant when I told her I thought we should go ahead and replace an embryo. I asked what she was waiting for. "Our success rates are as good as any in the published literature, and we don't really know how far along Edwards and Steptoe are, do we? If they happen to beat us to the finish line, we stand to lose a lot. First in the USA would be good, but nothing like first in the world."

So the next afternoon, I got Joyce Kennett on the phone, and asked how things were going at the U. I was more than pleased to hear the super-specialist professors had been no more successful than I'd been. I told Joyce there were some new developments in the field, and that if she'd like, she and James could come in and hear about them. She liked. We set up a meeting for the next afternoon.

They'd looked nervous six months before, but that was nothing compared to their appearance now. James shifted constantly in his chair, kept wiping the back of a hand across his mouth. Joyce was practically twitching. "I've got an interesting possibility for you," I said. "But before I say anything about it, I'm going to ask for your promise that you won't discuss it with anyone, even if you decide against it."

They turned puzzled faces to each other, then to me.

"It's a controversial procedure," I said. "Perfectly legal, but there are people who object to it on religious grounds, or on the basis of their own system of morals or ethics. I suspect they'd try to make life uncomfortable for any couple who decided to give it a go."

Joyce got it. "You're talking about in vitro fertilization, aren't you?"

"I need a promise," I said.

Another look at each other, then they both nodded.

"All right. Yes, I am talking about in vitro fertilization. I believe it's a good procedure, and eventually it's going to be routine. Right now, doctors all over the world are trying to get it done. An English team at Cambridge seems to have the inside track, but I've been working quietly with a very knowledgeable embryologist here. She's at the point now where she gets fertilization and embryo development in about half the eggs I recover."

Joyce was nearly off the edge of her seat. "How many embryos has she cultured?"

"Successfully? Twenty-two."

"And how is it you're involved? Why isn't this a University research project?"

I didn't try to hide my grin. "I could give you the stock answer, that I just don't know, but I've always been honest with you. I *do* know. Dr. Hearn, the embryologist at the U, is the equal of any scientist anywhere at doing these procedures, but the department chairman is as conservative as they come, so Dr. Hearn's been doing her work in private. The other half of the equation is the need for a doctor who's especially good at laparoscopy. That's where I come in, and I have no institutional rules to hold me back."

"But hey, wait a minute. Aren't you worried about what'll happen when that chairman at the U finds out?" The first words out of James.

"When the world looks at your smiling face and Joyce's, and the gorgeous baby in her arms, nothing Dr. Camnitz might say would mean a thing."

"If the baby *is* gorgeous," Joyce said. "What if I miscarry? Or worse, what if it has a terrible birth defect?"

"If you miscarry, no one will know anything," I said. "Women miscarry every day. And if there's a birth defect, well, about three percent of all babies conceived naturally have significant birth defects. The important question is whether the rate of abnormalities is higher after conception in a plastic dish, and there are two reasons to think not. One is that Dr. Hearn's cultured embryos have looked normal and had normal chromosomes. And second, all evidence indicates that when a very early embryo isn't developing right, it's miscarried."

Joyce nodded. "Of course. That's true in all animals. But, Dr. Sanford, what would this work cost us? You know we're not—"

I held up a hand. "The only cost you'll have will be hospital bills for the laparoscopy when I retrieve the eggs. No charges for my work, or Dr. Hearn's. But while we're talking about money, here's something to think about. The parents of the world's first IVF baby will be in a position to earn a bundle from endorsements of everything from baby food to diapers, never mind all the magazine and TV interviews. Remember the Dionne quintuplets, back in the 'thirties? Those little girls made their family's fortune. The first in vitro baby will get at least that much attention."

The longer I spoke, the more James frowned. "I wouldn't feature living in a fishbowl."

Joyce put a hand to his arm. "That would be our choice," she said. "I'm sure Dr. Sanford wouldn't release our names unless we agreed to it."

"No, I wouldn't," I said. "But the truth is, if I don't announce who you are, some reporter is almost certainly going to get into the hospital records and find out. On the other hand, a new house, an unlisted phone, and an agent should take care of the worst of it, and still keep money coming in."

"We *should* think about that," Joyce said.

"It sounds like you've already made up your mind."

James didn't sound as if he'd made up *his* mind. "You can go home and talk," I said.

Joyce waved me off. "I *have* made up my mind. I know enough as a biology teacher to be comfortable that there really shouldn't be any major risk to either the baby or me. And if I turn down the opportunity, what am I going to think when I read about some other woman who had more courage and ended up with a baby? I'm thirty-one, James. We've been married two years, and been through every investigation and treatment available. I'm at the end of my rope. If Dr. Sanford can do what they won't try at the University, more power to him. If he succeeds, I'll have the thing I want most in the world, and he'll make his career, fair enough. And as far as money's concerned, wouldn't it be nice to have that kind of security? I'm not going to let anyone else raise my child, which means I'd need to stop working."

James was a bright enough guy, but he had a good dose of the quirkiness you often see in paranoid schizophrenics. He picked at a fingernail. "Well, if that's what you want, Joyce…but I guess I'm nervous about you being a guinea pig." He turned to me. "You're sure this Dr. Hearn of yours has had enough experience? I sure wouldn't want her screwing up on my wife and baby."

More of James' schizophrenia. Suspiciousness, and a short fuse. Again, Joyce reached a hand to his arm.

I talked fast. "James, there are never guarantees any time a woman gets pregnant. But Joyce isn't going to be a guinea pig. The experimental work's all been done, and it's gone beautifully. And replacing the embryo is straightforward. We push a little fluid with the embryo in it up into the uterus through a tiny plastic catheter. Like giving an injection."

Again, Joyce and James looked at each other, and as couples seem to do, came silently to agreement. Joyce looked back at me. "When can we start?"

"When was your last period?"

She sagged in her chair. "I started three days ago."

"That's all right. While you go through this cycle, I'll keep Dr. Hearn in practice. Call me when you start your next period. We'll set up a schedule for the hormone shots to prime your ovaries, and arrange for the laparoscopy at the best possible time. Sound all right?"

Joyce smiled. "Yes."

James chewed his lip, and nodded.

I can't say it went entirely like clockwork. As uptight as Giselle was, I figured I might have to untie a knot or two in her knickers, and in fact, I did need to steer her around one bump in the road. But in my line of work, I'm used to anticipating and dealing with complications, and if I say so myself, I'm good at it. Six weeks after my talk with the Kennetts, I retrieved five ova from Joyce's bulging ovaries. Giselle took them from the operating room to her lab, and three days later, she had three apparently-normal embryos, two eight-cell, one four-cell. I got Joyce and James right in, and suggested we put all three into her uterus. That way, there would be three times the chance of an implantation, worth the risks of a multiple pregnancy. It took Joyce exactly no time to say, "Go ahead."

James chose not to watch the procedure, which was fine with me. I told Ruth Ellen, my nurse, that Dr. Hearn had developed a new procedure for treating sperm so as to make them more effective at attaching to eggs and penetrating them. She got Joyce into one of my exam rooms while I called Giselle, who came over the skybridge with a cart holding her dissecting microscope and a small incubator. While she set up at the side of the room, Ruth Ellen helped Joyce onto the table and into stirrups. I did a quick manual pelvic exam, then slipped in a vaginal speculum, checked the cervix, and gave silent thanks that it was perfectly straight. If it weren't, I'd have had to grip it with a tenaculum, a surgical instrument with two sharp points, not only uncomfortable for the patient, but also a stimulus that might produce a uterine cramp which could push the embryos right back out.

Ruth Ellen handed me a thin plastic catheter, the kind we use for intrauterine insemination. Slowly, gently, I passed it through the cervix. No resistance whatever, bingo. "All good, Joyce," I said. "Practice run perfect. Ready for the show?"

"Let's do it."

"She's a trouper," Ruth Ellen chirped, and patted Joyce's hand.

While I was doing the preliminaries, Giselle got the embryos ready for delivery. The night before, we'd gone into her lab, and I'd watched her rehearse the procedure. It involved attaching a one-c.c. syringe to a catheter, then drawing the embryos in five to ten microliters of fluid from the culture dish into the end of the catheter, and leaving a minute air bubble at the catheter tip. Straightforward, but delicate.

I'd thought I might feel nervous, but I was cool as a Popsicle as I took the syringe and catheter from Giselle's trembly hand. Still, I slid the catheter through Joyce's cervix as if it might explode under less-than-meticulous attention. As I pushed the plunger, I surprised myself by breathing out a huge "whoof." We'd pulled it off, done all we could. Now it was up to biological chance.

I left Joyce with Ruth Ellen while I walked Giselle out of the office and to the elevator. As I came back through the waiting room, James flew out of his chair, nearly knocked me over. "Did it go all right, Dr. Sanford? Is Joyce okay?"

"It went fine, and she's fine," I said. "Come on, I'll take you in. I'm going to admit her to the hospital overnight to keep her at strict bed rest with her head lower than her rear end. Let's give those little guys every chance to implant." Not that I really believed topside-down bed rest would do anything useful, but I was of a mind to dot i's and cross t's.

The next four weeks seemed like four months, waiting to do a definitive pregnancy test. I ordered weekly serum tests, the kind we used to help diagnose an ectopic pregnancy, and they were promising, very promising. But I didn't want to set Joyce and myself up for a massive disappointment. Finally, on September 8, 1976—I'll never forget the day—I ordered both a blood and a urine sample, check and double-check. Joyce was as bubbly as she was twitchy. "I know they're going to be positive," she said. "The last three days, I've been really green around the gills."

Could be just nerves, I thought, but my own stomach did a back-flip. I smiled. "Fingers crossed." A couple of hours later, the results were back: "Both serum and urine HCG levels consistent with normal pregnancy at six weeks menstrual age." That evening, Giselle and I had lobsters and champagne at Charley's Boathouse.

Next morning, after rounds, as I walked down the corridor to my office, a woman stepped into my path from the little nook outside the rest rooms. "Dr. Sanford, I need to talk to you."

She looked familiar.

"You don't know who I am," she said.

"I've seen you—"

"I'm Alma Wanego, the supervisor in Dr. Hearn's laboratory."

"Oh, sure. Of course. Sorry."

"That's all right. No reason you should have noticed me. I need a few minutes of your time."

I checked my watch. "I don't want to be late to my patient appointments. Can we talk later? Over lunch?"

"I think we'd do best to talk now, Doctor. I won't take more than twenty minutes." She gestured with her head toward the elevators. "Let's go down to the coffee shop."

Everything about her was severe. Her face looked chiseled out of marble, thin lips, tightly drawn, not a hint of a smile. Blue eyes cut from a glacier. Long blonde hair, waved down over her right forehead, every hair strictly in place. Poker-straight posture. Sharply cut gray suit with thin white stripes. Her tone and manner said she was someone not used to being contradicted or corrected. I was caught off guard by a feeling of strong sexual attraction, one that carried a warning: take on the Ice Queen if you dare, but if you fail, you die.

I nodded. "All right."

Once at our table, steaming cups of coffee between us, Ms. Wanego turned those twin blue jets of frost on me. "I'll be direct and clear, Dr. Sanford. To save you the time of playing what's-all-this about, I know what you and Dr. Hearn are up to. Remember that little incident in the lab on August 9? I saw all of it, including you rushing over and into Dr. Hearn's office, then off double-time to the supplies room, and then down the hall. I also happened to be standing outside the men's room a short while later. Are you with me?"

"I'm listening."

"So after everyone else left that afternoon, I found the project log in Dr. Hearn's desk. The patient for that day was coded as JK, so it was no problem to check the Puget Community Surgery Unit records and see you'd done a laparoscopy for lysis of adhesions on a Joyce Kennett. I kept my eye on Dr. Hearn, and three days later, when she ducked off into her alcove, wouldn't talk to anyone, then went rushing out with a wheeled incubator and a microscope, I followed her."

"You *followed* her?"

For the first time, I got a smile, but not one you'd want to see on the face of somebody who had the goods on you. "Yes,

I followed her. Right to your office. And then I counted ahead on the calendar. When Dr. Hearn got a phone call yesterday, and practically floated around the lab like a helium balloon, I called the hospital laboratory, told them I was your receptionist, and I needed the result of a pregnancy test on Joyce Kennett. She said she'd already given the result to someone, so I said we were a little uncoordinated right then, and could she please give it to me one more time." Another smile. "Congratulations, Dr. Sanford. The first IVF baby in the world."

She flicked the tip of her tongue across her lips. "That should be worth a lot to you and Dr. Hearn, not to mention Mr. and Mrs. Kennett. But a few words from me to Dr. Camnitz, and that would be the end of this collaboration, and probably also the end of Giselle Hearn's career. I imagine *your* reputation would also take a pretty substantial hit, especially considering that little accident you thought you'd covered over. But I know how to keep a secret. For ten thousand dollars, cash, my lips will be sealed."

The oddest thing. The way she was looking at me right then should've made me want to smack her in the face, but what I really wanted was to throw her to the floor, jump on top of her, and start tearing at her clothes. Her expression was an invitation to go at it, very hot and very heavy. Her modus operandi, I thought, and figured it must have won her a ton of arguments and negotiations. But I was not about to let this discussion go past the talking stage. The frying pan wasn't comfortable, but that would be one ugly fire to jump into.

I tried to play for a little time, shot my cuff and looked at my watch. "You said not more than twenty minutes, and—"

"That was for talking. Now, look. Don't even try telling me you have no idea where you'd come up with ten thousand dollars. That's ice-cream cone money to you, *Doctor*. You have two choices. Come across with the money, now, or I go straight to Dr. Camnitz's office. This is not negotiable. What's your decision?"

"Sorry," I said. "But I do have a couple of questions. When's the next time you'll be knocking on my door with your hand out?"

She clearly didn't like to be on the receiving end. "I said I want ten thousand dollars, and that's what I'll take. I keep my bargains. What's your other question?"

"What are you demanding from Dr. Hearn?"

"Nothing. I need to work with Dr. Hearn, and I'm not a stupid enough bird to foul my own nest. This matter will be entirely between you and me. Do you have any more questions?"

I pushed my chair away from the table. "There's a phone booth at the corner. I'll call my office and tell them I have an emergency."

◇◇◇

I didn't want to risk phoning Giselle at the lab, so I waited till evening, and called her apartment. "We've got a problem," I said. "With that, uh, complication we had on the way to getting Joyce Kennett pregnant."

I heard a gasp. "Oh, no. Look, Colin, I'll take the blame for that. I'll apologize to the Kennetts. I really should have done that when it happened."

"Wait, there's more. But let's not talk over the phone. I'll come right by."

◇◇◇

Giselle's apartment was only a few blocks from mine. She rang me in, then had the door open before I got up to her floor. "I made some coffee," she said.

I almost said we might want something stronger, but no need to get her more upset than she already was. "Good. Bring it on."

She listened quietly to my story. I thought just as well to spare her the sexual component of the exchange, but told her everything else. When I finished, she blew. "Oh, that snotty little creature. Sometimes it takes all I have to keep from giving it to her, bang, right in her arrogant, condescending kisser. Ten thousand dollars? I could kill her."

"But it's your lab, isn't it? Why don't you can her?"

"Hah. Good question. Look for the fine hand of Chairman Camnitz. When the job opened up, Gerry told me he wanted

Alma appointed. He said he thought she had what it took to keep a bunch of techs in line and working efficiently. She'd been a good tech, but I had real reservations about her management skills. Gerry wouldn't budge, though. The techs hate her, all of them. They file complaints, they threaten to leave, and one of them actually did quit. I spend way too much time trying to pacify them and bitching to Gerry, but he sticks to his guns. If he tells me one more time about cracking eggs and making omelets, I may kill *him*." She made a wry face.

"What do you think? Wanego said she keeps her bargains, and this would be a one-time payoff. Do you see that happening?"

"In a word, no. She'll be back, but not necessarily the next time she wants to buy something. With Alma, I don't think money is really the thing. She seems to get off on winning when she can rub the loser's nose in it, the harder, the better."

"Little sadistic, is she?"

"More than a little. That's where the staff gets the most upset with her. A supervisor's supposed to keep watch for mistakes or lapses in protocols, then use them as an opportunity to help the staff, to get them to feel even more involved in the work. But Alma…"

Giselle shook her head. "The more stupid, the more careless, the more negligent she can make someone feel, the more she seems to like it. I've seen her face get flushed when she's chewing someone out. She looks like a kid, sticking a pin into a worm, watching it wiggle, then sticking it again. My guess is that some time when she's not getting enough of a charge from making the techs squirm, she'll be back to you. That line about not wanting to foul her own nest? She's gotten this nest so foul it couldn't possibly smell worse."

"It wouldn't occur to her to go ask the Kennetts for a payoff, would it? Especially if she really was standing outside the men's room when James came out with the second sample."

"Whatever would give her the biggest tingle is what she'd do. But I still think I ought to apologize to the Kennetts. Maybe that would help a little."

"It wouldn't help at all. It'd be a disaster. Remember, I told James the first sample was inadequate, and if he could get us a second one, you'd do your best to make it work? He thinks you're a hero. All he'd have to hear would be that you dropped the first tube."

Giselle sighed. "I guess we'd better deal with Alma. I've got an idea."

Chapter Three

Baumgartner

My old man was a cop. He died three months before I was born, and if you don't think that's a weird thing for a kid to get his mind around, think again. It never even felt right to refer to him as "my dad."

From all I heard, he was a good man and a good cop. His name was Harry Baumgartner, but they called him Bulldog because of how he went after his cases. He'd tug at a piece of evidence this way, that way, every way he could think of, until finally he was looking at it from just the right angle, case closed. Which is why he died, or at least, why people figured he died. A whole family had been executed gang-style in their house, the investigation was going nowhere, and my father was driving himself and everyone around him nuts. Then one night, he told my mother he thought he had it, he only needed to make one more connection. He went out to get that connection, but he never came back. They found him three days later, floating in the Green River, south of Emerald. They never got his killer, and they never cracked the murder case, either.

My first memories are of my mother telling me about my father, what happened to him, and why. Ma did everything she could think of to make sure I'd never become a cop, which the shrinks told her later was about the worst tack she could've taken.

But I didn't join the force out of spite. All that talk from my mother started me reading crime stories, real ones and made-up. I read everything I could get my hands on, newspaper accounts of murders, books with genius private eyes like Philip Marlowe, Hercule Poirot, and Philo Vance, and I always tried to nail the bad guy before the detectives did. By the time I was fifteen, it was a rare book where the dick beat me to the killer. By my last year in high school, I was spending all my free time and then some hanging around our neighborhood station house. The cops knew who I was, and who my father was, so they put up with me. A young looey, Mel Richmond, took me under his wing, told me war stories, even let me ride around with him on night patrols. Finally, word got back to my mother. She told me if I ever became a policeman, she'd never talk to me again. She never has, either, thirty years now and counting.

In those thirty years, I've seen my share of homicides, but there's one case I'll never forget. The call came in a little after eleven in the morning, an apparent murder-suicide in a laboratory at the University Medical School.

By the time my partner, Roger Olson, and I got there, it was like all Niagara had busted loose. Two people were down, a man and a woman. She'd been shot twice in the chest, he'd shot himself up through the mouth, and the ER doc and paramedic who'd been called in were standing over the bodies, waiting for me to tell them they could officially leave. The first responders had done a good job of making sure nothing got touched or changed, keeping people out who didn't belong there, getting everyone who was in the lab when it happened seated quietly in the room next door. When Olson and I came in, one of the cops showed us a list of names, and some notes he'd taken. The woman was Dr. Giselle Hearn, the head of the lab, but no one knew anything about the man. One of the techs had heard an argument, the man and the woman shouting, and then there were three shots.

We called in the ME, the criminalists, and the photog, and were starting to find out who was who, and what they'd heard and seen, when a fat guy in a long white coat blew through the doorway in a cloud of expensive men's cologne. For a minute, he stood there like a moose in a car's headlights. Then he bellowed, "What's going on here?"

I walked over to him, and flipped my badge under his nose. "Detective Baumgartner, Emerald Police, Homicide," I said. "You are…?"

He looked down his nose, and made a major effort to pull in his gut and stand tall. "I'm Dr. L. Gerald Camnitz, the chairman of this department. I want to know what's going on—"

He shut up in a hurry when the doc from the ER stepped away, and he got a better view of the vics. "Oh, my God. Giselle Hearn?" He ran the few steps to her side, started to kneel and grab at her wrist, but I got to his arm first. "Please don't touch anything, sir."

It took some work to get him back to standing. He couldn't take his eyes off the woman. "My God, she's dead," he muttered, then raised his voice. "Who's that man on the floor there? Did he kill her?"

"Looks that way," I said. "My partner and I are going to try to sort it out. Meanwhile, the policeman over there will get you a seat for a little while. Soon as we're squared away here, I'll want to talk to you."

He didn't like that. "I have a full schedule of appointments the rest of the day."

"The policeman will walk you back to your office so you can ask your secretary to reschedule them."

"What? You're treating me like a prisoner. This is outrageous."

I looked over to the bodies on the floor. "No, sir, *that's* outrageous. This is standard investigative procedure. Don't take it personally." I motioned the cop over. He reached for Camnitz's arm. The doctor grunted at me, then stalked toward the door.

Chapter Four

Sanford

It was the nastiest medical situation I could remember. I gave Amy Dickenson, the postpartum charge nurse, a quick heads-up before we went into Joyce Kennett's room. As we walked to Joyce's bedside, her round face creased into a smile. I took her hand. "How're you feeling?"

"Oh, much better than I expected. I've hardly needed any pain medication. I'm so glad you talked me out of a c-section."

She'd been concerned over possible hazards to the baby of labor and vaginal delivery, and wanted to "play it safe." But the idea of so-called premium babies has always bothered me. Is any one human life, no matter how difficult it was to conceive, more valuable than any other? I told Joyce that sections have risks of their own, both to mother and baby, and that I wouldn't take a step off Labor and Delivery from the minute she came in until she was holding her baby. Her labor lasted only seven hours, and the delivery was as uneventful as her pregnancy had been.

"And she's already been up and walking, several times."

Amy's enthusiasm over a few strolls to the bathroom and nursery came across as forced. I gave her a hard look. "My patients don't have episiotomy pain. They all walk right away." I coughed, squeezed Joyce's hand. "We do have a problem, though."

Cheer drained from her face; her free hand shot to her throat. "What's wrong with my baby?"

"Nothing at all. The baby's fine. It's something else. Do you know why James went to talk to Dr. Hearn?"

She was clearly puzzled. "Well, yes. He wanted to thank her for the work she did…" Her voice faded as she looked at Amy. "You know, what she did to help us get pregnant. That was all right, wasn't it?"

I grimaced, couldn't help it. "Joyce, I'm sorry. I just got word that James shot Dr. Hearn. And then he shot himself."

She grabbed at my white coat. "Are they…I mean…"

"I'm sorry," I said again. "At least from what I've heard, they're both dead. I wanted to come see you before you heard it from anyone else."

Joyce released her hold on me, put both hands to her eyes, and began to weep silently. But then lowered her hands, looked at Amy, and without the slightest waver in her voice, said, "Ms. Dickenson, would you excuse us, please? I'd like to talk to Dr. Sanford privately."

Amy nodded. "Of course." She practically flew out of the room.

As the door clicked shut, I thought Joyce was going to wail like a siren, but no. She stared at me for a moment, then said, "I didn't want to talk in front of her…oh, Dr. Sanford, I can't believe it. James was so happy about the baby." She choked, coughed, took a deep breath, brushed hair off her cheek. "He said he wanted to thank Dr. Hearn for giving him to us. He was so excited…I wonder if he forgot to take his medications this morning."

"Did he often forget?"

"I never gave him the chance. I was there to remind him every morning at breakfast." She shook her head. "But I wasn't there today. And he was so wound up with excitement all day yesterday."

I considered not saying what was in my mind, but decided to go ahead. "If he got himself a gun beforehand, he must have had something on his mind."

Now, tears came, a flood down her cheeks. "He's always had guns. He thought he needed them for protection. I didn't know until we were engaged, and when I told him I wasn't sure I liked the idea, he got upset. So I backed off. I mean, he did have a permit and all. He carried a gun everywhere, wherever he went."

I'd wondered why he came to every office visit wearing a sport jacket. "How could he have gotten a concealed-weapons permit? He's been a psychiatric patient for more than twenty years."

Words worked their way out between choked sobs. "I don't have any idea. I guess they don't check all that hard."

"Did his psychiatrist know?"

Helpless shrug. "Dr. Hammacher never talked about James' condition with me."

"Of course not. Sorry."

She swallowed hard. "Dr. Sanford, you've got to cancel the press conference. There's no way I can handle the publicity right now."

"Already canceled. But Joyce, listen. The police want me to come over to the lab. I'm sure they're going to ask me a lot of questions, and when they're done with me, they'll be asking you at least some of the same questions. We don't want to let the cat out of the bag, so we'll need to be sure we give them the exact same answers."

Panic covered her face.

"Don't worry. I've got it figured out. One of Dr. Hearn's lab projects was something called Density Gradient Separation, an experimental procedure to make sperm more efficient at fertilization. For now, let's tell the police I got her to do a Density Gradient Separation on a sample of James' sperm, and I inseminated you with it. You can handle that, can't you?"

She sighed. "I guess I'll have to. Oh, I wish I could manage that press conference. I know how much it means to you, and it's more important to me now than it ever was. Without the money from the publicity..." She started to cry again.

"Don't worry," I said. "You're going to get full living expenses for you and..."

"Robbie. Robert Jackson Kennett."

"Right, for you and Robbie. I promise. Meanwhile, it won't hurt to wait a bit—better all around, in fact. By the time you get yourself in hand, there won't be anything else going on to distract the reporters."

She gnawed at her lip. "Yeah. All right."

I patted her hand. "I've got to get along. Let the police catch up with us separately. I'll go over to the lab now, see what I can find out."

She started to cry again, silently. "Thank you so much, Dr. Sanford. I don't know what I'd do without you."

"Don't even think about it. Let me do the worrying. Now, what's the name of the procedure Dr. Hearn did?"

"Density Gradient Separation." She made a poor attempt at a smile, then washed it away in a flood of tears.

"Perfect," I said, gently as I could. "Be back later. I'll take care of everything."

My mind moved at least as fast as my feet as I hurried across the skybridge to the U Medical Center. No mulligans in this game. I'd need to do something about Joyce's office records, and then, at the delayed news conference, if anyone asked about Density Gradient Separation, I'd go a little shamefaced, and explain it had been a necessary lie to protect my patient when she was so vulnerable. And if that led someone to ask why they should believe me now, I'd smile benignly and open the log I'd stashed under my file cabinet. After I'd made a small revision.

The Department of Obstetrics and Gynecology was Pandemonium. All up and down the hall, secretaries, lab techs, doctors milled about. Some were crying. I worked my way through the mob to the end of the administrative corridor, where I turned left into the research wing, and went up to the third door on the left, next to the brass plate that read REPRODUCTIVE GENETICS.

A gangly young policeman moved to block my entrance. "I'm sorry sir, you can't go in here."

I nodded understanding. "I'm Dr. Colin Sanford, Dr. Hearn's associate. Is it true she's been—"

"Sir, I can't discuss anything with you. I need to ask you to leave."

I flashed the smile I'd intended to use on the reporters right about that time. "The wife of the man who did the shooting is my patient. A detective called my office and asked me to come over."

"Mr. Baumgartner?"

"That's the name my office manager gave me."

The cop looked like someone who'd picked up on a strong odor of fish, but he pointed down the hall. "Detective Baumgartner's interviewing people in the department conference room and the room next door to it. You know the way?"

"Yes. Thank you."

◇◇◇

I walked down to the end of the hall, and into the conference room. Three techs, two women and a man, huddled at one end of the long table; at the other end, Laurie Mansell, the supervisor, sat with Gerry Camnitz. Their conversation was so intense, they didn't notice me until I walked up to them. Camnitz's face fairly glowed. His blood pressure must've been off the charts. "What are *you* doing here?" he barked at me.

Little shrug. "I heard something terrible happened, and since it concerns one of my patients, I thought I ought to check it out."

Camnitz's eyes bugged. "One of *your* patients?"

"A postpartum. I delivered her yesterday, and I just heard her husband shot Giselle, then killed himself."

Ms. Mansell, slack-jawed, paler than any anemic patient I'd ever treated, looked up at me. She nodded several times, an automaton on low-wind. "I told the police detective, I was in my cubicle next to Dr. Hearn's office, when I heard shouting, Dr. Hearn's voice and a man's. The man—Mr. Kennett—yelled something like, 'What do you mean, second sample?' and then

Dr. Hearn said she was so glad the second one was adequate, she was upset when the first one wasn't…and then they were both shouting. Dr. Hearn screamed, "No. Don't. Listen," and right after that, I heard two shots. I didn't think, just ran to the doorway and looked inside. Dr. Hearn was on the floor, blood…Mr. Kennett looked straight at me, and I've never been so scared in my life. I thought I was dead for sure. I tried to turn and run but I couldn't, it was like in a nightmare where you're stuck in place, and can't move. But then…I'll never stop seeing it the rest of my life. He put the gun in his mouth and pulled the trigger."

I closed my eyes for a moment. "How did you know it was Mr. Kennett?"

"I didn't, not then. But the police found out somehow. Oh, Dr. Sanford, it was so awful. You must be beside yourself, how close you and Dr. Hearn were, all the time you spent here with her…"

Mansell's face went slack, cat caught in the cream pitcher. Camnitz looked like a balloon being dangerously overfilled with air. He glared at Mansell, who shrank back into her chair, then turned and waved a sausage-finger in my face. "Colin, what is she talking about? Why were you spending 'all that time' here with Giselle?"

I shoved his hand away. "Get your finger out of my nose, Gerry. The police detective called me over, and besides, I need to do what I can to help my patient. Don't give me—"

I shut up as a stocky, balding man in a brown suit walked into the room with a young woman in a white coat; I recognized her as another of the lab techs. She was near-hysterical. The man spoke to her softly, then with a gentle hand on her back, directed her to the group of her colleagues. "Miss Stephens?" The man's voice was a rich bass, almost musical, a human tuba. "Could you come with me, please…wait a minute." He held up a hand to Miss Stephens, and looked at me. "Who are you, sir?"

"Dr. Colin Sanford. My patient is the wife of the man who shot Dr. Hearn. You called my office and asked me to come by."

"Right. He walked over to me, opened a billfold to show a metal badge. "Bernard Baumgartner, EPD, Homicide. Thanks, Doctor." He extended a hand.

I gripped it. "I guess you want a word with me."

Baumgartner scanned the room. "Yes, I do, as soon as I'm finished with the lab personnel. I'll have to give your patient the news, and I thought the two of us—"

"I've already talked to Ms. Kennett," I said. "She's taking it as well as I could've hoped."

Baumgartner's face went into lockdown mode. "Didn't your office manager tell you to come right over here? Immediately?"

"Barbara did tell me that," I said. "But my responsibility to Ms. Kennett takes precedence in a situation like this. I'm ready and willing to cooperate with you in any way I can, but not at the cost of compromising my patient's care."

Baumgartner's face softened. He looked like a man trying to solve a complicated jigsaw puzzle. I thought he was about to say something, but instead, he scratched at the front edge of his retreating dark, curly hair. Then he said, "Where can I find you later?"

"In my office. Puget Community Tower, Suite Twelve-o-one. Can you tell me about what time?"

He checked his watch. "Five o'clock?"

"Fine. I'll be waiting for you." No trouble there, I thought, since I'd canceled all my appointments for the day. And that would give me plenty of time to get my thoughts in order.

"Thank you." Baumgartner turned back and nodded to Miss Stephens, whose face suggested the lion was about to lead her into his den.

The instant the door to the adjoining room closed, Camnitz wheeled around to face me. "He's not the only one who wants to talk to you, Colin." He launched an eye-dagger at Laurie Mansell. "Would you please excuse us, Mrs. Mansell?"

She scuttled to the other end of the table, and slid into a chair near the techs.

Camnitz turned his back on the group, then leaned toward me. He steepled his fingers, aimed them in my direction. "I've heard a rumor here and there about you and Giselle, that you might be collaborating on some work, but never anything, you might say, substantial enough that I thought I should pursue it. But the look on Mrs. Mansell's face just now? You and Giselle *were* up to something, weren't you? On top of a murder-suicide in my department, do I need to deal with a secret research project? Can you imagine how embarrassing that could be? Now, I demand to know just what was going on between you and Giselle."

I thought about whether I ought to deny everything, tell him Giselle and I had been friends, and Laurie had misinterpreted my visits. But there was nothing he could do to me, so why should I set myself up for him to call me a liar when I announce my success? "Sure, Gerry. I've been supplying Giselle with human oocytes to study for chromosome errors at fertilization."

"*What*? You know my opinion on human embryo research. How dare you—"

"Giselle said you and she had reached an agreement."

"We did no such thing." He looked like an overgrown, over-weight baby with colic, flailing his arms, sputtering. "You know good and well I'd never permit that work in my department. Did you ever see approval papers from the Institutional Ethics Committee?"

"That wasn't my business. That was Giselle's concern."

Camnitz pounded one fist into the other. "How many oocytes did you get for her?"

"I didn't keep count."

"Approximately, then."

"Gerry, where are you going with this? I don't know, maybe fifty or sixty, over the past year."

"And you got them where?"

"Christ, Gerry. From ovaries. Where do you think oocytes come from?"

He swallowed hard. "*Whose* ovaries?"

"Surgical patients. I retrieved ova incidentally at laparoscopy."

"After informed consent, I assume."

"You're over the line. All the procedures were done at Puget Community Hospital. You have no authority there."

"But you involved yourself in a study of live human embryos in *my* department."

"The study was Giselle's. If you want to know the details of what she did with the ova, go look in her lab log. I was just a humble practitioner helping a university professor with her research."

Camnitz laughed, not a pleasant sound. "'Just a humble practitioner,' my foot. You've never in your life been humble about anything. How did this association come about?"

"Giselle called me one day, asked me to come to lunch, and told me she wanted to extend her studies from mice to humans. She said she picked me because I'm the hands-down best laparoscopist in Emerald."

"And you were generous enough to agree to recover eggs for her. Nothing in it for you."

"She told me I'd be second author on any papers that came out. Look, Gerry, I've had enough. I have no way of knowing what went on between you and Giselle, but nothing I did was illegal, or a violation of any of my institution's rules or guidelines. If you want to pursue this, let's go public with it. I'll say what I just told you, and then you can try to explain to news reporters, prospective faculty members, the dean, and a whole country-full of OBGYN chairmen why you're such a misguided reactionary that a respected member of your department felt she had to do reasonable and important research on the sly." I sprang from the chair so suddenly, Camnitz jumped. "So long, Gerry."

A few minutes before five, Barbara Renfro knocked lightly at my office door, then pushed it open. "Dr. Sanford?"

I raised my eyebrows, a silent "What's up."

"Detective Baumgartner is here to see you."

"Oh, right. Thanks, Barbara." I got up, walked around the desk to the door, and extended a hand to Baumgartner. The detective looked tired, hair mussed, eyelids at half-staff. He gripped my hand. "Thanks for making yourself available."

"No trouble." I pointed to the chair opposite the desk. "Take a load off. Care for a drink? Coke, Pepsi, juice?"

He shook his head. "Thanks. I'll try not to take too much of your time."

"Whatever you need."

"I talked to Ms. Kennett. Poor woman, what a thing to happen to someone after she's had a baby. You were right, though, she's bearing up well." He paused, and I could've sworn I heard gears humming inside his head. "But it might surprise you to know how many well-meaning people throw monkey wrenches into police investigations. When a police officer tells you to come directly to the lab, that's what you should do."

"I'm sorry if I caused a problem by going to see my patient," I said. "But I still think I had an obligation to do it. For a doctor, the needs of a patient have top priority."

The gear noise got louder. "Well, I guess we all have our own ideas about priorities. Let's leave it at that."

No reason not to give him the last word. "All right. Joyce definitely is a tough cookie, Mr. Baumgartner. Infertility's a hard row to hoe, going month after month, hoping whatever treatment you're getting will be the one that works, and then comes the next menstrual period. Not every doctor takes that into account, but I've always given full attention to the emotional sides of the situation. I think that's one reason my success rate with infertility patients is as good as it is. Some patients get terribly depressed, but I watch for any signs of trouble. Catch it before it gets out of hand."

Baumgartner regarded me from the corners of his eyes. "Do you watch the husbands, too?"

I kept my smile secret. "Yes, of course. Too many gynecologists get a sperm sample from the husband, and if it's normal, they ignore him from then on, and basically just treat the wife.

But my approach is always to treat the couple, and given that James carried a diagnosis of paranoid schizophrenia, I made certain to talk to Dr. Hammacher, his psychiatrist."

"Your idea or the Kennetts'?"

"Mine. Expert consultation. I'd have insisted if I'd needed to, but Joyce and James had no problem with it. Dr. Hammacher said he didn't think there was a contraindication to James becoming a father. His condition was borderline, and ever since he'd had a breakdown, oh, twenty years ago, he'd taken his meds religiously and stayed away from alcohol, and he'd done very well. He was a little peculiar here and there, but so are a lot of people, and as best I could tell, he was handling the infertility workup better than a lot of so-called normal men. I can't begin to imagine what happened."

Baumgartner sighed. "That's what both Dr. Hammacher and Ms. Kennett told me. Ms. Kennett said her husband went over to thank Dr. Hearn for doing a procedure on his sperm that was supposed to help her conceive, something about separating the sperm. Can you enlighten me about that?"

"Sure. The Kennetts had been through both my clinic and the University's, almost two years of the usual tests and treatments, but nothing worked. I knew one of the projects in Dr. Hearn's lab was a procedure called Density Gradient Separation. You set up a tube with layered solutions of silica particles, the densest layer on the bottom, the thinnest on top. Then you place the sperm above the top silica layer, and centrifuge the tube, which brings the fastest-moving sperm into the bottom layer. Inseminating with that sub-sample theoretically uses the sperm with the best chance of getting to an egg and fertilizing it. Dr. Hearn told me that as far as she knew, no one had done a trial in humans, but results in mice seemed encouraging, and we couldn't see any risk to giving it a try."

Baumgartner nodded. "Seems like it was very encouraging for the Kennetts." A little grin curled the side of his mouth. "Makes me wonder, though. Isn't that kind of like asking a man to get a woman pregnant right after he runs a marathon?"

I laughed. "Think of it like this. A guy in condition to run a fast marathon is going to do better in any race if a bunch of slow, out-of-shape runners aren't all around, blocking his way. We figured we'd try it, what could we lose? And I guess we won, except for what happened out past the finish line."

"That's one way to put it. The lab supervisor told me that right before the shooting, she heard Dr. Hearn and Mr. Kennett arguing, something about a second sample that had worked when the first one hadn't. Ring any bells with you?"

I shook my head, shrugged. "No, but I'm a clinician. I don't begin to know the ins and outs of lab protocols. Sorry."

"Okay. Do you have Ms. Kennett's chart handy? I'd like to take a look at it, just for the record."

I checked my watch. "Office staff's gone by now. Hang on, I'll go out to the file storage."

A few minutes later, I was back, shaking my head. "I'm sorry, I can't seem to lay my hands on it."

Baumgartner's smile was wry. "Not quite in your job description?"

"I thought I could find a chart in my own office, but it's not in the alphabetical storage. I also looked through the piles of charts at the check-in desk, and it wasn't there either. I don't know where else it could be. Do you want me to call my office manager? I'm not sure she'll be home yet, but—"

Baumgartner waved off the question. "Nah. If anything comes up, I might ask you to find it for me, but right now, I don't think it's worth bothering your staff. Dr. Hammacher thought the excitement of the birth might have unglued Kennett, that maybe he went out and celebrated a little last night, and then, on top of that, maybe he didn't take his pills this morning. According to the doctor, putting a gun into the hand of a paranoid schizophrenic is like putting a dynamite detonator into the hand of an epileptic. He said if he'd had any idea Kennett owned a gun, he'd have been sure to get him to turn it in. If, if if." Well, thanks for your time, Doctor."

"Glad to help. You know where to find me if you need to talk to me again."

I walked Baumgartner through the empty waiting room, into the outer corridor, where he shook my hand, and headed off toward the elevator. I went back to my office, locked the door behind me, then took a key from my pocket, opened my center desk drawer, and pulled out a thick Manila folder labeled KENNETT, JOYCE/JAMES. Good thing I'd thought to grab it from alphabetical storage earlier, when I came back to the office from the lab.

I laid the folder on my desk, flipped pages until I came to the one I was looking for. Smart move to have all office visits on separate pages. Not only did that make it easy to find the record of a particular visit, it also made it a snap to get rid of a visit you didn't want anyone else to be aware of. Anyone else like lawyers, I'd thought, when I started that practice. I'd never imagined police.

I opened the two-pronged metal clasp at the top of the chart, and carefully pulled off all the pages through the two I was looking for. Then I took a pad of medical charting paper from a desk drawer, copied the date from the first page of the two originals, and wrote a careful description of the way I'd supposedly explained Density Gradient Separation to the Kennetts. On a second clean sheet, I copied the date from the second original page, and composed an account of insemination with treated sperm. If I could've doctored Giselle's log entries that easily, I would have, but I knew I couldn't copy her hand, and besides, her notes had no page breaks. I'd think of something, though. I had to.

I re-read both new chart notes, slipped them in place of the originals under the more recent chartings I'd pulled off the clasp, and worked them all back on. Then I took the two original pages to the file cabinet, tipped the cabinet, and stashed the originals inside Giselle's log book. More insurance than I needed? Not if Baumgartner decided to come back for another shot at the chart.

On my way out, I stopped at file storage, behind the reception desk, and pushed the chart in, a few spaces from where it should've been. "That's why I couldn't find it," I murmured, as if to Detective Baumgartner. "It had been misfiled."

Time for a good workout at the gym. Let the fuss die down, a few days, a week at the outside. Then I'd retrieve the original pages, put them back into the chart, and reschedule my press conference.

Chapter Five

Baumgartner

Melville Richmond, the guy who took me on patrol when I was seventeen, became Emerald's youngest-ever Chief of Police in 1955. Trying to live up to his expectations for twenty-two years was not always the easiest thing, but I knew that without Mel's interest in me, I'd probably be putting in eight long hours, five days a week, at a desk in some insurance agency. I could count on a firm pat on the back when I got something right, a hard kick in the ass when I didn't. If I was a good cop, a lot of the credit had to go to Mel. I'd have done anything for him.

So, eight o'clock on a Friday night, there we were, sitting in his office, talking about this case. Mel has a habit when he's nervous, he picks up a pencil and makes like a one-armed Gene Krupa with the eraser. All the time I filled him in about the case, he was beating out prizewinning riffs on the top of his desk. He wanted every little detail, and when I finally finished, he put down the pencil and smiled. "Sounds pretty straightforward, doesn't it?"

"I'm not sure. I've got to think about it a little."

He shrugged, then held out his hands, palms up. "A head case who shouldn't have a gun but does, forgets to take his pills, then blows away a doctor and himself. What's to think about?"

A few things. One, he didn't keep his pills in any sort of daily counter, so we don't know for sure he didn't take them. Two, his wife said he went over to thank the doctor for doing the lab procedure that got her pregnant. Three, the woman's doctor is this little guy with an ego the size of an elephant's dick. I left word for him to come right over to the lab to talk to me, but he first stopped to see the wife and tell her what happened, and then, when I talked to the wife, she seemed nervous as hell. Four, the doctor couldn't quite manage to find her chart for me to look at. Is that enough?"

Mel leaned across the desk. "Bernie, why do you get yourself so worked up over stuff that doesn't matter? Seems reasonable the doc would want to talk to his patient when he found out her husband was dead. The wife was nervous? What did you want from her, right after she found out her husband killed someone, then shot himself? And I've had my chart get lost in a doctor's office when I've had an appointment, haven't you?"

I shook my head. "I just don't think it's as clean as it looks."

I saw it in his eyes, just for a second, but it was there. Once upon a time, Mel Richmond had been Mr. Straight-from-the-Shoulder. But the last couple of years, coming up on retirement, he'd gotten to be more than a little careful not to piss off anyone who might respond by pissing on him. It hurt to see that. I tried to be as gentle as I could. "Mel, I think you and I can do better if I know the whole story. Is there somebody who's unhappy about this case?"

He took a deep breath. "Horace Bancroft."

There's always a reason for everything. Bancroft was a big-time lawyer, and a member of the U Med Center Board of Directors. "What's his problem? Seems like he'd want a murder-suicide in the Med School cleaned up."

Mel grabbed up the pencil, started a new riff. "Well, I'm sure he does...but he doesn't want...you know how it is, Bernie. The papers and the TV reporters have field days on stuff like this, and the longer it goes on, the more lurid it gets. Bancroft hauled the mayor in here to tell us both he wants the case wrapped up quick and quiet. The med school lives by its reputation as a primo research and care center, and Bancroft thinks a juicy murder-suicide in the OB Department isn't exactly great promotional strategy. And then…this is between us, Bernie. Bancroft's son-in-law, the OB chairman—"

"Dr. Camnitz."

Mel looked surprised. "You know him?"

"I've seen his picture in the paper, front and center with Bancroft and their wives at every society shindig in town. He ran in on the scene right after I got there. Puffed-up, patronizing windbag."

Mel made a face, nodded. "Camnitz told Bancroft there was talk that the doctor who got killed might've been doing some very controversial work on human embryos under the table. He said if that gets out, it could be a major black eye for the department and the school."

"More major than a murder-suicide?"

He leaned across the desk toward me. "Bernie—"

"What? Are you saying you want me to go sit down and write this up as a nuthead who forgot his meds and went over the edge?"

The pencil snapped in Mel's hand. He looked at it like it had broken of its own will, to embarrass him. "No, Bernie. That's not what I'm telling you. I'd never order you to cover over a case you thought needed looking at. What I *am* going to do is take Olson off, and give it to you as a special assignment. Get what you need from the crime-scene crews, then you're on your own. I don't want to take any chance that someone in the department might talk out of school. And stay away from the press. Take a week or so, then let's talk about it again. But in the meanwhile, I don't want Horseshit Horace dragging the mayor into my office again. Fair enough?"

I got to my feet. Christ, I was tired. I gave Mel a good fish eye. "What could be fairer?"

He smiled. "Thanks, Bernie. I knew I could count on you."

◇◇◇

"Bernie?"

Irma, my wife. I took a deep breath. "What?"

She slammed down the book she was reading. "Bernie, what the hell am I going to do with you? I keep thinking, maybe as you get older, you'll mellow out a little, but you just get worse and worse. You didn't come home till after nine o'clock. Dinner was like shoe leather."

"I'm sorry, Irma, I'm a cop. I don't punch a time clock when I'm on a murder-suicide. After I was through at the scene, I had to go talk to the suicide's wife and the wife's doctor, then drive out in the boonies to tell the victim's mother her daughter had been shot to death."

"No, that's wrong. You didn't *have* to do any of it. You've been eligible for retirement for almost a year. You could be taking things easy, enjoying life. Reading books. Working in the garden. You could be home for dinner on time every night. We could go on a cruise, let people wait on us hand and foot. That actually might be nice."

"Irma, how many times do we need to go through this? Can you just about see me on a cruise, pacing the deck of a ship like a caged animal, except for when I'm doubled over the rail, turning my stomach inside out? And I did call to tell you I'd be late, didn't I?"

"You want a medal for that? To go along with your thirty-year ribbon? God damn it, Bernie, all you think about and all you care about is cops and robbers. You come in three hours late, then you don't say Word One all through dinner, and for an hour now, you've been stretched out in that goddamn recliner, staring at the ceiling like you're trying to burn holes in it with your eyes. It's only your body that's here, and as for me, *I* might as well not have a body, for all the interest you show in it any more." She grabbed her book, jumped up out of her chair, and let the book fly. I dodged left; it whizzed past my ear, hit the headrest, bounced to the floor. "I'm going up to bed," she shouted. "You're probably going to fall asleep right where you're sitting, anyway."

A minute later, I heard the door slam upstairs. The whole living room shook.

Irma's Hungarian, and she's got that real Hungarian temper. The least little thing sets her foaming at the mouth. Her mother was like that, too. In twenty-four years of marriage, Irma and I must have set some kind of record for good, loud fights, but right then, I was glad she settled for taking herself off to bed. I didn't feel like cranking it up. I was tired, I was disgusted, and I was thinking. This case didn't smell right.

Chapter Six

Baumgartner

Next thing I knew, the sun was in my face. I shook my head awake, then checked my watch. Five minutes to eight. As I threw the recliner handle forward and the chair snapped upright, my back registered a serious protest. Damn, getting too old to sleep nights in a chair.

Upstairs, the bedroom door was closed, whether still or again. I tiptoed into the bathroom, cleaned up. Downstairs, a quick note for Irma, "Had to go in, back when I can," on the kitchen table, and I was out the door.

Sadie's Luncheonette, in the little strip mall a few blocks from our house, does a nice breakfast, and they leave a man alone to think while he eats. By the time I was done, I knew where I was going to start. I went out to the phone booth at the corner, opened my pocket notebook, and dialed Laurie Mansell's number. Her husband told me she'd drawn Saturday duty in the lab. Good. I thanked him, walked out of the booth, got in the car, and drove off toward Pill Hill.

The day before, Ms. Mansell had looked like the skin on her face was tightened with thumbscrews, but now she was a cute little blonde with dimples that made me want to put my fingers in them and twirl. She stiffened when I told her why I was there, but said yes, of course she'd be glad to help however she could, and she had about forty minutes before she needed to do the next procedure. She took me into her cubicle, then studied me across the desk. "You don't like the smell in here, do you?"

"You're sharp. No, I don't. It reminds me of the autopsy room. But you don't work with flesh here."

"Sure we do. We have to kill mice—we call it 'sacrificing'— to get the eggs out of their ovaries. Then, there are our tissue culture fluids, which have a lot of protein in them, sometimes even blood serum." She shrugged. "We get used to it."

"That's what they say in the autopsy rooms too." I cleared my throat. "Let me ask you a few questions. Ms. Mansell. Some of them, we may have talked about yesterday, but don't worry about that. Start with Dr. Hearn. She was the…what? Head of the lab?"

"Officially, she was the Director and Principal Investigator. Except she was the only investigator."

"Who's in charge now?"

"I guess I am, since I'm the supervisor. Dr. Hearn's grants are still in force, and Dr. Camnitz, the Department Chairman, wants to keep her experiments going while he tries to find another research scientist who could step in, maybe under a joint appointment with another department."

"Dr. Hearn didn't have any postgraduate students?"

Mansell licked at her lips. "Not any more…I mean, she once did. But she was pretty tough on them, and word got around, so for the past few years, no one's applied."

"Hmm. What was the nature of her work?"

"Early development in mouse embryos. Her main interest was looking into what causes chromosomes to behave abnormally at fertilization."

"Like in mongolism."

"Right, except now it's called Down Syndrome. That's where the embryo gets an extra Number Twenty-one chromosome. It's the most common chromosomal aberration you see in human babies."

"So you fertilize eggs in a test tube, and watch to see what happens?"

"In a petri dish, actually. That's a flat, circular plastic culture dish. Embryos grow better in those than in test tubes. We also study embryos from natural fertilization, so we can compare different things at different stages, right up to where the embryos would implant into the uterus."

"Do you do any work on human embryos?"

Mansell threw a hand to her mouth, but couldn't stifle the snort. "Not in this lab. Dr. Camnitz won't allow it. He says there's too much controversy over the ethics, and we need to wait till it all settles out. He and Dr. Hearn had some real shouting matches. She told him if no one did the work because they were afraid of the controversy, it never *would* get done. One time she got really fried, and said it was lucky Dr. Camnitz wasn't Galileo's chairman…"

I leaned forward. "What're you thinking?"

"I'm just wondering."

"Say it."

"Well, it's something I'm not sure of, and I wouldn't want to get someone in trouble."

"If it entered your mind, spit it out. Sometimes those maybes turn out to be important."

She drew a deep breath. "I think it's possible Dr. Hearn *might've* been doing human work on the sly. One of the OBGYNs at Puget Community Hospital was always coming over to see her, and it occurred to me that he could have been bringing her some kind of samples. They'd go into her office and shut the door, then after he left, she'd go off to her little alcove around the corner, and work there for a while. The alcove has a small sterile hood, a dissecting microscope, and a tissue-culture incubator, which Dr. Hearn always kept locked. She was the only one who had a key."

I scratched at my chin. "What's the doctor's name?"

Mansell hesitated. I made a come-on motion with my hand.

"Dr. Sanford. Dr. Colin Sanford."

"Interesting. Dr. Sanford and Ms. Kennett told me Dr. Hearn did some kind of procedure to make Mr. Kennett's sperm work better. Know anything about what that procedure could have been?"

"Oh." I saw a light go on. "It might've been Density Gradient Separation. That's been a minor line of research in the lab for the past year or so. We kept finding white blood cells in the mouse sperm we were using to fertilize eggs, which meant the samples were infected, and since there are reports that centrifugation with specially-treated silica particles can separate white cells out of semen, we tried that, and it worked. But Dr. Hearn noticed something else. Not only did the treatment get rid of the white cells, but the most active sperm migrated into the densest silica layer. So she wondered if we could use the procedure to weed out weaker sperm from a sample so the healthier ones would have a better chance to fertilize the eggs. We've just recently begun to look at it in human sperm."

"Was that the work Dr. Hearn did in the alcove there?"

"I don't think so. She wouldn't have needed the sterile hood and incubator. Those things make me think more of tissue culture.

Tissue culture, tissue culture. "And Dr. Hearn had the only key to that locked incubator?"

"Yes."

"So, no one's opened it since yesterday?"

"I don't think so."

"Can we take a look at it?"

She practically flew out of her chair. "Sure, if you want."

I followed her from the office, around a corner into a small alcove, then past a black workbench with a water faucet and sink at its center. In the far corner of the room was what looked like a plastic sheet. I walked over and tried to peek through it. "That's the sterile hood," Ms. Mansell said. "For tissue culture. You put on sterile gloves and a sterile gown, lay the petri dish on the heating plate inside to keep it at body temperature, and then stick your hands through those holes in the plastic sheet to do the manipulations." She pointed to a small metal container on a shelf at the side of the hood, attached to the wall from below with steel bars running at forty-five degree angles. "That's the incubator."

I tried to twist the handle on the door, no luck. "Anything about this incubator that might clue us in on the work Dr. Hearn did in here?"

She shook her head. "It looks like an ordinary tissue-culture incubator with the usual maintenance and backup systems for carbon dioxide and temperature."

"All right. I guess I'll have to hunt up the key. Can you tell me any more about the connection between Dr. Hearn and Dr. Sanford, and the work she was doing in here? Weren't you or anyone else curious?"

Mansell frowned, creased her forehead. "Maybe a little, mostly because of Dr. Hearn's fights with Dr. Camnitz. But it's not unusual for a PhD scientist to work with a clinician to get samples for one line or another of research. They do it all the time."

"How about the fact that she worked alone in this alcove and kept the incubator locked? Didn't that strike anyone as odd?"

"Well, sure. But look, Mr. Baumgartner. This was Dr. Hearn's lab. She treated the techs well, but I told you before, she didn't have any grad students because she could be pretty nasty if you got her back up. And frankly, if she was doing work she didn't want Dr. Camnitz to know about, no one in the lab would've cared. Dr. Camnitz is…can I speak off the record?"

I sighed. I can't remember the last interview where somebody didn't ask to speak off the record. "I'll do whatever I can to see that you don't get embarrassed, but I can't make any promises."

She fidgeted, then let out a little laugh, pure nerves. "I guess I wouldn't want Dr. Camnitz to know I'm saying this. Nobody in the lab likes him, he's such a stuffed shirt. As far as he's concerned, the lab exists for the glory of Dr. Camnitz. We joke that it's the first item in the supervisor's job description to make sure all the help—that's what he calls us, 'the help'—don't forget it for a minute. Nobody in the lab would have said or done anything that would get Dr. Hearn in trouble with Dr. Camnitz, or even worse, get them caught between Dr. Hearn and Dr. Camnitz."

"How long have you been supervisor, Ms. Mansell?"

"Since last September."

"Did the old supervisor leave?"

"You could say that." Another nervous laugh. "She didn't come in to work one day, and no one ever heard from her after that. So they made me temporary supervisor, then after Alma... Alma Wanego had been gone a couple of weeks, they hired me permanently."

"This Alma Wanego never showed up again? Fell off the edge of the earth?"

She nodded vigorously. "Yes."

"Didn't anyone look into it?"

"You mean like file a Missing Person Report?"

"Like anything. When somebody disappears, usually people try to find her, for one reason or another."

"I know Dr. Hearn called her house the day she disappeared, and then a few days later, but all the landlady knew was that Alma didn't come home one day, and she hadn't seen her since. I guess Dr. Hearn didn't think there was any reason to go to the police. Alma was a funny duck, Mr. Baumgartner. We all thought she'd most likely gone off somewhere on a whim."

"Didn't she have any family? Friends? Someone who'd notice she was missing, and go looking for her?"

"I don't have any idea. She never talked about any family, or any friends, for that matter. She was pretty much a loner."

"Was she a good supervisor?"

Little pause, then Mansell's face creased into a crooked smile. "I guess you could say she kept the trains running on time."

"At the cost of executing an engineer or a conductor here and there?"

Mansell took a moment to chew on her lip. "Actually, one tech did leave. Alma could be snippy, and it didn't take much to get her dander up. She didn't tolerate any backtalk, and you didn't question anything she said. Never."

"Interesting. Did she and Dr. Hearn get along?"

"Alma knew better than to mess with Dr. Hearn."

"Did Ms. Wanego do any work here in the alcove with Dr. Hearn?"

"No. Absolutely not. No one did, not under any circumstances. I remember one time when Dr. Hearn was working in here, and I was doing a procedure with Alma around the corner, in the workroom. The other techs were in the main lab, one door down. We heard Dr. Hearn yell, 'Shit' and 'God damn it.' Alma ran in to see what had happened, but she came back faster than she'd gone in. She told me she'd seen a broken glass tube on the floor, with fluid all around it. Then we both heard Dr. Hearn talking on the phone extension in there. We couldn't make out words, or who she was talking to, but then she slammed down the receiver, came through the workroom like a house on fire, charged into her office, and slammed the door. Alma went back into the alcove, just for a few seconds, and when she came back, she said the mess was cleaned up, and the pieces of the tube were in the wastebasket." Mansell took me by the elbow. "I can show you where we were."

I followed her into the adjoining workroom. "See how from here you can look into the hallway? Next thing we knew after Dr. Hearn ran out, Dr. Sanford came tearing through there, toward Dr. Hearn's office, and a few minutes later, we saw them both going back the other way, toward the supplies room. Dr. Hearn looked *really* upset. We thought Dr. Sanford was trying to calm her down."

"Then what?"

"Nothing, at least as far as I know. A little while later, Dr. Hearn was back in the alcove, and spent pretty much the rest of the day there. She never said boo about what happened, and I sure wasn't about to ask her."

"How about Ms. Wanego. Did you talk to her about it?"

"Just once. A couple of days later, I said something like, I wonder what that fuss in the alcove was about, and she shut me right down. Told me walls have ears."

"Can you remember when it happened?"

She closed her eyes, pursed her lips. Her forehead looked like corrugated cardboard. "It was the first week of last August, when we had that terrible heat wave. Everybody was on edge. Right around when Dr. Hearn's accident happened, the techs were complaining to Alma about a janitor making too much noise, working in the hall outside the lab. Then someone made a stink about a blocked drain in the men's room. It was crazy."

"Okay. And you became supervisor in September?"

Mansell nodded. "First temporary, then permanent. Alma took a few days off the week before Labor Day and through the holiday weekend, so I was kind of in charge then. And she was back for...let's see." Mansell closed her eyes, counted on her fingers. "Right, four days before she disappeared. She came to work that Friday, but never showed up over the weekend or the next Monday."

"Did she seem different in any way before she vanished? Worried? Unhappy?"

Mansell shook her head. "Not that I remember."

"Okay. Now, you've got me curious about something. You made it sound like Ms. Wanego didn't have a very good attitude for a supervisor. Why did Dr. Hearn appoint her?"

Mansell's lips moved, but for a few seconds, nothing came out. I waited. Finally, she said, "Technically it was Dr. Hearn's decision, and I was in line to get the job. But Dr. Hearn told me Dr. Camnitz ordered her to give it to Alma. Dr. Hearn did get me a raise, though, and she said we should both hang in and give Alma all the rope she wanted, that she'd hang herself for sure...I guess that's not the best way to put it, but that's what she said."

"But why would Dr. Camnitz think Ms. Wanego was better qualified for the job than you?"

"I don't know. Maybe Dr. Camnitz could tell you."

"Sometimes you get a better answer from the sergeant than you would from the general. Look, Ms. Mansell. My station house is no different from your lab. When strange things happen, people talk about them. Now, here's a department chairman ordering a lab director to appoint someone to supervise a lab full of people who dislike her. I can't believe no one in the lab wondered why, and no one talked about it to anyone else."

"I don't know if I want to spread gossip."

I extended both arms. "Spread it all over me."

She couldn't hold back a little laugh. "All right. The word was, Dr. Camnitz and Alma were having an affair. Satisfied?"

"I'm getting there. Was it 'They must be having an affair, why else would he have insisted she get the job?' Or was there anything specific?"

Mansell picked at her teeth with the point of a pencil. "Well, for one thing, Lois Rockford—she was the supervisor before Alma—Lois told me she once brought Alma up for insubordination, but Alma got off with a warning, which really bugged Lois. So she went to Personnel, and they told her 'somebody with influence' had gotten involved, and made it pretty clear who that somebody was."

She frowned. "Also, Alma took a lot of short vacations, a few days here, a few days there, and they always seemed to be when Dr. Camnitz was away too, usually at a medical meeting. In fact, the time she took off right before she disappeared was one of those. I remember because the techs complained to Alma that two of them had scheduled time off for the Labor Day weekend far in advance, and for Alma to also be away would mean the two techs who weren't scheduled off would have to work around the clock to keep experiments going on schedule. The techs filed a complaint with Personnel, but by the time it got attended to, Alma had already disappeared."

"To no one's great sorrow."

"No one that *I* knew, anyway."

She started to get up. "I'm sorry, but I really do have to get to work now."

"That's fine. You've been very helpful. One more quick question. Do you have Ms. Wanego's address, where she used to live?"

"Yes, that'd still be in the files. I'll get it for you."

"Thanks. Then I'll leave you alone." I fished a card out of my wallet, put it into her hand. "If you think of anything else you'd like to tell me, please give me a call. And in the meantime, I'd like you to keep what we've talked about strictly to yourself."

She nodded. "I will, Mr. Baumgartner."

"And don't worry about Dr. Camnitz hearing anything of what you've told me."

Finally, a genuine smile. "I'd really appreciate that."

Twenty minutes driving uptown took me to the Sheepskin District, with its narrow streets and small frame houses, most of them rented to students, junior faculty, and staff. The address I had for Alma Wanego was on Northwest Forty-Sixth Street, between Nineteenth and Twentieth, a yellow frame two-story with a waist-high wraparound porch. I rang the bell three times before I heard someone call, "Just a minute, be right there."

Finally, a young woman opened the door and peered through through the screen, shading her eyes like the light bothered her. She wore a light blue blouse, nothing underneath, and a pair of red shorts. No shoes.

"If you're selling something, forget it," she said.

I pulled out the badge, held it up to the screen. "Detective Baumgartner, Emerald Police," I said. "Can I come in and ask you a few questions?"

"What about?"

"Alma Wanego."

"She doesn't live here any more."

"I know that. Look, Ms…"

"Corrigan. Katie Corrigan."

"Ms. Corrigan. I'm sorry to bother you, but I'm investigating a serious crime, and I need to talk to you."

She mugged impatience as she unhooked the latch on the screen door. "Did something happen to Alma? I haven't seen her since last September. Did you guys re-open the case, or something?"

"Or something. Okay if I come inside?"

"Sure, if you don't mind it's a little messy."

"If I had a problem with messes, I wouldn't be in police work."

I followed her into the living room. 'A little messy' didn't quite say it. The room was a hodgepodge of dirty dishes and glasses, scattered books and papers. T-shirts, shorts, and a bunch of female underwear were all over a sofa with a torn green corduroy cover. Katie tossed a brassiere and a pair of almost-nonexistent panties onto the floor, grinned, and motioned me over. "Have a seat."

I sat at the end of the sofa. Katie tilted a wooden chair forward, dumping probably a hundred sheets of paper, then sat. Her breasts bulged above the top of her low-cut blouse. She was a full-bodied woman, olive skinned, with huge deep brown eyes over a nose with a prominent bridge and wide lips. I pointed at her copper hair. "Except for that, you look more like a Caterina Columbini than a Katie Corrigan."

Katie shrugged. "My mother was Italian. She always did call the shots."

I wondered if she'd put it that way on purpose. While I was thinking about it, she used both hands to rake her hair back behind her ears. "What can I do for you, Mr. Bumgarter?"

That struck me funny; I laughed. Which set Katie laughing, too. The air in the room seemed to clear. "I'm hoping you can give me some information." I said. "We're taking a look at Alma Wanego's disappearance."

"Now? It's been more than half a year."

I nodded. Sometimes things come up. Did you move in here after Alma left?"

"No. There's two bedrooms upstairs, and Mrs. Harrison, that's the landlady, she rents this place out to two women at a time. Alma was here before I came, and it'll be two years in September since I moved in."

"So you were here with Alma for just about a year before she disappeared."

"Simple arithmetic, yeah. Hey, did you find her body, or something?"

I shook my head. "Have you heard anything from Alma since last September? Anything at all?"

"Not a word. After she was gone a month, Mrs. Harrison asked me to help pack up her stuff, and she rented out the other half of the apartment to somebody else."

"Where does Mrs. Harrison live?"

Katie jerked a thumb over her shoulder. "Right next door. She likes to keep a watch on what goes on around here."

I did a slow sweep of the room with my eyes.

"No sweat, it's cool for another week. The old battle-ax is off visiting her sister in Michigan. Besides, the plaster walls're real thick in these old houses. There's a lot you can get away with if you just keep the windows shut."

"I'm sure. Who's the new renter? Is she around?"

Katie snorted. "You kidding? Patty's a pre-med. She was off to the library the minute it opened, and she won't be back till they throw her out at midnight. I wouldn't want to be a pre-med for anything. Not with the hours they gotta work."

"What's your major?"

She made a face. "I majored in Psych for two years, but my grades weren't good enough and I lost my scholarship. So now I'm a secretary in the Psych Department. I'm trying to save up and go back and finish school."

"What happened to Alma's things after you and Mrs. Harrison packed them up?"

"We stored them in the basement. Mrs. Harrison didn't want any legal crap if Alma showed up and wanted her stuff. It's a full basement, and the boxes hardly even took up a whole corner."

"What did you and Alma talk about? Guys? Family? Hobbies? I'm looking for anything that might give me some idea why she disappeared."

Katie shook her head. "Alma and I weren't real close. Frankly, she was a pretty weird person. She had this look that got you to thinking maybe she could read what was in your mind, creepy, you know? And she could be pretty sarcastic."

"Did you ever meet any of her friends or her family?"

"She never did say much about herself, but I do know her parents died in a car crash a long time ago. And I never heard anything about brothers or sisters."

"Any boyfriends?"

"Not that I knew about. But there *was* this one thing…"

I shifted my ass away from a spring that was threatening to pop through the sofa cushion and give me the goose of my life. "What's that?"

"See, Alma had this habit of going off for maybe three days here, five days there, without saying anything to anybody. And then, like out of nowhere, she'd be back. Once, when I asked her where she'd been, she gave me that so-what look and said she'd gone fishing. Please. Alma didn't like the out-of-doors, never went camping or anything like that. She said if God wanted us to sleep on the ground in tents, He wouldn't have given us mattresses and box springs."

"But when she was gone a week, two weeks, a month, still nobody called Missing Persons?"

A dark red smudge spread over Katie's cheekbones. "Mrs. Harrison said she figured Alma must've decided to beat her out of the next month's rent, so she didn't see any reason to go to all the bother of reporting her missing. I guess maybe *I* should've put in a report, but I didn't want Mrs. Harrison to get pissed off and kick me out. Now, I'm feeling a little bad about it."

"Don't. We've all got things we wish we could do over. Do you remember anything about those times she was away? You said they weren't for very long. Was there anything that linked them together? Time of the month or year? Did she ever say anything about them, besides the bit about fishing?"

Slow shake of the head. "No…nothing really. I never thought a lot about it, or kept track. Why would I? I'm pretty sure the last one was right before she disappeared, but that's the best I can do. Sorry."

"That's okay. You can't tell me what you don't know."

"What do you think happened to her, Mr. Baumgartner? Do you have any idea?"

"I wish. Tell you what, Katie. Can you show me where Alma's things are stored? That might be a big help."

Katie grinned. We were friends, now. "Sure, but let me get some shoes on first. I don't want to walk barefoot in that basement. There's mice."

◇◇◇

The concrete basement was damp and cold, and the only light came from an unshaded ceiling fixture to the side of the furnace, switched on from the foot of a treacherous steep wooden stairway. Without the flashlight Katie carried, it would have been the easiest thing in the world to go down those stairs ass over teakettle. She led me to the far end of the room, and pointed at a small pile of cartons. "That's it."

I peered into the corner. "That's all of it? Only six cartons?"

"Yeah, there wasn't much. Alma's room looked like a nun's cell. Just the bed, chair, desk, and a little dresser that came with the room. Nothing hanging on the walls. Like I said, she was different."

"Okay. Let's take a look. You mind holding the flashlight for me?"

"No, it's fun, actually. I mean, being part of a police investigation. Where do you want to start?"

I thought about whether I ought to get a warrant, but Mel wanted the work done quietly, didn't he? "Let's start at the bottom," I said. "I'll unpile the boxes, then go through them one at a time, and stack them back up."

The first two cartons were full of underwear, socks, blouses, jeans, slacks, and dresses. I looked over each article, checked the pockets, shook them over the floor. "Wow, you guys're pretty compulsive," Katie said.

"We damn well better be," I grunted, then packed the clothes back into the cartons and set them against the wall. As I pulled the lid open on the third carton, Katie leaned forward to look, and started breathing into my ear. Her breast pressed against my shoulder. Thirty years earlier, I'd have been distracted. I rummaged through five empty pocketbooks and four pairs of shoes, then closed the lid and tossed the box onto the pile.

The fourth box looked more interesting, stuff that probably had been in the desk. Pencils, pens, erasers, pads of paper, envelopes. Who did she write to? A screwdriver and a small hammer. Couple of bus passes. A passport. "Whoa," I said. "Let's have a look here."

Katie aimed the flashlight at my hands. I turned the blue plastic cover, and looked at the picture inside. You don't expect a passport photo to be flattering, but no mistake, Alma Wanego was or had been a good-looking woman. Very Nordic, light hair, fair skin, thin lips tightly closed, so her mouth looked like a surgical incision. But it was her eyes that really got me, staring so hard into the camera that I had trouble pulling my own eyes free. This was someone who could be a cross to bear *and* a bear to cross.

I ran a finger down the pages with entries, then looked at Katie. "This was issued eight years ago, and through 1974, she made only one foreign trip, to Bermuda. But in 'seventy-five, there was a trip to Mexico and one to England, and last year there were three, France, then England, then Norway. All of them short, none more than a week."

"Yeah, well, that's what I was telling you," Katie said. "And those aren't near-all the times she was away. I don't get it. I mean, this house is okay, but if I could afford to do all this traveling to Europe and places, I sure wouldn't be living here."

I smiled. "Maybe she wasn't paying for the trips."

Katie giggled. "At least not with money."

"No. But look here. The last trip, the one to Norway, was August thirty-first, with a return on September sixth. That was just five days before she disappeared. Do you remember anything from then?"

Katie knitted her brows. "Not really...wait, yes I do. When she came back, it was on a holiday, Labor Day. Was that the sixth?"

I shrugged.

"Yeah, I remember that because my sweetie and I went to the coast for the holiday weekend. When I got back, Alma was there, and when I told her where I'd been, she laughed, sort of snotty. Then I said something about how my weekend wasn't cheap, and I was gonna have to eat Spaghetti-O's for while. That made her laugh again, and she said, 'I'm not going to have to worry about that.'"

"'I'm not going to?' Or 'I'm not going to have to?'"

"Pretty sure it was 'not going to have to.' And then she flipped me the smug mug."

"Real tease, that Alma."

"Not the nice kind of tease, either. It was always like she was laughing at you. I figured, well, maybe she found herself a boyfriend or a sugar daddy, good for her."

I slipped the passport into my pocket. "Let's look at the last box. Jeez, heavy."

The reason for that was obvious as soon as I opened the carton. I pulled out a Remington manual typewriter, set it on the floor. Then I reached back into the carton, and came out with a wooden box about a foot long, four inches high. Katie shrugged when I held it up to her. "Yeah, I remember that. It was up on top of her closet shelf, behind the typewriter. Mrs. Harrison and I almost left it there, we didn't see it at first."

I pulled at the lid, but it stayed shut. I squinted at the small slot surrounded by a metal ring, a bit below the edge of the lid. "It's locked."

If a woman who seemed not to give a hoot in hell about material possessions had thought enough to lock something inside this box, I definitely wanted to see it. But not in front of this particular audience. I set the box on the floor, off to the side. "Aren't you going to open it?" Katie said. "I thought you guys could open up whatever lock you wanted."

I shook my head. "I don't think I can get into it without doing some damage, and I don't like to damage peoples' property. I'll take it with me, and get it opened cleanly."

Katie pouted. "Meanie."

"How'd you feel if the cops broke open a box of yours, instead of taking a little time to get the right key? Let's see what else is here."

As it turned out, there was only a small lamp, an alarm clock, and a radio. I put them and the typewriter back into the carton, then hefted it up to the top of the pile. "Thanks, Katie," I said. "I appreciate your help."

She jutted a hip, turned a crooked smile on me. "Maybe I'll see you again?"

"You never know."

◇◇◇

My usual procedure would've been to take that box to the station and get one of the lock-and-key boys to pop it open, but Mel said he didn't want people talking up this case around the station. Okay, Mel. I got into the car, turned the key in the ignition, and drove off.

Fifteen minutes later, I pulled up in front of Iggy the Key's Lock Shop, on Sixty-fifth Street, just off Ravine Boulevard. Another minute, I was inside, mysterious box in my right hand. I smiled at the hello I knew I was about to get.

Iggy was behind the counter, working on a lock. As he looked up, his bland expression of welcome to a customer morphed into surprise, then into his trademark left-sided grin. The right side of Iggy's mouth doesn't move. It's called Bell's Palsy. The nerve that supplies the lower part of the face on one side sometimes stops working, nobody knows why. "Hey, Mr. B, how you doin'?" Iggy crowed. "It's been a while. You got a job for me, or is this a social visit?"

Irwin McKeesport, a.k.a. Iggy the Key, has been my friend and occasional Guy Friday for more than five years. When it came to appearances, God was not overly kind to Ig. Besides having a dead facial nerve, he was barely five-two, with close-set beady eyes that made him look snakey, a honker that would've given Durante jealousy fits, and cheeks that were relief maps of a teenager's long-lost Battle of Acne.

But Iggy's the best lock-and-key man in Emerald, hands down. I got to know him when I was going after a scuzzbag who'd been getting into places he had no right to get into, departing with choice items of high market value, and more often than you'd expect by chance, finding a woman on the premises and leaving her with the most disgusting, sadistic injuries I've ever seen.

Then, one morning when I came into the station, here was this round little character with a half-paralyzed face, waiting for me. Iggy broke down and cried while he told me about the creep who'd been putting the screws to him to get doors open, and the six-inch purple bruise he showed me over his right kidney was evidence enough of the way the bastard worked. "He told me if I didn't make him keys, he was gonna kill me, inch by inch," Iggy said. "You know, tweezers and ice picks and shit. But I can't stand what he's doin'. One of these times, he's gonna kill one of them poor women. If you gotta lock me up, go ahead, but just get him stopped." Then, Iggy told me where the next attack was going to happen.

I told Iggy to get the guy his key. Next night, when the weasel slipped the key into the lock, I was waiting for him.

Iggy was double-dip grateful to me for getting the sadist off him, and for getting *him* off without jail time or even a court appearance, and he's returned the favor many times over. Cops do well to have a guy like that in the wings. Better yet is knowing they can trust the guy.

"Not a social visit, Iggy," I said. "I've got a job for you. Interested?"

He rubbed his chin, then looked at me, all squinty-eyed. "I ain't never gonna say no to you, Mr. B. You want something, all you gotta do is say what. And you notice, I ain't asking any questions."

I laughed. "You've got a way with words." I set the wooden box on the table in front of him.

The little guy had you-gotta-be-kidding-me all over his face. He jabbed a finger at the box. "Mr. B, I don't believe this. You need the help of a professional to get this piece of shit open?"

"I could crack it with a knife blade, or stomp it into splinters, Ig. But I've got no idea what's inside, and whatever it is, I want to find it in the right number of pieces. And I need to have the job done very privately."

Doubt spread across Iggy's pan. "It ain't gonna blow up on me, is it?"

I shrugged. "No idea what's inside. Tell you what. Get me a key, then stand back, and *I'll* open it."

He marched off, not another word, down the stairs into the basement. Inside three minutes, he was back, holding up two flat keys. "If at least one of these don't do the job, I'll eat that box." He slid the first key into the slot, wiggled it, twisted his wrist. "Close." Then he withdrew the key ever so slightly, and worked it gently back and forth. "I can feel...yeah." The key spun 180 degrees. He threw the lid open.

We gawked into the box, then at each other. "Dip me in shit," Iggy whispered. He chugged out from behind the counter, threw the lock on his front door, turned the cardboard sign to CLOSED, and pulled down the shade behind it. Then he came running back to stand beside me and rubberneck over the box. "Whew, talk about long green. How much d'you think that is?"

I pulled a handful of bills out of the box, riffled the stack. "All hundreds," I said. "Let's start counting."

It took only a few minutes. "I've got fifty-four," I said. "How about you?"

"Forty-six." Iggy pulled a grimy handkerchief from his pocket, wiped at his forehead. "That's ten K even."

"Not what you'd find when someone's been dropping change into a piggy bank. Smells like a payment."

Iggy nodded. "Question is, was it one gonna be made, or one received?"

"Could be either. This was in a carton with stuff from a woman who vanished about eight months ago. No idea whether she got the money or was going to give it, but either way I can't see her leaving it behind if she decided on her own to go off where nobody could find her."

Iggy jerked his head in the direction of the box and the two piles of hundred-dollar bills. "So now what?"

"So now you get me a key that any moron can use to open or lock this box."

Iggy pulled the key he'd used out of the lock, held it up to the light, and squinted. "Piece a cake. I can fix this one in two minutes."

"Good. And after you do that, I'm betting you've got a spot out back with a good heavy lock where we can stow this box away."

He froze. "You're gonna leave that dough here? Ten grand?"

"Trust me, Ig. I need to leave it in the safest place I can find. Who's going to have a better lockup than you?"

He shook his head, then picked up the box. "Come on, I'll show you where. I don't want to worry if I die from a heart attack or a stroke or something, and you can't find it, you'll beat the crap out of me."

Chapter Seven

Baumgartner

"Bernie, God damn it to hell. Talk to me."

I blinked at Irma across the living room, in the antique rocker. Her mother's chair, her mother's daughter. Another minute, she'd be blowing fire out of both nostrils. "What do you want me to say?"

"How about telling me where your head was. What were you thinking about? A case, right? *Your* case."

"My case, yes."

"Surprise, surprise. So tell me about your case. I can't stand another whole evening of you just sitting there, like I don't exist."

"I could never think you don't exist. And I'm sorry, but you know I can't discuss an open case with you."

She snorted. "Yeah, I know. I just thought, maybe once… forget it. Do you think tomorrow you'll be permitted to tell me what you think of the tulip fields."

Oh, shit, I forgot. "Irma, I'm sorry again. I've got to go up to the Medical Library tomorrow and do some research."

"For your case, right?"

"Right."

"So it doesn't matter you promised we'd go up to La Conner tomorrow and walk through the tulip fields."

"Yes, it matters. Problem is, I made the promise before this case hit. I really *am* sorry, Irma, but I need to pick up some background in a hurry. We can go see the tulips next weekend."

"Next weekend? In case you haven't noticed, today's April thirtieth. The tulips are all but done. The biggest tulip fields outside of Holland are an hour's drive away, and as far as we're concerned, they might as well be in China. We put off going last weekend and the weekend before because you had too much work to do. And please don't tell me, 'I'm a cop.' Say that, and I'm going to lose it. I'm sick and tired of being married to the Emerald Police Force. By the time they finally kick you out, we're going to be too old, too sick, too whatever to do anything else."

"Irma, how many times do we need to go down this road? I live to investigate crimes, and right now what I want most of all is find out why some poor schizo shot a lab scientist and then killed himself. Can't you understand that?"

Irma swallowed hard, then started talking like an automatic machine. Imagine moving out of a howling wind into the eye of a hurricane. "Bernie, I just felt something snap. When I first met you, I thought the way you were dedicated to justice was sexy as hell. You went after me in bed the way you went after your bad guys. Back in 'fifty-three, people really did believe marriage was for life, and I bought it, one hundred percent. But in twenty-four years, a person learns fanatics are no picnic to live with. You're only fifty-two. You've still got time. Don't give yourself a heart attack. If life gives you lemons—"

"Irma, don't tell me to make lemonade. Please? If I quit the force, what I'm going to make is bile, and I'll taste it every minute of every day. Cop work is what counts for me. Anything else would be just passing time till I fall over dead. I think *I'd* probably shoot myself if all I had to look forward to every day was the ocean out past the rail of a cruise boat. Look, maybe I can get done at the library early enough, and we can run up to La Conner afterwards."

Irma jumped out of her chair. "That's it. I give up. You could at least spare me the lies. We both know you're not going to be home early tomorrow. Fine. Enjoy yourself. But count me out. I swear, you're going to drive me to…do something."

I opened my mouth to tell her I wished I could give her what she wanted, but before I could say a word, she stomped off, into the kitchen. A few minutes later, she came sailing past me in the other direction, didn't look at me, just barged up the stairs. Then the bedroom door slammed.

Chapter Eight

Baumgartner

I wouldn't have said it to Irma, but a library wasn't really the place I'd have picked to spend a whole nice Sunday. I was there at nine o'clock, and the place was deserted, so it was easy to buttonhole one of the librarians, explain what I was looking for, and have her get me started. She checked through indexes in magazines called *Nature* and *Lancet* and *The American Journal of Obstetrics and Gynecology*, and inside of an hour, I had a pile of magazines with articles about Sperm Density Gradient Separation, and research on eggs and embryos.

Only two articles were on Density Gradient Separation, and they said less than I'd heard from Laurie Mansell the day before. I was through them inside fifteen minutes, then went on to the write-ups about eggs and embryos.

Not that it was easy going, but after my talk with Mansell, I could follow the gist of the work. There was a lot about fertilizing mouse eggs that had been treated with different chemicals, or too much carbon dioxide, or not enough oxygen, or the wrong temperature, and then looking at the chromosomes in the embryos, to see which stuff made a mouse embryo get too many chromosomes, or too few.

From what I could understand, human eggs and embryos were even fussier than mouse tissues. The culture medium had zero room for errors in measuring out all the different chemicals that went into it. The water had to be sterile, and come from a certain company. The petri dish had to be a particular brand, or else something in the plastic would kill the embryos. The temperature had to be right on, same for the carbon dioxide concentration. Almost every article ended with something like, "These findings will need to be corroborated by more extensive studies." Which was going to be tough, given that human eggs were so hard to come by.

Toward mid-afternoon, my eyes started to go glassy, but then I noticed something. A lot of the articles were written by a couple of guys named Robert G. Edwards and Patrick Steptoe, or occasionally, Steptoe and Edwards. Some of their work had to do with how chromosomes in embryos looked and behaved, but it was obvious that their real interest was a procedure they called in vitro fertilization, where they fertilized eggs in the laboratory, then kept the embryos alive and developing normally in an incubator. Edwards and Steptoe said some day, doctors would treat infertile couples by taking an egg from a woman and sperm from her husband, mixing them together, then putting the embryo into the woman's uterus. In other words, "test-tube babies." That, I'd heard about, on TV and in newspapers.

All of a sudden, I was wide awake. I separated out the articles by Edwards and Steptoe, and went through them again, more carefully. Most were research pieces, and a lot of the stuff was pretty technical, past what I could understand. But what came through loud and clear in the most recent articles was that Edwards and Steptoe had been able to grow embryos right up to the point where they'd be ready to implant in a uterus.

I looked through a couple of Review Articles, and those filled in some blanks for me. Edwards and Steptoe made the point that "test tube baby" isn't the right term, because fertilization and those first few days of embryo development take place in plastic petri dishes, the same as in Dr. Hearn's mouse experiments. Edwards had done work on mice, too, which sounded like carbon copies of Hearn's experiments. Also, Steptoe, the guy who got the eggs for Edwards, was some kind of gynecological superstar with an instrument called a laparoscope, which he used to take eggs out of a woman's ovary without having to cut open her belly. I filed that away for future reference.

At that point, I went up to the desk where my librarian-friend was sitting, staring at the ceiling, and asked if she could find me more articles on in vitro fertilization. She did, in spades. There were pieces in scientific journals, more of the same like I'd been reading, but there were also little books, transcripts of conferences about in vitro fertilization, where scientists talked about their experiments and the general state of the research, and the effect that work was going to have on society.

One doctor with a lot of initials after his name thought artificial fertilization techniques were going to be the end of family life as we know it, and we should never, ever, use them, but another doctor with the same number of initials said it would be a great thing for infertile couples, so we should hop on the stick and get it done. Some of the writers were in favor of in vitro fertilization because it would let people be born who otherwise would never exist, but others worried that the procedure might produce defective babies, and since there wasn't any way to test it out without actually doing it, we should be smart enough not to try it at all. They kept using the word "hubris," which I finally went and looked up. Pretty heavy stuff.

Seven in the evening by the time I left the Medical Library. I hadn't stopped to eat all day, I had a killer headache, and my eyeballs felt like they'd gotten a rubdown with 1500 grit sandpaper. But I knew a whole lot more than I had the day before. One thing I knew for sure. This was the hottest field in medicine. A one-way ticket to Easy Street was ready and waiting for the first doctor who produced an in vitro baby. That doc would die with a gold spoon in his mouth, and he'd know that people would be talking and writing about him five hundred years in the future. Something like that could really pump up the head of a guy like Sanford.

◇◇◇

Irma was going to throw a fit. Earlier in the day, I thought maybe I could get through the research stuff in time to run her up to La Conner and see the tulips. But from the minute I glommed onto in vitro fertilization, I couldn't think about anything else till I walked in the door of my house. "Irma, I'm home," I shouted, and got myself ready for the barrage. But nothing happened. I shouted again, still no answer.

I ran up the stairs, looked in the bedroom. No Irma. She wasn't in the bathroom, either. So I went back downstairs, into the kitchen, and there was a note on the table. "I went up to La Conner with Henry Streator."

Henry Streator is one of my brother-cops. He lives a couple of blocks away. Irma got to be friends with Henry's wife Bessie, mostly on an I'll-listen-to-your-cop's-wife-sob-story-if-you'll-listen-to-mine basis. The four of us would go out to dinner, maybe a movie, once every week or two. But then last year, Bessie died, dropped dead on the street one day, only forty-eight years old, and since then, Irma hasn't been able to do enough for poor Henry. I dropped the note back on the table, and went out to get some food.

Chapter Nine

Sanford

I wiped a napkin across my mouth, then looked at my mother, down at the end of the table nearest the kitchen. "Good dinner, Mom."

Which it was anything but. 'Inspired' is not a word I'd ever use to describe my mother's cooking. That evening's slab of unseasoned cod, broiled to near-rubber, took even more than the usual amount of water to get down.

Mom humphed. "If you'd managed to pay a little attention to Carmel, you'd be getting good meals every night."

My mother's never been able to see more than one side to either a story or a person, and the side she sees when I'm involved is never one favorable to me. "Carmel was a labor room nurse," I said. "She knew what it would be like, married to an OBGYN."

Mom tightened her lips. "She still had a right to *some* of your attention. You could have at least taken in a partner."

One of the red highways on my mother's map. "I did, Mother, twice, in fact. It didn't work out."

"Because you didn't want it to work out." She pointed toward Dad, who hadn't said a word in the past ten minutes. "Your father had partners, and when they were on call, he was off. Why couldn't you ever let another doctor deliver one of *your* patients now and then?"

"I've told you, Mom, things are different now. Pregnant women like to know that barring some emergency, *their* doctor will deliver their baby, and they tell all their friends that's the way it goes in Dr. Sanford's office. When Dad was practicing, the University docs wouldn't set their hands on a patient if they could possibly avoid it, but now they're trying to sell themselves to the public as genius professors. I've got to be able to compete with that."

Dad aimed the points of his fork in my direction. "You could've been a professor yourself, Colin. You had a brilliant record in med school."

Brilliant enough, but no amount of time in a research lab, boiling urine to isolate abnormal body chemicals, could compete with treating patients like the Russian woman I followed in labor during my residency. Except for the nurses, who came and went every eight hours, I was her only human contact during thirty hours of fear and pain. After I finally delivered her of a healthy eight-pound son, she gripped my hand with both of hers, and asked, "What you' name, Dr. Sanford, you' first name." "Colin," I told her. "C-O-L-I-N." She pointed to the baby in the bassinet. "That *his* name," she said. "Colin Yushenko." Then, there was the young Mexican woman whose baby's heart rate dropped out during her final stages of pushing. I rushed her into the delivery room, put on forceps, pulled the baby out, unwrapped the cord from around its neck, and resuscitated it. The husband worked in a bicycle shop, and next day, he showed up at the hospital with a beautiful ten-speed bike that he insisted I accept, or he would be offended. "I thank God you were my wife's doctor," he said. "I bet no other doctor coulda saved my baby, and don't try and tell me different." So I didn't try.

I pushed my father's fork down to the table. "Dad, we don't need to go through this again. Those hypocrites at the U tee me off, that's all. There's not one of them who can say honestly that my patients would be better off with him than they are with me."

"You're smug, Colin," said my mother. "You think you're better than other people. You should be ashamed, the way you ignored Carmel. But you're not ashamed of anything. Not even that you make money by killing babies, or that your misbehavior robbed the world of a great genius."

The killing-babies bit started some six years back, when I became the first doctor in Emerald to do amniocentesis for the detection of fetal genetic abnormalities. To my mother, that was guilt by association, since the abnormal fetuses would be aborted. As for the other issue, she'd never stopped blaming me for what had happened to my brother, Victor. He was some kind of prodigy; from the age of two or three, my parents had had a private tutor for him. He was going to be tearing college curricula apart by the time he was ten. But he never got past five.

She sat rigid, as always, eyes hidden behind dark glasses. She'd started wearing them after Victor died, because she didn't want people to see her crying, but she'd never gone back to clear lenses. Sometimes when I was a kid, I'd go up to the attic and look through old picture albums, and I was always taken aback at how vivacious my mother had looked. For as long as I can remember, though, her skin has been sallow, and her face expressionless, as if smiles came under heavy rationing nearly forty years ago, and the restriction was never lifted. "I guess maybe I should be, Mom," I said quietly.

Dad gave me a look that said, "Thank you." Then he cleared his throat, his usual introduction to a change of subject. "That's quite a commotion they've been having over at the Medical Center. Terrible."

Mom got up, began to clear plates. Dad talked on. "I'll bet you're glad to be at Puget Community. The people in the University OB Department must be going crazy."

"There's plenty of spillover, Dad. The woman was a Puget Community patient. And if you want to talk specifics, she's *my* patient."

"*Your* patient. For heaven's sake. How is she taking it?"

"About the way you'd expect."

"Do you have any idea why her husband—"

"No. None at all."

Dad straightened in his chair, the better to look down at me. "I'm sure this has been hard for you, Colin, but you don't need to bite my head off."

Mom glided between us to pick up my plate, and gave me another unforgiving look, whether because I'd spoken to my father in that tone, or because I'd lived and Victor had died. Maybe both. "Sorry, Dad," I said. "I really have been pretty tense. I've got no idea why Mr. Kennett went over the edge."

Dad shook his head. "I don't envy you having to deal with her right now."

I shrugged. "Part of the game. While she was in the hospital, I practically lived in her room, and now that she's gone home, I'll go see her there every day."

"She's not home alone, is she?"

"Her mother's staying with her."

Dad drummed fingers on the table, early warning of something coming. "I read in the paper that the scientist who was murdered had done some sort of fertility procedure for the killer's wife. Might that have had anything to do with it?"

I couldn't tell my father the procedure was Density Gradient Separation, not with what I had in mind to announce as soon as I could. One thing to lie to news reporters and cops, another thing entirely to sail a whopper across the dinner table to my father, then have to repudiate it a week later. "I don't see how," I said. "It worked, didn't it? And according to Ms. Kennett, her husband went over to thank Dr. Hearn."

To all intents and purposes, my mother, at the far end of the table, was fully involved in slicing her infamous white cake with cream cheese icing, but I knew better. Behind those dark glasses, she was a recording machine, capable of repeating a ten-minute discussion verbatim. Like those musical geniuses who can listen to a tune played on a piano, and repeat it, note for note, mistakes and all. I remembered a winter day when I was six or seven, and started to walk across a frozen pond near our house. After a few steps, there was a loud creak. "Watch out, kid," a man called from the edge of the pond. "You're on thin ice."

"If Mr. Kennett had had any concerns or problems, I'm sure he'd have come to me," I said, one eye on my mother. "He and I had developed a close relationship, all through the workup and the pregnancy. He'd never even met Dr. Hearn."

Dad looked like a man who'd just noticed a fly in his soup. "I gather you don't want to tell us about this fertility procedure."

I didn't dare speak into the microphone of that recording machine at the end of the table. "It's not that I don't want to," I said, and I've never spoken truer words. "But right now, I can't. Ms. Kennett is pretty fragile, and I promised her I wouldn't speak about it to anyone until she's gotten herself back together."

My father knew bullshit when he smelled it, but I had him tied up. No way would Dr. Arthur Sanford ask me to violate a patient's confidence.

"If I ever can talk about it, you'll be the first to know," I said. "And I think you'll be impressed."

"Hmmm." Dad scowled as he passed me a slice of cake on a plate. I waited for my mother to remind me I could be enjoying white cake with cream cheese icing every night, had I only shown Carmel a little consideration. But she stayed quiet. She knew when silence would serve her purpose better than any words.

Chapter Ten

Baumgartner

Irma must've had herself a nice long tiptoe through the tulips. By the time she got back, I'd had dinner, taken a shower, and gotten into bed. When I heard her come into the bedroom, the clock on the night table said eleven-twenty. I pretended to be asleep.

When the alarm went off in the morning, she didn't budge. Usually, that bell sends her straight up in the air, but she was going to take her turn at faking sleep. I shaved, got myself some breakfast, and headed out.

I stopped at the station, checked the preliminary autopsy reports on Hearn and James Kennett. Like I'd figured, negative and negative. No tumors or any other pathology in what was left of the shooter's brain, and except for holes in her chest, heart, and left lung, the vic's body was entirely normal. I thought of stopping to update the chief, but decided I really didn't want to see him right then, he probably didn't want to see me, so why not make both of us a little happier on a Monday morning.

◇◇◇

Now that I'd learned what I had about in vitro fertilization, I zeroed in on that locked incubator in Dr. Hearn's inner sanctum. I could have buttonholed someone at the station to open sesame for me, but again, Mel had been more than clear about working quietly. So I drove over to Iggy's shop, and got him to close up for a couple of hours.

Laurie Mansell took us into her office, where I introduced her to Detective Irwin. "I need to look inside Dr. Hearn's locked incubator," I said.

She began to fidget, trying hard not to stare at Iggy. "I don't know…" She twiddled her thumbs against her forefingers, bit on her lip. "Aren't you supposed to have a search warrant or something?"

"Not if I have probable cause, and not if a delay might impede the investigation of a crime scene. If that material happens to get taken away or altered before I've had the chance to examine it, I'm afraid you'd be facing a charge of obstructing a police investigation. Neither one of us wants that."

Any time or money Ms. Mansell might've spent in tanning parlors was wasted. She steadied herself against the edge of her desk. "Don't you think it would be better for you to speak to Dr. Camnitz? I'd hate for him to get sore at me."

I shook my head. "I need to keep the investigation low-key, and I'm not ready to talk to Dr. Camnitz yet. If he ever bothers you over this, give me a call, and I'll take the heat." I pointed to Iggy, standing next to me, sympathy all over his ugly face. "Detective Irwin'll have us inside that incubator in two minutes, tops, not a scratch on it, and after we've seen what's in there, he'll lock it back up. If any of your staff asks why we were here, we didn't tell you." I smiled. "Why don't we just do it, and get it over with?"

Two deep breaths. I thought she might bite through her lower lip. "I guess so."

◇◇◇

I'd learned from those research articles on tissue culture that the point of locks on biological incubators isn't to prevent theft, but to stop some idiot from opening the door and screwing up the temperature or the amount of carbon dioxide in the air. So they're not terribly sophisticated. Iggy had this one open almost instantly. I peered inside. Two wire shelves, bottom one empty, but the top shelf held a small round plastic container with a cover. I looked at Ms. Mansell. "What's that?"

"A petri dish."

"What's in it?"

"I guess some kind of tissue culture. I'd have to look under a microscope."

There was a small binocular microscope on the worktable behind us. I pointed at it and shrugged. Mansell nodded, then took an envelope from a cardboard box next to the incubator, carefully slipped a pair of latex gloves out of the package and onto her hands, rinsed off the powder with a little sterile water. Then she took the petri dish from the incubator, sat at the microscope, put the dish onto the viewing platform, turned on the scope, and lowered her eyes to the oculars. She moved the dish side to side, front to back. Finally, she frowned and shook her head. "All I can see is fragments. Dead tissue."

"No idea what it was?"

"Knowing what Dr. Hearn worked on, I'd have to guess it was some egg or embryonic tissue, but I can't say more than that." She stood, then motioned me to the seat.

I peered through the eyepieces. "Looks like tiny little brown dirt particles, floating in water."

"Not water. Culture medium."

"Could it be analyzed to find out exactly what's in it, and then we'd know what she was culturing?"

"'Fraid not. For one thing, the culture media for experiments in this lab are pretty similar, just small differences here and there, depending on whether you're dealing with eggs, sperm, embryos, or other tissues." She looked at a paper label on the cover of the dish. "And for another thing, it's been in here for five days. By now, the composition of any culture medium is going to be very different from what it was at the start."

I bent to look at the label. Below the date, 4/27/77, "SW" was printed in neat block letters. "Recognize this handwriting?" I asked.

Ms. Mansell nodded. "Dr. Hearn. She's...she *was* the only one in the lab who used a fountain pen."

"Okay, thanks. You can put it back now." I gave Iggy the nod. "Close the box up again for her. One more thing, Ms. Mansell. What kind of records did Dr. Hearn keep of the work in this lab?"

"Oh, she was a stickler for complete and accurate records—which was good, don't misunderstand me. There's a log for every experiment in the lab, three specific lines of investigation, so three logs. Dr. Hearn held weekly review sessions where we went over all the logs, and if there were any mistakes, we'd pick them up." She pointed toward the main lab. "They're all out there. Do you want to look at them?"

"Only if they have anything to do with the work Dr. Hearn did in here."

"I'm sure they don't. Part of my job is to keep day-to-day tabs on the logs, and if there had been any of this room's work recorded, I'd have seen it."

"You never saw a log for the work she was doing in this room?"

"No. But I can't believe she didn't keep one. I'd guess she might have stored it in her desk, but I know you went through her whole office Friday. I don't know where else it might be."

How about with Sanford, her co-conspirator? "Ms. Mansell, before I leave, I want to take a better look around in here."

"Do you want me to stay?"

"Yes, if you don't mind. You might pick up on something Detective Irwin and I miss. I'd also like to look through Dr. Hearn's office again. Just to be thorough."

We spent an hour, found nothing. I drove Iggy back to his shop, then turned around and went back to the Med Center. By a quarter to twelve, I was at Sanford's reception desk. I showed my badge and ID to a receptionist with a blue and white name tag, SALLY, and told her I needed to speak to her boss. Her eyes bugged, jaw plunged. Standard response. "Wow. Is this about Mr.

Kennett and Dr. Hearn?" Pure New York, a recent immigrant to the great Pacific Northwest.

"Good guess. Could you please tell the doctor I'm here."

"Sure." She picked up the phone receiver, pushed a button, then said, "Dr. Sanford, there's a Detective Baumgartner here who wants to talk to you about…oh, hold on, I'll ask him." She looked back to me. "Dr. Sanford says he's with his last patient for the morning, and can you please wait till he's done? He says it won't be long."

I nodded. "Thanks."

◇◇◇

I'd waited thirteen minutes when the door to the back corridor opened, and Sanford came through behind an overstuffed dyed blonde in a calico dress meant for someone twenty-five years younger and fifty pounds lighter. By appearances, she had not gotten the best news from the doctor. She wiped at her eyes. Sanford rested a hand on her arm. "I'll see you and your husband first thing in the morning," he said. "And if either of you comes up with anything that won't wait till then, just call. If it's after office hours, the answering service will put you through."

"Thank you…so much." The woman looked like he'd just tossed her a life preserver and hauled her onto shore. "I can't tell you how much I appreciate…you're not *like* most doctors."

Which got her a twenty-four carat smile. No way Sanford's dentist was on food stamps. "We'll beat this thing," he said. "See you tomorrow." Then he walked over to me. "Mr. Baumgartner. Has something new come up about Dr. Hearn?"

When I stood, I had a good five inches on him. "I've got a few questions. Can we go in the back?"

"Of course." He waved a hand toward the corridor. "Would you like me to send out for some lunch?"

"Thanks, but let's just stick to Q and A."

Back in the office, Sanford closed the door behind us, then walked around his desk and settled into his recliner chair, hands up behind his head. Napoleon on his throne. From where I sat, opposite him, I could see half the city through the window. Twelfth floor, what was the rent on this office? I whistled. "Nice place."

I thought he was going to purr. "Thanks. I try to make it relaxed and comfortable. Openness is reassuring."

This guy could drown a person in eyewash, but he wasn't the first I'd gone up against, and the ones who came before him were now wearing zebra suits. "I appreciate you giving up your lunch hour to talk to me, Doctor."

He opened his eyes wide, spread his arms, palms up. "My patients always come first, and Ms. Kennett is my patient."

Time to roll. "Dr. Sanford, I may repeat some of the questions I asked Friday. I hope you'll bear with me."

"You're the doctor."

I sat back, stretched my legs, took a deep breath. "Have you come up with any thoughts at all about why Mr. Kennett might've gone off the deep end?"

"No. He had that breakdown twenty years ago, but since then, he seems to have done very well." Sanford paused just long enough for me to open my mouth to ask the next question. "But in any case, as I told you Friday, I relied on the opinion I got from Dr. Hammacher, James' psychiatrist. I have several notes from him, in fact, starting before the pregnancy, and going right on through till shortly before delivery."

"Okay. Had Mr. Kennett and Dr. Hearn ever met before Friday? Did they know each other?"

"I'm quite sure they didn't."

"He'd never talked to her before?"

"I don't think so. I don't know why he would have."

"All right, let's go on. This Density Gradient Separation you did for the Kennetts—you said that was a first, right? It hadn't been done on patients before?"

"Not as far as I know. But since there was nothing else to offer the Kennetts, it seemed reasonable to give it a try."

"So, was that a favor Dr. Hearn did for you? Did she owe you for something?"

"Of course not. She didn't owe me anything. The reason the private hospital and the University Medical Center have such a close physical relationship is to make it as easy as possible for doctors in practice to work with scientists, both to support research, and so patients can get the best possible care."

"But you and Dr. Hearn *have* been working pretty closely for a while, haven't you? You were getting her human eggs to work on in that private alcove of hers."

Just for an instant, his body went stiff, and the hint of a glow spread over his cheekbones. He swallowed, then had to clear his throat before he could say, "Who told you that?"

"Doesn't matter," I said. "It's true, isn't it?"

He shrugged. "Yes, it's true. So what? Every now and then, I retrieved some human eggs for her to do experiments on. I guess if you want to look at it that way, those ovum retrievals were my quid for her quo of doing an occasional clinical procedure for one of my patients. As I said, that's why the Medical Center operates the way it does. It works to everyone's benefit."

"And 'every now and then' was how often?"

"I didn't keep count. When I was doing a laparoscopy, say, to cut adhesions or to tie tubes for birth control, I'd also retrieve some eggs from the ovaries."

I filed that in the back of my mind, right next to what I'd read the day before about the way Dr. Steptoe went about retrieving eggs. "Did you get permission from the women to do that?"

"I could hardly do it without their consent. I gave them injections of hormones for a couple of weeks beforehand, to ripen the eggs so some would be ready to ovulate at the time of the procedure. Ova that haven't gone through that development can't be fertilized. Then I got sperm samples from medical students, and Dr. Hearn did her studies."

"Which were what?"

"She was interested in conditions that might cause abnormal chromosome behavior at fertilization. I can't tell you more than that. I'm not a geneticist."

"But what you *are* saying is that she worked on human embryos. Live human embryos that could've developed into—"

"If they'd been able to implant in a uterine wall, yes. But there's nothing illegal about this research. It's being done all over the world."

"Isn't there some sort of Ethics Board in your hospital that's supposed to review procedures like that?"

"No. We're a clinical, community hospital. We have a Practice Standards Committee that reviews cases where treatment may have been inappropriate or inadequate, but if a doctor wants to help further medical research and the patient has no problem with it, we don't see any need to tie our own hands with bureaucratic red tape."

"How about at the University? Don't they have an Ethics Board or Committee that researchers are supposed to go to for approval of research on human tissue? Especially on human embryos?"

"Yes. There is an Ethics Committee at the U."

"Did Dr. Hearn present her work to that board?"

"I don't…no, she didn't, and I'll tell you why. Even if the Committee had given unanimous approval to that sort of project, Gerry Camnitz still wouldn't have permitted it to be done in his department."

"Why not?"

Sanford looked like he'd swallowed a mouthful of sour milk. "Because Camnitz has six inches of moss growing on his back. God forbid that some religious nut or conservative ethicist might get on TV or in the newspapers, and accuse Dr. L. Gerald Camnitz of permitting experiments in his department that Dr. Mengele would have loved."

"Could that have gotten you into any trouble, too?"

Sanford shrugged. "I only supplied her ova and sperm samples. What she did and how she did it wasn't my concern."

I broke out laughing. "Come on, Dr. Sanford. First you talk about Dr. Mengele, then you say you were only providing Dr. Hearn what she needed to do *verboten* experiments?"

"Nothing she did was '*verboten,*' except according to Dr. Camnitz. I told you before, work on human embryos is not in any way illegal." He made a show of glancing at his watch. "What are you getting at?"

"I'm wondering whether Dr. Hearn did any work on Joyce Kennett's eggs."

"I told you, she did Density Gradient Separation on James' sperm."

"Yes, I remember you said that. But what I asked you was whether she also did any experimental work on Ms. Kennett's eggs?"

"No," Sanford said. "Is that clear enough?"

I got up, walked to the window, stared at the city twelve stories below, then turned to stand over Sanford. "Wasn't there a problem with one of your…Dr. Hearn's experiments a while ago? Something about a tube that she dropped on the floor and broke?"

He got to his feet, but still had to look up to talk to me. "I don't recall anything of that sort."

I held up a hand. "Before you perjure yourself—"

"We're not in court, Mr. Baumgartner."

"No, we're not. But we may well be headed that way. And if you repeat in court what you've just told me, you'll be perjuring yourself. Before we go any further, I'm going to tell you there were witnesses who do recall that accident, very clearly, in fact. They say right after the accident, Dr. Hearn called you, and practically before she hung up, you were over there. You both went into her office, then came out a few minutes later, and hustled off down the hall. Does that help you remember?"

Sanford walked a few steps off, studied the ceiling. "Yes…I'd forgotten. It was some time ago, and it wasn't important. Giselle had a little bout of the clumsies, dropped an experiment and ruined it. She was a very serious woman, totally dedicated to her work, and she was worried I'd be angry at her for wasting the tissue I'd retrieved. I told her not to worry, accidents happen, and I wasn't the least bit sore. She went back to work, I came back to my patients, and that was that. She just needed to vent."

"What was it she dropped that got her so upset?"

"I told you, I don't know exactly what she did. It was one of her experiments in progress, studying chromosomes at fertilization. She dropped a specimen, and that was the end of the experiment. That's all I can tell you." He glanced at his wrist again. "I really would like to grab a sandwich before my afternoon patients."

He stepped to the side; I matched him. We must have looked like two tomcats circling each other, looking for an opening. "Dr. Sanford, I don't want to inconvenience you. Could we please take a quick look at Ms. Kennett's chart? Then I'll get out of your hair."

"We couldn't find that chart on Friday. What makes you think—"

"I think a doctor who pays so much attention to his patients' well-being isn't going to settle to have a chart vanish permanently."

Sanford made a disgusted face, then marched to the door. I rode his wake into the waiting room, behind the reception counter, and up to the chart storage rack. He worked his fingers into the row of hanging charts. "K…K-E…N-N…damn, still not here. Sorry."

"Think one of your office workers could find it?"

"They're on their lunch break in the staff room."

"Can you get one of them out?"

He tapped a well-manicured nail on the counter. "Mr. Baumgartner, my staff works hard. Barring emergencies—and this really isn't one—my receptionist is supposed to have an hour free to eat lunch and relax. She's still got twenty minutes. Come on, let's go down to the cafeteria and have a sandwich. Then we'll see if she can find the chart. I have nothing to hide."

Twenty minutes later, Sanford and I marched up to the reception counter. Sally flashed just the right smile to her boss and his cop guest. Sanford cleared his throat. "Mr. Baumgartner and I want to look at Ms. Kennett's chart, but I can't find it in the rack."

Sally jumped to her feet. "Bet I can find it for you." She turned to the chart rack, then started to paw through it. After a few seconds, she cried, "Ah," and pulled a folder from the rack. "Here it is, Doctor. It was misfiled by a few names."

Sanford took the chart from her. "Thank you, Sally."

The young woman grinned at me. "This happens a lot. We've all learned, if you can't find a chart, don't give up till you've checked at least ten names on either side of where it should be. Usually, it's off by only one or two."

I tipped an imaginary hat to her. "Good work, young lady. Dr. Sanford's lucky to have such great help." I crooked a finger toward the office. "Let's have a look."

Back in Sanford's inner sanctum, I asked if it was okay for me to sit at the desk to look through the chart. He told me to be his guest. I flipped pages to the last entry. "'Prenatal visit, thirty-nine weeks,'" I read out loud. "Looks like everything was hunky-dory." I paged back past the first prenatal visit on September 26, to a one-line confirmation of pregnancy on September 8, then to a handwritten operative summary from August 6. "'Post-Pergonal and HCG regimen. Laparoscopy, lysis of adhesions... pre-ovulatory ovaries, tubes, uterus, all normal, save for small number of adhesions at right and left tubo-ovarian junctions, which were easily lysed.'" I looked up at Sanford. "Would you mind translating for me?"

"Sure. It means she'd gotten hormone shots to time ovulation to the procedure, and the ovaries were on the point of releasing eggs, perfect timing. And she had a little scar tissue around the ends of the fallopian tubes, where they come up to the ovary to receive eggs at ovulation. That scar tissue can block an egg from getting into the tube and being fertilized. So I lysed—cut—it away."

"Where's it come from, the scar tissue?"

Sanford shrugged. "Could've been an old inflammation, say from a mild case of gonorrhea. Or appendicitis. Or a condition called endometriosis, though I didn't see any specific evidence of that. Sometimes, we just don't have any idea. Whatever caused it, it's not an unusual condition."

"But she had a long history of infertility, and got workups by you and the University doctors. Didn't anyone ever look for scar tissue before?"

"That's a yes-but. She had a radio-opaque dye injected up through the uterus and into the tubes, to see if it spilled out the far ends. But that's not awfully precise, especially if the adhesions are mild, which hers were. An open operation to look for adhesions would be excessive, but laparoscopy has reached the point of being useful for that."

"Laparoscopy…that's that new 'Band-Aid' surgery, right?"

He chuckled. "You've got it."

"And you can do it?"

"No one else in Emerald, including the University faculty, has my background or experience."

"What? You mean to tell me you're the only doctor in town who can do laparoscopy? That nobody at the U—"

"Oh, they can *do* it." Sanford practically drooled contempt. "Talk to people at the U, they'll tell you they're the last word. But I learned the technique from Guiseppe Allegri, who happens to be the world's authority. If a woman in this city needs laparoscopy and goes to anyone but me, frankly, she's out of her mind."

Amazing, the load of brass this guy schlepped around between his legs. "You told me before that you used laparoscopy to get eggs for Dr. Hearn when you were cutting adhesions on patients. But you didn't take any eggs from Ms. Kennett, is that right?"

"The chart doesn't say I did, does it?"

I took a deep breath. "Dr. Sanford, it's a bad idea to crack wise to a cop who's looking into a homicide. I take my work as seriously as you take yours. Now, the chart says you gave Ms. Kennett the same hormone shots Dr. Edwards and Dr. Steptoe use in their experiments, and I'm betting if I check back, I'll find out they were also the same shots you used in your experimental women before you took their eggs. So, did you or didn't you take eggs from Ms. Kennett at this procedure?"

He put on his best thinking cap. "To the best of my recollection, no. If I had, it would've been in her chart. In her case, I was timing ovulation to give the treated sperm the best chance to fertilize eggs in her body. It would've been silly to inseminate her if she wasn't going to have eggs ready to be fertilized."

"Okay. Thank you. Now, if this procedure took place on August 6, and Ms. Kennett had her baby April 28, unless that baby was premature, she must have conceived right then. Your sperm treatment must have worked."

He made no secret of how pleased he was with himself. "I like to think so, but it really could have been any number of things, or even a combination. Maybe cutting away the adhesions freed up the tubes to let an egg enter from the ovary. But I've got to admit, there's a joker in that deck. Almost any infertility treatment, even the crackpot stuff, has a decent conception rate right after it's done. Some people think it's psychological, but no one really knows. Whatever, Joyce did conceive in that cycle. Sure, I'm curious about what actually did the job, but I don't think Joyce or her husband cared."

"Was there anything else you did? To help her get pregnant?"

"Like what?"

"Like anything. Anything else either you or Dr. Hearn did that you haven't told me about."

Sanford shook his head slowly. "No…there was nothing else." He gave his watch a long look.

"Dr. Sanford…"

He waited.

"Did you know a woman named Alma Wanego?"

"Wanego? That name's not familiar."

"She was the supervisor in Dr. Hearn's lab until she disappeared one day last September. You never heard anything about that?"

He made such a production of thinking, I wanted to tell him to go down to the Rep and see if he could get a part in their next play. "Yes…yes…I do remember something about a supervisor who vanished, and they had to replace her. But I have nothing to do with the running of that lab, and it made no impression on me.

"All the times you took eggs over there for Dr. Hearn, you never met Alma Wanego?"

"I didn't take eggs over there. Dr. Hearn came to the operating room so she could get the eggs as soon as I'd recovered them from the ovary. I did take sperm samples from the medical students over to her, and from time to time we'd get together to talk about how things were going, and whether we needed to make any changes in the clinical protocol."

"Dr. Hearn was never busy doing something else, so you had to deal with another lab person?"

"No. We planned our meetings for when she'd be free."

"And she never sent anyone else to the operating room to pick up the eggs?"

Sanford's laugh had a sharp edge. "And take a chance someone might leak information that could get to Dr. Camnitz?" He shook his head. "Besides, the first steps for culture after retrieval are critical, and Dr. Hearn was as compulsive as they come. I don't think she'd ever have trusted anyone else to do that work."

"Doctor, how far along in pregnancy does a woman have to be before her pregnancy test turns positive?"

"There are blood tests and urine tests. Blood tests can be suggestive very early on, but the gold standard for both tests is six weeks after the last menstrual period. That's four weeks after conception."

"Six weeks, four weeks…okay, then. Dr. Hearn's botched experiment happened right about the time your patient, Ms. Kennett, got pregnant, thanks to the sperm preparation, the lysed adhesions, psychological reasons, whatever. Cut to four weeks later, early September. Ms. Kennett's pregnancy test turns positive, and the supervisor in the laboratory vanishes."

Sanford shrugged extravagantly. "So?"

"So, you think it's just a coincidence that strange things happened at two key points in Ms. Kennett's pregnancy?"

"I'd say you're reaching, Mr. Baumgartner. Sorry."

I slammed the chart shut. "Okay, Doctor, thanks. I appreciate the time you've given me."

"I hope I've been able to help."

"Oh, yes." I extended a hand, we shook, then Sanford led me to the door. As he reached for the knob, I stopped. "Shoot, I forgot. One last thing. I hear you had a press conference scheduled last Friday, but you canceled it."

Sanford frowned. "Where did you hear that?"

"From a reliable source."

Actually, I'd heard it while I was waiting for Sanford to finish his morning appointments. A woman was dropping a load on Ms. New York, the receptionist, about how her weekend had been ruined by the vaginal bleeding that was supposed to have been taken care of on Friday, but they'd had to re-schedule her because of a press conference Dr. Sanford had set up. Yes, the receptionist said, she was awfully sorry, and on top of everything, Dr. Sanford had had to cancel the conference.

"So, what *was* that conference all about?" I asked.

Sanford turned on the sad-eye. "I guess it really doesn't matter now. It was going to be for Dr. Hearn to announce something she'd discovered in her work. She thought she'd made a major breakthrough."

"And you've got no idea what this major breakthrough was?"

"Only in a general way. Something to do with the cause of Down Syndrome. That's all I know."

"Isn't there a record of the work Dr. Hearn did in that alcove. Don't scientists keep notes? Details of their experiments as they go along?"

"Sure they do. I saw the log Dr. Hearn kept on our collaborative work, but I never looked over the data."

"And you have no idea where it might be."

Sanford shrugged. "My best guess would be that she kept it in her desk."

"You're saying the press conference was to announce Dr. Hearn's work, which you only knew about in a general kind of way, but it was going to take place in *your* office. Why didn't Dr. Hearn schedule it at *her* office?"

"Two reasons. For one thing, Dr. Hearn didn't want to have Gerry Camnitz playing bull in her china shop. Camnitz has no control over what I do in my office. And for another, bringing reporters and photographers into my office does wonders for my patient lists. Get it?"

I nodded. "Another little quid."

"You could put it that way. Now, if you don't mind, I'm already five minutes late for my first afternoon. I hate to keep patients waiting."

I pulled a piece of paper from my pocket pad. "If you want to get hold of me for any reason, here's my beeper number."

Amusement crept across his face. "I didn't know police detectives use beepers."

"This one does," I said. "It rings right through to me, and it's always on. Round the clock, seven days a week."

He smirked. "Just like me. Maybe we're not as different as I've been thinking."

I pushed the paper into his hand, then walked out without saying another word. Sooner or later, he'd say something that would sink his ship like the Titanic. We were maneuvering through my waters, but he didn't know that. Guys like him never see the iceberg till they hit it.

I browsed magazines in the waiting room outside Puget Community Hospital's Operating Suite. After three issues of *Time,* two of *Sports Illustrated*, and half a copy of *Sunset,* a slim, middle-aged woman in green scrubs walked in. Roots of gray hair showed toward the front of her O.R. cap; her eyelids drooped. She looked past the two couples and one elderly woman in the room, then approached me. "Mr. Baumgartner?"

I nodded.

"I'm Judith Mortensen. I hear you want to talk to me."

"If you don't mind." I looked around. "Is there somewhere more private?"

"Of course. We can use Dr. Aronoff's office. He's on vacation this week."

◇◇◇

Ms. Mortensen closed the door behind us, then pulled off her scrub cap and shook her hair free. She smiled, but it took effort.

"Hard case?" I asked.

She nodded. "Cabbage. Seven hours."

"Cabbage?"

Mortensen laughed. "Sorry. Medical jargon. C-A-B-G, coronary artery bypass graft. A five-vessel special."

I almost asked if the operation came out all right, but decided to leave well enough alone. "Thanks for letting me take your break time."

"No trouble. I'm off duty now."

"I'll try not to make you stay too late. I'm interested in a particular case of Dr. Colin Sanford..." I paused as the nurse's face brightened. "I see you know Dr. Sanford."

She laughed. "Dr. Sanford makes certain everyone knows him, and knows how good he is. He'd be insufferable if he weren't so darned charming. He's kind of like a little boy. I once tried telling him he'd do better if he didn't brag so much, and he told me, 'If you can do it, it's not bragging.' Then he gave me that smile."

I knew the smile she meant. "The case I'm interested in was a laparoscopy last August on a woman named Joyce Kennett. The Operating Suite record has you listed as the nurse for the procedure. Do you remember it?"

Mortensen looked like she was dredging up material from a deep well. "Kennett..." She tapped a fingernail against her front teeth. "Kennett, Kennett...oh. Isn't that the woman whose husband just killed one of the lab workers at the U?"

"Yes. She was one of Dr. Sanford's infertility patients. He did a laparoscopy on her last August, lysis of adhesions between the fallopian tubes and the ovaries. Does that help?"

She went back to the dredge. Lines formed between her nose and mouth. Her lips twisted with effort. Then, she shook her head. "I'm sorry, Mr. Baumgartner, but no, I really can't. Dr. Sanford does so many laparoscopies. And it was almost a year ago."

"Nine months, to be exact."

She didn't make the connection. "That's still a while to remember a routine case. Was there something special you wanted to know? Maybe that would ring a bell."

"Try this. Do you remember whether Dr. Sanford took some eggs from Ms. Kennett at that procedure for a research project he was involved in?"

Mortensen frowned. One more time to the dredge. "No, I'm really sorry. I've got a faint memory of being there, but I can't recall any specifics. And Dr. Sanford was doing so many ovum retrievals. For a while there, it seemed as if he was running his patients through a production line. Every week, two or three more."

I perked up. "You say he *was* doing a lot of them?"

"Yes. But then he slowed down, a lot, and I'm pretty sure that happened in August…yes, I remember thinking, people must be going on vacation this time of year."

Wasn't that interesting. I thanked Ms. Mortensen, and went on to my next stop.

The desk clerk in Medical Records motioned me up to her cubicle. "I've got the charts you want, sir, all of Dr. Sanford's surgeries for the past two years. I'm sorry it took so long."

I stared at the four piles on the table opposite her desk. "Looks like you had a lot of digging to do."

"Oh, yes. Dr. Sanford probably does twice as many operations as any other doctor on the staff. Everyone says he's a whiz, and he's always so *nice*. If I ever need GYN surgery, I'll have him do it for sure."

I nodded. "Okay if I sit here and go through them?"
"Sure. If you need any help, just holler."

An hour and a half later, I said thank you to the clerk, tucked the notes I'd written into my pocket, along with the copy she'd made of one particular page, and walked out of Medical Records. Sanford had been busy, all right. Between January 21, 1976 and August 6, 1976, he'd tried to retrieve eggs from fifty-five patients. Forty-one attempts had been successful, including that August 6 patient, whose name happened to be Joyce Kennett. After that, there'd been only eighteen more retrievals, the last one during the week before Ms. Kennett had her baby, and the name of the patient, Sandra Wellington, fit the initials on the petri dish label in Dr. Hearn's locked incubator. Ms. Wellington's indication for laparoscopy was "grand multiparity," which the helpful clerk told me meant she'd had a lot of kids. Made sense, since her procedure was a tubal ligation. No infertility treatment to look for there.

I'd have loved to go right back to Sanford's office, lay Joyce Kennett's op report on his desk, and ask him to explain it. But I felt sure he'd tell me it must be a mistake, the transcriber got a couple of records confused, and I should go chase my wild geese someplace else. Better to lay back for now, give him enough rope that he'd work himself into a tangle that even he couldn't talk his way out of. Sanford needed his patients, his colleagues, his office staff, surgical nurses, department clerks, *everybody*, to think he was a genius-doctor who could do what no other doctor could. I'd have bet my last nickel he'd been going hellbent for election to be the first doc to make a baby by in vitro fertilization. But something went wrong.

Three-thirty, plenty of time left in the day to try to connect some dots. I went across the skybridge, past the Office Tower, to the University Med complex, and followed signs to the

Administration Office. The secretary reeked of that musky-smelling stuff women started dousing themselves in during the hippie years. When I asked where I'd find Personnel, she pointed toward the door. "Catch the elevator right outside here to B-floor, then turn left, take the first left after that, and you'll be right in front of Personnel." I thanked her, walked out, and took the elevator down into the bowels of the building.

Interesting how eager most people are to help a detective dig up dirt. Something a little different to break up those eight big ones every day at a desk, and it makes for great cocktail party chatter. Before I was done talking, the poker-faced Assistant Director of Personnel had snatched up a pencil and a pad. "Just give me a list of the names you need, sir. I'll get you the folders right away."

I thought she might fall on her face, trying to navigate off to the storage area on those five-inch heels. But she was back in record time, charmingly flushed, and holding out a pile of manila folders. She pointed to a table next to the door. "You can sit there if you'd like, sir. And if you need anything else, just let me know."

I said a polite thank-you, walked to the table, sat, and fanned the folders out in front of me. Okay, I thought. Who wants to go first?

No one answered, so I decided to start with Dr. Colin Sanford, MD. His folder had a red tab, which meant he was medical staff, not an employee. Dr. Sanford was forty-two, divorced, no kids. His father, Arthur Sanford, was a doctor too, retired, living up north, in Shorebeach. Nothing in Sanford the Younger's file jumped out at me. He was a clinical associate professor of OBGYN on the university teaching faculty, with full admitting and surgical privileges at both University Hospital and Puget Community. He went to med school in New York, interned and did his residency at Bellevue, finished in 1964, then came back out to Emerald and opened his office. I figured he must have gotten done with his training just in time to beat the

'Nam draft. Guys like him always seem to dodge past stumbling blocks that trip up everybody else.

Next was another red tag, Louis Gerald Camnitz, MD, MPH, Professor and Chairman, Department of OBGYN. Camnitz was forty-eight, married to Susanna Bancroft Camnitz, two grown kids. He'd spent his whole professional life at Washington Public University, undergrad work, med school, internship, residency, faculty member, and had been named Chairman two years ago. His specialty area was gynecologic cancer.

I opened the third red-tagged folder. Giselle Davida Hearn, PhD, born January 8, 1933. Divorced. Father was dead, mother had a rural mailing address out in Holcomb County, as well I knew. Remembering how the poor old woman had looked when I gave her the news about her daughter, I started to tear up. Crappy way to wind up your tour of duty on the planet. I swallowed hard, then went back to the folder. Dr. Hearn had a BS in Biological Sciences, University of Oregon, 1955, and an MS, 1957, and a PhD, 1961, both from the University of Chicago. She stayed on the faculty at Chicago till 1968, then came to Washington Public University as an associate professor. Her string of publications was a mile long, all about chromosomes and what made them do what they shouldn't at fertilization. High-level medical science, and clear she was a star in her field. I did pause for a bit to think about the divorce, but it had been seventeen years earlier, 1960, while she was still in Chicago. Not likely to be a factor in this case.

Now, I came to the blue tags, the employees. Loretta Jill Mansell. Age thirty-three, married, two kids, nine and seven. BS in Biology from Washington Public University, taught high school for a couple of years, then had the kids, and after that, got a job in the Reproductive Genetics Lab. By all accounts, she was an excellent worker, and was promoted to supervisor the past September. Again, nothing out of line, off the charts, or off a wall. This was looking like the most boring assortment of normal people I could find anywhere.

I picked up the last folder, another blue tag. Alma Elizabeth Wanego. Ms. Wanego had turned thirty-six a week before she disappeared. She had a certificate in laboratory procedures from South Puget Community College, and had started working at the Reproductive Genetics Lab two and a half years before, but in the eight years prior to that, she'd gone through four different jobs. Laid off at one of them, and quit the other three, one because of "irreconcilable differences" with her supervisor, the other two for "dissatisfaction with the work." The last of those jobs was in a Urology lab at the University of Oregon Med School. Less than a month after she was canned there, she was on board at Washington Public University, where, in her first four months, her supervisor brought her up twice for insubordination. Both times, though, she got off with a warning. But then the supervisor left, and her job went to Wanego.

It got even more interesting. After Wanego's promotion, there were three complaints from other techs that they'd been on the wrong end of "inappropriate and unwarranted chastisement." She also tried to get a housekeeper, Charles Rapp, fired for not carrying out an assignment to fix a plugged-up drain, but in the end, he was transferred to the Anatomy Department. That complaint against Rapp had been filed in early August, 1976. And then came the punch line. Wanego had been hired in the first place on the recommendation of one Loretta Mansell.

I pushed back from the table, scraping the chair on the floor, and jumped to my feet. The Personnel AD looked up from her desk. "Sir?"

"Sorry," I said. "But how fast can you get me copies of these records?"

She was at her Xerox machine practically before I was done talking, and had copies in my hand in less than ten minutes. I thanked her again, then took off, out the door. After five now, but maybe I could catch Mansell before she left work for the day. I also wouldn't have minded having a chat with Mr. Rapp, the transferred housekeeper, but he worked a seven-thirty to four shift. Tomorrow.

The Reproductive Genetics Lab was dark, all doors locked. I put Mansell on the next day's list, along with Rapp, then took a few steps toward going home. But with what I'd found out since Friday, I thought it might be interesting to talk to Joyce Kennett again.

Chapter Eleven

Sanford

I had a late-afternoon delivery, so it was close to seven by the time I pulled into a parking space in front of Joyce Kennett's house. The four concrete steps up to the front door were crumbling; for that matter, the place could've used a couple coats of paint. James hadn't been much of a DIY guy. But with the payday Joyce was looking at, she'd have no trouble getting her house spiffed to the nines. Or she could up and move to any neighborhood she might fancy.

I took the steps carefully, then rang the bell. A woman's face appeared through the small window in the door, then the door opened, and a short, round gray-haired woman in a white pants suit that made her look like the Michelin Lady greeted me. "Why, Dr. Sanford, hello." Her smile faded into uncertainty. "There's not any…problem, I hope."

"Not at all, Mrs. Enright. Just checking up, making sure Joyce is doing all right."

The woman's eyes widened. "You're making a *house call*?"

Of course. "When it's not possible or reasonable for my patients to come to me, I go to them." I lowered my voice. "Especially considering the circumstances. And I'm glad you could come out. Having you here will make all the difference for Joyce."

Mrs. Enright made a go-away motion with her hand. "What else is a mother going to do? My husband can look after himself for a little while. Please, come in. Joyce is resting, but I think she's awake. That policeman really wore her out."

"Policeman?" Now I was doubly glad I'd come by. "I thought the police were finished with Joyce."

We walked through the living room and down a short hallway. "I don't know why he was here, Doctor. Joyce was so tired afterward, she didn't want to talk. She just said he asked her some of the same questions as he did Friday, but pushed her harder on the answers. He was in with her for almost an hour, then said he'd be back if anything else came up. He only left about fifteen minutes ago."

At the doorway to the bedroom, Mrs. Enright threw an arm across my chest. "Joyce, dear," she called. "Dr. Sanford's here to see you. Are you decent?"

"Yes, Ma. I'm beyond reproach."

Mrs. Enright rolled her eyes. "That girl. She's always been so sarcastic, even when she was little."

I laughed, then walked in, and up to the bedside. "How'd it go today, Joyce?"

Big sigh. "Okay, I guess." She glanced at her mother. "Having Ma here is huge. She says she's going to give Robbie all his night feedings."

I bent over the baby, sleeping in the bassinet next to the bed. "Beautiful baby, look at that head of hair. But then, I only deliver beautiful babies."

Joyce smiled politely; her mother gushed, "Oh, Dr. Sanford."

"And that little bit of jaundice he had looks much better now. All the tests for blood-group incompatibilities that the pediatricians did were negative."

Joyce smiled. Mrs. Enright turned her eyes upward. "Thank God."

"It was pretty much a formality," I said. "Especially since it was a first baby, the odds of a problem were very low. But it's nice to be sure."

Mrs. Enright shook her head. "When it's your only grandchild, anything less than sure isn't good enough."

"No argument. Joyce, are you doing all right with pain? Any problems with your breasts?"

She shook her head. "I've got them bound, and I'm putting ice on them. I haven't needed any pain pills at all. I think things are…as good as they can be."

Mrs. Enright tried unsuccessfully to keep back tears.

"Stop that, Ma," Joyce said. "You're going to start up my waterworks. That police detective really wore me down." Her voice quavered. "He wanted to know all about James and me, whether we were having any problems, how James felt about the pregnancy and the baby, whether James had any hangups about the sperm separation process, whether I'd met Dr. Hearn…I thought he was never going to stop."

"Hmmm. He was in my office the whole lunch hour, asking questions."

Joyce turned to her mother. "Ma, I'd love a cup of tea. Would you mind?"

"Why should I mind? What do you think I'm here for? Dr. Sanford?"

"I'm not much of a tea drinker, thanks. In any case, I'll need to get along soon."

Mrs. Enright waddled out of the room and around the corner into the corridor. When her footsteps died away, I whispered, "Does she know? About the procedure?"

Joyce shook her head. "I've never mentioned a word about it to her or anyone else."

"Good. We want to keep it under wraps until we're sure the police are finished. I can't imagine it'll go on much longer."

Joyce gazed at the window next to the bed, its brownish dried water line framed by dime-store flowered chintz curtains. "I've got to admit, I'm on the edge," she murmured. "James didn't have much life insurance, no pension or anything like that, and we never had money we could put away. Then, there were all those medical bills that insurance wouldn't cover because they were for infertility work."

Her voice grew shakier. "Dr. Sanford, I'm scared. I can't get my job back. My mother wants me to 'come home to Topeka,' and live with them, but just thinking about that could make me suicidal." She nodded toward the baby. "I'm looking at twenty years' hard labor, having to put Robbie in some cheesy day-care center where he'll catch all the colds and upset stomachs the other kids have, then pass them along to me. And where am I going to get money to send him to college? Would it really make any difference to the police if we went ahead now? A press conference *wouldn't* be easy for me, but I think I could suck it up and get through. I need to see the color of that money."

My mind went into overdrive. "You say you've got some insurance. How long is it going to hold out?"

"Six months, tops. But—"

"All right then. No reason to panic. If we come out with our press conference while the police are still poking around, they're going to wonder about some of the things I had to do in a hurry, to protect you. Like hiding Dr. Hearn's log book, and changing your chart to say all we did was a sperm treatment. But if we wait till they close the case and move on, it shouldn't be a problem to quietly put the original pages back into the chart, and say I found the log book someplace where Dr. Hearn had hidden it. We want the reporters to focus on you and Robbie, no distractions. Believe me, I want to make this announcement as much as you want me to."

Before Joyce could answer, Mrs. Enright came into the room, a teapot in one hand, cup and saucer in the other. "Here you are, dear," she said to Joyce. "Chamomile. It'll do you a world of good."

She set the cup and saucer on the little table next to the bed, on the side opposite Robbie in his bassinet. As she began to pour, Joyce and I exchanged a look of suppressed amusement, a conspirators' handshake. "I'll be on my way," I said. "Your daughter's doing fine. You don't need to worry about her."

Mrs. Enright passed the teacup to Joyce, then executed a little bow. "Will you be coming back to see her."

"Count on it." I started to the door, but stopped after a couple of steps, and called over my shoulder, "Was the detective who came to see you named Baumgartner?"

Joyce nodded.

"That's right," said her mother. Bernard Baumgartner. I remember thinking, 'BB.' Why?"

"Just curious."

Chapter Twelve

Baumgartner

I was hungry when I said good-bye to Joyce Kennett, but as I drove home, my mind was grumbling louder than my stomach. Lab accident, special sperm treatments, vanishing lab supervisor, murder-suicide, all tied together in time through the same small group of people. Hard to write off as a line of coincidence.

And was I really supposed to believe Sanford was doing all that work to get eggs for Dr. Hearn so he could say he was the right-hand man for a University research scientist? And that he'd scheduled a press conference for the day after Joyce Kennett's baby was born so Hearn could announce a research breakthrough that Sanford didn't know a whole lot about? More applesauce than I could swallow.

Cops who live thirty years on the job have above-average peripheral vision. As I approached a street-corner bar, I picked up on some action. A fancy dude, was laying it heavy, both fists, to a woman. I swerved into a parking space, hustled out of the car and across the sidewalk. The guy took one look at me, dropped the woman, and took off around the corner. I thought of going after him, but decided better to help the woman, who had collapsed to the pavement, sobbing and groaning. I knelt beside her, cupped her chin in my hand. "Take it easy, Ma'am. I'm a policeman. We'll call you an ambulance, you'll be all right."

She was a mess, face swollen, blood running from the corner of her mouth. I wiped it with my handkerchief. "Please don't leave me alone," she whispered. "He'll come back and kill me."

"No way," I said. "After we get you taken care of, we'll make sure he doesn't bother you or anyone else anymore."

She tried to smile, but couldn't carry it off. "Thank you… thank you so much," a murmur I could barely hear.

If I was hungry before, one foot inside the house, and I was starving. Hungarian goulash. Irma's mother had made sure her daughter learned to cook right. I hustled into the living room, slung my folders onto the couch, my gun along with them, then trotted into the kitchen. Irma was stirring a pot on the stove with a big wooden spoon. I walked over and grabbed her bottom. "Hey, there."

"Hello."

One word that froze me on the spot. "Something the matter?"

She took way too much care setting the spoon into the pot. "What were you doing all this time?"

"What do you mean, 'what was I doing?' What do I do for a living?"

She tossed a long look up at the clock over the sink. "Till after eight o'clock at night?"

"Till whenever I can get away. I worked my case all day, then on the way home, I ran into an assault, a man beating up a woman, and I didn't really think I ought to ignore it because I'd be late for dinner. Not exactly like I'm having an affair or something."

Wrong move. She wheeled around. I could see on her face, in her eyes, from the way she was standing, this was now a lost cause. "Damn you, Bernie," she shouted. "You *are* having an affair. Over thirty years now, you've given every minute of every day of your life to the Emerald Police Force, and I'm sick of it. Sick…of…it. Do you hear me?"

Like I might not hear her, the way she was yelling. "Yes, I hear you, but—"

"But nothing. "God *damn* it, Bernie, if it's not one thing, it's another. But it's always *something*." She wheeled around, grabbed the spoon out of the pot and slung it straight at my face.

I ducked. The spoon sailed past my ear, splattered goulash on the wall behind me.

"There's always something more important than coming home in time to have a bowl of goulash that's not vulcanized." She stamped a foot; a drinking glass tumbled off a shelf, shattered on the floor. "Bernie, you son of a bitch, you had no *right* getting married. I could put on a see-through negligee and prance around in front of you, and you'd just stand there, trying to figure out what I'm up to. Getting a good fuck once in a blue moon wouldn't be interesting enough for you."

It'd been a long day, Sanford wise-assing me, now this. "What're you saying, Irma? That I'm supposed to get all worked up over Henry Streator's cold leftovers? I mean, if you want to talk about having an affair."

Don't bother telling me I shouldn't have said that. Irma looked like she had a open air hose up her butt. We just stood there for I'm not sure how long, glaring at each other, till Irma whipped around and grabbed the pot off the stove. I made a move toward her, but saw I was going to be too late, so I turned and dodged left, but she read me perfect, scored a dead-on hit with that pot. If it was a bullet, it would've blown my heart into powder. "There's your dinner," she shouted. "Get down on the floor and lick it up. You might as well enjoy it because that's the last meal you're getting from me." She slammed the pot to the floor, then ran out of the room and up the stairs. A minute later, I heard a door slam.

So there I am, standing in the middle of the kitchen, dripping goulash all over the floor. I walked over to the sink, brushed off what I could, rinsed my hands, face, and arms. I felt like I'd been cranked through a wringer. I pulled a dishrag off the rack under the sink, got down on the floor, and started mopping up goulash. I figured when I was done, I'd go up and apologize for what I said about her and Henry, but what to say about my work and her feelings about it, I didn't have a clue.

Then I heard Irma come back into the room. I looked up from the goulash puddle, and found myself staring into the barrel of a handgun—*my* handgun, to be specific. I was on my feet in nothing flat.

"Take one step, and I swear, I'll shoot." In a voice like a violin string. Tighten it one more tiny turn, and snap!

I held out my hand. "Irma, give me that gun."

She pointed it at my right knee. "Stay away. Come one step closer, and you'll never move that leg again."

Her eyes had the look you see in people an inch away from shooting a hostage or jumping off a bridge. Try to reason with them, and everyone ends up dead. Part of me wanted to rush her and knock the gun away, but the cop in my noggin got the upper hand over the hothead who'd made the dumb remark about her and Henry. I tried to distract her. "Well, I sure am glad I showed you how to defend yourself if somebody came in here and I was away."

Which did exactly nothing. "You'd better *be* away, in a hurry. I'm not kidding, Bernie. You've been making me crazy for way too long, and tonight you sent me all the way. Now, get yourself out of this house, and stay out."

The hothead started a move, but the cop threw a quick stranglehold on him. "Look at me." I held out my arms. "I can't go out like this. At least let me take a shower."

"No shower. No nothing." She stepped to the side, clearing a path to the door, then whipped the gun around and put the end of the barrel to her temple. "On three," she snapped. "If I get to three and I can still see you, I'm gonna fix it so I never have to look at you again. One…"

A picture flashed in my head, blood and brain all over the wall and the floor, and a homicide cop covered in goulash, trying to explain things to the first-response guys.

"Two…"

I could see her finger tighten. "All right," I shouted. "That's what you want, I'm going." I turned and ran out the door, pausing just long enough to grab up my folders from the couch. All the way through the house, I listened for a gunshot. I don't think I took a breath till I was outside, on my way down the sidewalk.

An older man and woman passed me, going the other way. I thought their necks were going to snap right off. "It's the latest style," I said. "Straight from Paris. You like?"

As I watched them hustle away, I think I smiled. But now, what? Sleep on a park bench, then go out in the morning and do interviews in my filthy shirt and suit? Have to do better than that. Who on the force could I trust to not ask questions and keep their mouth shut? No one. Even my friends wouldn't be able to resist yukking it up about something like this.

Then I had it. I brushed off as much stew as I could, stepped around the bunch of crows who were already fighting over the little solid bits, jumped in the car, and drove off.

◇◇◇

When Iggy opened the door, he looked me up, down, and up again. I started to laugh. "What's the matter? You've never seen a man wearing Hungarian goulash before?"

He didn't want to smile, but couldn't help it. "I don't ask questions that ain't none of my business, Mr. B. You want to come inside?"

I stepped into his living room. "My wife got a little annoyed with me."

"Well, I'd sure hate to see what she'd do if she got a lot annoyed."

"I'll tell you. She'd grab my gun and let me know that if I didn't leave, one of us was never going to do anything ever again."

Iggy worked his tongue around his mouth. His face asked a hundred questions, but all he said was, "Well, I'm guessin' you need some new duds. Only thing is, I ain't got clothes gonna fit you. I'm like half your size."

"Could you go out and get me some stuff to wear?" I looked at my watch. "Bergstrom's is open for almost another hour. If you wouldn't mind."

"'Course not. I'll go right on down. But not to make too much of a point, what're you gonna do about money?"

I pulled my wallet, peeled bills, put them into Iggy's hand. This should cover the clothes. Irma and I keep separate accounts, checking and saving, and what I can draw on ought to hold me for a while."

Iggy grinned. "You always think of everything, Mr. B."

"If I always thought of everything, I wouldn't have run my mouth to my wife like I did."

Then I thought of something else. With Irma holding my gun, I'd need to pick up a new piece. Not likely anyone in this case was going to make me draw, but you never know. I was pretty sure Iggy either had a gun on hand or could get me one in a hurry, but if I had to use that nonofficial gun in the line of duty, things would get very ugly, probably uglier for Iggy than for me. I'd have to come up with a better idea.

"Well, hey, Mr. B. Nobody's perfect. Where you figuring to stay?"

"Get a room at a motel, I guess."

"Bah. You can do better'n that. You come to the right place." The little guy jerked a thumb back over his shoulder. "My living room there ain't exactly the Ritz, but the sofa bed's okay, there ain't no bugs, and the rent's cheap. But hey, listen, I better go down and get you them threads, before Bergstrom shuts down for the night."

"Right. I wouldn't get very far tomorrow, trying to grill people in my underwear."

Not often that cops talk about a case with a civilian, but every rule's got its exception. Iggy was holding evidence for me, had opened a lab incubator, was getting me wearable clothes, and now he was offering me a place to stay. If I screwed up, he could be the perfect fall guy if Richmond decided to turn the spotlight off the force. Iggy was almost at the door; I called him back. "Before I pitch a tent here, you need to know why," I said. "It goes a long way past a pissed-off wife and a pot of goulash. When you get back, I'll bring you up to speed, and you can decide then if you want to have me staying in your house."

Iggy's face—half of it, anyway—usually has a look on it that says he's thinking something is funny, but now he got as serious as I've ever seen him. "You can tell me whatever you want, Mr. B, and nobody's gonna get it outa me, not even with needles under my fingernails. Or, you don't have to tell me nothin' at all. Wasn't for you, I'd be doin' my ten to fifteen right now, and stuff like that, I don't forget." He made a grand gesture, taking in his entire living room. "Make yourself at home."

Chapter Thirteen

Baumgartner

Too bad I never thought to set an alarm. By the time I opened my eyes, sunlight filled the room. Almost nine—Iggy'd be on his way to work. I jumped off the couch, and while I shaved with the razor my host had left on the sink for me, I drank some of the coffee he'd been kind enough to leave in the pot. Then I scrambled a few eggs, washed them down with the rest of the coffee, and got myself dressed. Iggy knew clothes. With what my new suit cost, plus a few shirts, couple ties, underwear and socks, I could've taken a Caribbean vacation. But I had to admit, I looked like one of those guys in the fashion magazines.

So, first things first. My wallet was damn near empty. I won't say the thought of floating myself a loan from the box with ten thousand dollars in it didn't enter my head. But whatever dumb things I've done in my life, I'm proud that I've never gone on the take. I drove back to my neighborhood, to the Greenacres Branch of First Savings and Loan, just five minutes' walk from my house, and pulled seven hundred from my savings account. It crossed my mind to stop in and see if Irma had cooled off any, but the mind-cop told me to let it rest.

Next, I dropped down to the station, swung into Mel Richmond's office, and asked if he wanted a quick update. He gave me five minutes. He wasn't pleased to hear I'd left ten thousand dollars "in a safe place," but when I asked if he'd like me to bring it in and check it through, he shook his head in a hurry.

"I'm sure that money came from Sanford," I said. "I'd love to find out where he does his banking, and look for a tenK withdrawal last September. If I could squeeze him with that, I think it'd open a bunch of doors."

Krupa with a pencil on the desk. "You'd need a warrant."

"Mel…"

"Okay, Bernie, I'm sorry. I know you know that. What I'm saying is, I'd rather you find some way to get what you need without doing something the newsies might pick up on. But if absolutely nothing else works, and you're positive you've got to have a warrant, please come to me, and let me handle it directly."

With a judge you can count on to keep it quiet in the interest of public safety, I thought. "I hear you, Mel. One more thing before I get out of your way. I need for you to get me a gun." I flashed my lapel back to show the empty holder.

His lips moved, but nothing came out.

"You've got to go with me on this," I said. "Part of trusting me to do right by you on the case. I don't think you'd want me to answer the questions I'd get, requisitioning a gun through channels."

Picture a guy whose son just asked him for money to take his girlfriend to see a doctor. "Bernie, this isn't going to come back to bite me, is it?"

Judgment call. I couldn't see Irma using my gun to hold up a liquor store. And with me out of her sight, she wasn't about to shoot herself, either. Sure, I could be wrong, but it sounded like a smart bet, and if Richmond wanted to tie one of my hands behind my back, it didn't seem unfair for him to take a small risk to keep my one free hand working as well as it could. "I don't think so, Mel."

He hesitated a few seconds, then picked up the phone. Ten minutes later, I was outside, with a full holster, leaving Mel to take on his next headache of the day.

◇◇◇

Granted, I was not supposed to make any waves, but since everything I knew about the goings-on in Hearn's lab had come from Laurie Mansell, and since it had been on Mansell's recommendation that the Supervisor from Hell had been hired, I thought it might be interesting to hear how other people in that lab had seen things. Ms. Mansell didn't look overjoyed to see me as I came through the door, but she was cordial, and told me I could use her office to interview the four techs.

The first three gave carbon-copy replies to all my questions, no deviations off the shorter accounts they'd given me right after the Kennett-Hearn disaster. They'd been at work when they heard shouting, then gunshots, and then the lab went nuts. When I asked about the accident the prior August, none of them remembered anything. Not unreasonable, given that Mansell had told me she and Wanego were working adjacent to the alcove, and the other techs were a room away.

The fourth tech was George Altgeld, a nice looking kid, deep blue eyes, big nose, lots of dark hair curling over his ears. Tall, muscular, spine straight, all his movements smooth, graceful. Most people look uncomfortable when they get called in for a police interview, but this guy didn't appear to be the least bothered. I decided to try a different tack with him. "Where do you work out?" I asked.

Which got me a conditional grin. "How'd you know I work out?"

"My job."

He shrugged. "I go to the Emerald Athletic Club, down on Westland Avenue. It's close enough, I can run over during lunch hour."

"So, how was it, working for Alma Wanego?"

Life's just one non sequitur after pork chops. He blinked. "Huh?"

"How'd you like working for Alma Wanego? What's complicated about that?"

Altgeld tried to figure out where I was coming from. I motioned with a hand: Give.

"Well…okay, you want to know, I can tell you pretty quick. It was a bitch. *She* was a bitch. I got it worse than anybody else, right from Day One, but I've got some pride, and I decided she wasn't going to send me out with my tail between my legs." Now, he grinned with all his heart. "And I'm still here, and she's not."

"You got it worse than the other techs? Why?"

"Why do you think?"

"I don't know," I said quietly. "That's why I asked you."

He ran his lips through a quick set of push-outs. "Okay, then. Here's how it was. I'm the only male tech, and Wanego didn't much like men. No, let me say it straight-out. I don't think she ever saw a pair of balls she didn't want to bust. Talk was, she had something going with Dr. Camnitz, but I never could buy that. If Wanego ever had a heart, it would have belonged to Laur…"

If he could have swallowed that last sentence, he would have. "Ah, shit," he muttered.

"Mansell?" I asked. "Her heart would have belonged to Laurie Mansell?"

Altgeld sighed. "That's what I said."

"But Laurie Mansell's married and has two kids."

Bingo. His face broadcast contempt for the dumb old cop. He wiped the back of his hand across his mouth. "Hey, this stuff happens nowadays. A gay guy or woman gets married, and thinks that'll take care of things, but it doesn't. They know they're playing on the wrong team."

"Any proof?"

"If you mean did I ever see them in the sack together, no. But the two of them always worked on the same projects, and, well…little things. The way they'd sometimes touch each other. The way Wanego talked to Laurie, nothing like how she talked to the rest of us. And since Wanego got the job here because of Laurie, and then got promoted over Laurie to supervisor, you'd figure Laurie'd be pretty pissed off, wouldn't you? Well, she never said a word about it."

"Sounds to me like if she had, she'd have been out the door before the word was out of her mouth," I said.

Altgeld nodded vigorously. "Yeah, sure. But there were other things. One day, I walked past where they were working, and Laurie pulled out a book of matches to light a burner, then dropped the matches on the desk. They were from the Venus Lounge."

The Venus Lounge was a lesbian spot on Wesley Street, up on Capitol Hill, the major gay section of Emerald.

"And one time, when I came back early from my workout, Wanego and Mansell had their heads together over a petri dish, and they jumped like I'd goosed them. I pretended not to notice anything, but Wanego had a smear of lipstick on her kisser, and she never wore makeup."

"Did you ever talk to the other techs about this?"

"No way. I'm not dumb enough to lie to a cop who's asking me questions, but for all I hated Wanego, and I'll tell you, that was plenty, I'd never want to do anything to hurt Laurie. I could care less if she swings both ways. It's her business, and besides, she's a sweetheart. *She* should've been made supervisor in the first place, not the Witch of the Northwest. I'd work for Laurie anywhere, any time. Hey, I sure hope you're not going to do anything to hurt her."

"I don't want to hurt anyone," I said. "For what it's worth, I'll do my best. I'll also do what I can to make sure she doesn't know the information came from you."

He looked relieved. "I'd really appreciate that."

I'd talked to the techs from behind Laurie Mansell's desk, but when I asked Ms. Mansell to come in, I moved to the visitor's chair. She settled in, smoothed her skirt, and asked whether my interviews had been helpful. "Sometimes we don't know right away," I said.

Which set off a wobbly little smile. "I understand."

"Now, I've got a question for *you*. How did you feel when Ms. Wanego was promoted past you to be supervisor?"

She shook her head and waggled her palms. "Oh, I guess a little resentful."

"Just a little?"

A shrug. "Yeah. No point making a big deal about it."

"Even though she'd gotten her job here in the first place because of your recommendation?"

Her mouth formed a neat O. "How—"

"It's in her file at Personnel. How'd you happen to know her?"

She could tell where I was headed, but wasn't about to come along if she could help it. "I met her, oh, five years ago, at the Annual Convention of Cytogenetics Lab Technicians. We got to talking, and she said she wasn't happy where she was working. I thought she seemed very competent, and I knew one of our techs was moving to Denver, so I spoke to Dr. Hearn, and she said why didn't I have Alma put in an application."

"And the rest is history. Ms. Mansell, you're not leaving anything out, are you?"

"I don't think so...like what?"

"Like why you happened to meet someone at a convention, then gave her a strong enough recommendation that she got a job in your lab, and before her suitcase was unpacked, everybody in the place hated her. And then, when this person nobody could stand got to be the next supervisor, jumping right over your back, you felt maybe only a little resentful."

"Mr. Baumgartner, what are you trying to say?"

"That it is odd you weren't bothered more when you were passed over, and that you seem to be the only person around who wasn't put off by Ms. Wanego's lack of interpersonal skills."

"There was no point being bitter. Dr. Hearn explained to me that Dr. Camnitz had insisted Alma be appointed supervisor, and there was nothing we could do about it. But she did manage a little raise for me." Mansell sighed. "And anyway, I got along with Alma all right. She had another side that not many people could see."

"But you could."

Ms. Mansell's face went the color of beef in a butcher's display case. She opened her mouth, but nothing came out. I paused, felt like a bastard, but pushed ahead. "Do you have another side, too? One that fit with Ms. Wanego's."

Up out of her chair, just this far from tears. "You don't have any right—"

"Venus Lounge."

Like I'd shot her. She fell back into her chair, slumped. Tears started.

"I'm sorry," I said, and meant it. "Why don't you tell me what really happened at that convention?"

She pulled out a handkerchief, dabbed at her eyes. When she looked back at me, it was with an expression I've seen before, one that says I'm finally about to hear the real story. "I was at the bar in the evening with a few friends. Alma came up and introduced herself, and then, when my friends took off, she asked would I like to come up to her room and talk. I knew… of course I knew. The way she'd been looking at me. So, I went with her. Later, she told me she was hunting for a job. I talked to Dr. Hearn…and I've told you the rest."

"Not all of it. If what you've been telling me is true, how was it that Ms. Wanego was carrying on an affair with Dr. Camnitz?"

"It was Alma's idea, strictly business. Lab techs work on soft money, and if a grant runs out and the investigator can't get a renewal or a new grant, some techs are going to be out of work. Alma said she could get job security for the two of us, and she'd give me half the raise that'd come with the supervisor's job. With that and the raise I got from Dr. Hearn, I was actually making almost as much as Alma."

"Did she follow through on her promise?"

"Every month, like clockwork." Mansell started to cry again, quietly. "We made a little ceremony out of it. Once a month, on payday, we'd go out and have a nice dinner, and then go back to her place, or get a room. I told my husband we had monthly lab staff dinner meetings, and every now and then, I said there was a weekend retreat." She covered her face; her whole body shook. "He was always...so...nice about it."

I pulled a couple of tissues from the box at the corner of her desk, and pushed them into her hands. "I can't begin to imagine how tough that was."

She nodded, wiped her eyes, then blew her nose. "If my husband *wasn't* so nice, I'd have told him what was happening, and maybe Alma and I could've found our own place. But I loved my husband—I still do. I couldn't stand the thought of losing him *or* Alma. Going to a motel felt so cheap, though, and planning visits around that snippy little roommate of hers was a real nuisance."

"Katie Corrigan?"

She nodded. "She didn't like me."

"Why not?"

"Well...I can't say for sure, but I think maybe she had a little crush on Alma, herself."

I remembered Katie telling me about her expensive Labor Day weekend at the coast with a boyfriend, right before Ms. Wanego had vanished. Maybe Mansell was being overly sensitive about the person she had to work around to visit Wanego. I apologized for having made her so uncomfortable, said I didn't have any more questions right then, and left her trying to get herself together before she had to face her lab crew.

Cops develop thick skin. They have to. But some stuff still gets through. I've known guys who were cheating on their wives, and a few women who were sneaking behind their husbands' backs, but I'd never met anyone in Laurie Mansell's situation. I could imagine, a little too easily, how I'd feel if Irma told me she was leaving me for another man, but what if it was for a woman? Would that be different? Better? Worse? I didn't know.

While I waited for the elevator, a thought hit me. Katie Corrigan didn't tell me she'd gone to the shore with her boyfriend. She said she went with her sweetie.

◇◇◇

The Medical School's Office of Continuing Medical Education was next to the Dean's Office, three stories down from the OBGYN Department. The young Latina woman behind the desk flashed teeth as I came through the door. "Yes, sir. Can I help you?"

"I hope so," I said. "I'm Dr. William Francis, I do OBGYN. I'd like some information about a conference that was held in Norway last September."

All the time I talked, she watched me. When I finished, she asked, "Are you on our staff, Dr. Francis?"

"That's in process," I said. "I've just moved here…" I looked toward my wedding ring, felt a little catch in my throat, good timing. "…for my wife's health. She's got a condition, and she's not doing well with the Minnesota winters. I just picked up staff membership papers, and I thought as long as I was here, I'd check into that September conference. Might be a good one for me to go to this year, you know, get to touch base with some of the old friends I had to leave behind in the snow."

The clerk was all sympathy. "Sure, sure. I understand. Let me go check the files." She sashayed across the room to a file cabinet.

In less than two minutes she was back, waving a color brochure in my face. "This the one you're thinking of?"

I scanned the two pages. Society of Gynecological Cancer Surgeons…September 2-5, 1976, Oslo, Norway…best time of year in Scandinavia…beautiful Midnight Sun Hotel. I nodded to the clerk. "Right, that's it. They don't have this year's brochure yet, do they?"

"Oh, no, sir. Much too early for that. But if you'd like, I can make you a copy of this one."

"That'd be great."

◇◇◇

I got a handful of coins at the cafeteria, then slid into a phone booth in the corridor and dialed the phone number on the brochure for the beautiful Midnight Sun Hotel. After a long sequence of bings and bongs as I dropped quarters, dimes, and nickels into the slots, I heard that funny ring they use on phones in Europe. When a man filled my ear with a string of words starting with something that sounded like "Midnight Sun," I said, "English, please. Do you speak English?"

The Norwegian accent was thick as cream cheese, but no trouble understanding him. "Ah, yes. I beg your pardon, sir. What can I do for you?"

"My name is Dr. Gerald Camnitz. I attended the Cancer Surgery Conference at your hotel last September."

"Yes, Doctor?"

"I know it's been a while, but I just noticed something I need to check on. My wife made some charges to the room, and I'm not sure all of them are valid. Is there a way you could check the bill for me?"

"For that, sir, you would need to speak to someone in the Business Office, but I regret they are now closed for the day. They'll open at eight in the morning. Can you call back then?"

"Yes, thank you. What time is it in Oslo now?"

"Nearly eight in the evening, sir."

Coming up on eleven a.m. here, nine hours' difference. "Thank you for your trouble."

"We're always glad to be of help, sir."

I found Charles Rapp in the Anatomy Department, working a mop across a laboratory floor, between two rows of stout tables with tarps draped over their tops. I tried not to think about what was under those covers. "I'm looking into a missing persons case," I said, and held my ID out to him. "Can I ask you a few questions?"

Rapp leaned the handle of his mop against the wall. "Don't mind taking a break." He swung a finger around the room. "Christ on a crutch. These med students, it's like they were brought up in a barn. They drop a Kleenex or a gum wrapper, they ain't gonna bother to pick it up. Let the goddamn janitor…

excuse me, the goddamn 'housekeeper' do it. Bet their mothers never made them clean up their room. Sometimes I even find a finger on the floor, or a piece of guts, or God knows what. Can you believe that?"

"Sure, why not? They're in training to be doctors. Soon as they've learned how to get a good table in a restaurant, they take a course in how to make sure someone else picks up after them."

He took a moment, then cut loose a horse laugh. "You're okay." He pointed toward the professor's desk at the front corner of the room. "Let's take a load off."

"Suits me."

Rapp settled into the straight-backed wooden chair with an "Ooomph." I perched on the corner of the desk. "Whaddaya wanna know?" he asked.

His voice was like ground glass in a mixer. He was a big man in his mid-fifties, with gray eyes and scanty straight gray hair on top. A thin scar ran from the corner of his left eye to the angle of his jaw. A faded tattoo of an anchor decorated his left biceps. Navy, World War Two. "I understand you've worked here for a half-year, little more," I said.

"Here in Anatomy? Yeah. But I been pushing brooms and mops for Washington Public U coming up on eighteen years."

"And before Anatomy, you worked in OBGYN, right?"

"Ten years."

His eyes told me exactly what he was feeling. "And you didn't leave there by your request."

"No. That cunt, Wanego…sorry, Detective."

"A rose by any other name," I said. "Don't worry about it."

The right corner of his mouth turned upward. "Yeah. Well, she was some piece of work, all right. Tried to get me fired for not opening up a clogged washbasin fast enough, and didn't give a flying fuck that a doctor countermanded her order."

Countermanded. Yep, Navy. "Why did a doctor countermand her order?"

I thought Rapp might spit on the floor. "How'm I supposed to know that? I figured he wanted me to finish putting up the fire extinguisher and get all my crap cleared outa the hallway. That's what I was doing when Wanego grabbed me. Wasn't my place to ask questions, but it seemed like a doc would outrank a lab supervisor." He snapped his right hand to his forehead in a crisp military salute. "I thought when I got outa the Navy I was done havin' to say, 'How much and how high, sir?' when an ensign not old enough to shave said 'Shit.' At least in the Navy, you know who outranks you, but here, it seems like everybody outranks everybody else, but for goddamn sure, they all outrank me."

He blew out two lungfuls of exasperation, shook his head. "Yeah, that Wanego, I never in my life seen the likes of her. Good-lookin' woman, I'll give her that, but I wouldn't have stuck it to her with a ten-foot dick. She chewed me out every which way to Sunday, and next morning I was down to Personnel. They didn't want to hear nothing I had to say, just told me I had a clean record up till then, and they thought it'd be better if I didn't work around Wanego no more. I felt sorry for Miss Walker—she was the head of Personnel. Everyone knew she had the Big C. She told me she'd assign me to Anatomy, so I said thank you and that's fine. And it's as good here as any other place, lot better'n some. Anything else I can tell you?"

"You do know Ms. Wanego doesn't work in Reproductive Genetics any more?"

I watched Rapp closely, but saw no sign of nerves, or even concern. Satisfaction, yes, and a little amusement. "Yeah, I know. I figured Wanego's this missing person you're looking for. 'Bout a month after she socked it to me, I heard it around that she walked out on her job and never came back, and nobody was sounding broken up about it. Maybe she made a mistake and took on somebody got more clout than a janitor. I sure hope so, the bitch. I just wish I was around to see it when she got hers."

Not all the people who say they like surprises really do. They'd rather think they're in control. But surprise was Sanford's game. He had to prove over and over how much cooler he was in an emergency than anyone else. He *was* good, no argument, but all I'd done so far was pitch him batting practice. Now I was warmed up. Time to see what he'd do with some nasty curves, sliders down and away, high heat under the chin. I figured Joyce Kennett was my best bet for a setup pitch.

◇◇◇

I drove the car out of the hospital garage, up to Sunset Bluff, across Seventy-first Street, and parked in front of the Kennett house. Ms. Kennett's mother opened the door. I gave her a nice smile. "Hello, Ms. Enright."

"That's *Mrs.* Enright. I'm not one of those women's lib people."

Like I'd propositioned her. "*Mrs.* Enright."

She was starting to look like caring for a new mother and a newborn baby was wearing on her. That nest of gray hair hadn't had a meeting with a comb or a brush any time recently, and her face said whatever I was selling, she was not interested. "I hope you're not going to bother my daughter again, Mr. Baumgartner."

From somewhere in back, I heard the baby crying. "I'm afraid I am," I said, gently as I could. "Something new has come up, and I need a few minutes of her time."

"Joyce is very tired," she barked into my face. "Men think taking care of a baby is no big deal."

I stepped past her, into the living room. "I don't know about 'men,' but I do know looking after a newborn baby is no walk in the park. I'll make it as short and easy for your daughter as possible."

She made a noise like an engine shutting down, then closed the door and turned away. "I'll go get Joyce."

"Thank you, Mrs. Enright."

As the women came back into the room, the baby in Joyce Kennett's arms let out a top-decibel howl. Ms. Kennett glanced at her mother. "Would you mind taking Robbie?"

Easy to see the old woman didn't want to miss the show. "Will you be all right, dear?"

"Please, Ma. I'm sure the detective won't hurt me. Take Robbie back and see if you can calm him down."

Mrs. Enright took the baby, turned like a soldier and marched off. Ms. Kennett motioned me to a faded red armchair. "Would you like to sit?" She pulled a little maple rocker up beside me.

As we settled in, I said, "Nice-looking baby."

"Sometimes more than others. What can I do for you, Mr. Baumgartner?"

"I'm sorry to bother you again so soon, but a couple of new things have come up. You told me yesterday that Dr. Sanford got Dr. Hearn to do a new procedure on your husband's sperm, then used that sperm sample to inseminate you. Right?"

She nodded automatically.

"And he did that insemination where?"

"In his office, three days after he broke up my adhesions. Dr. Hearn brought the treated sperm over, and Dr. Sanford inseminated me."

"Then your husband would have met Dr. Hearn, at the procedure."

"Actually, he didn't. James never liked to come into the examining room, he said it made him uncomfortable. So he waited outside. It was just the two doctors, the office nurse, and me."

I took in a quick breath. "Those eggs Dr. Sanford took from you during your laparoscopy? What did he do with them?"

She answered way too fast. "He didn't take eggs…I mean, why would he do that? I needed them to conceive at the insemination."

"That's why I'm asking," I said. "It doesn't sound logical. Was Dr. Hearn in the operating room?"

"Not that I saw. But—"

I waved off the rest of her answer. "Right. You were under anesthesia. Asleep."

"Yes. But I can't imagine why she would have been there, and I never heard anything about him taking my eggs. Did he tell you he did?"

"It was in the operating-room records," I said. "Now, one other thing. There was an accident in that lab at the time Dr. Hearn and Dr. Sanford were working on your case. Something about a laboratory container that Dr. Hearn dropped on the floor. She was really upset, and called Dr. Sanford to come right over. Did you hear anything about that?"

She shook her head emphatically. "Dr. Sanford never said anything about an accident."

But now, he'll have to, won't he? I thanked Ms. Kennett for her time, and left.

Chapter Fourteen

Sanford

I was in the examining room with a patient when Lettie, the receptionist, called to tell me Joyce Kennett was on the phone, and it was urgent. I excused myself, ran into my consultation room, picked up the receiver, and made an instant diagnosis of acute freakout. "That police detective was just here again."

"Baumgartner?"

"Yes. He said he knows you took eggs out of my ovaries at the laparoscopy."

"Did he say how he knew, or why he was interested in it?"

"He said it was in the hospital records, and no, he didn't say why he was interested. But he asked me if I knew why you took the eggs."

"And you said?"

"That I had no idea why you'd take my eggs because I'd need them to be inseminated. I couldn't tell if he believed me or not."

"Perfect, Joyce. If he comes back again, make sure you stick to the same story. I gave you hormones to make you ovulate at the right time, did the laparoscopy and cut away scar tissue, then James gave a sperm sample to Dr. Hearn. Dr. Hearn treated the sample, I inseminated you with it, you got pregnant, end of story."

"But there's more." Her voice shook. "He said right about that time, there was some kind of lab accident where Dr. Hearn dropped a container and called you to come right over. That didn't have anything to do with James and me, did it?"

"Bah." I chuckled into the phone. "No, absolutely not. Dr. Hearn was a perfectionist, which is what you want in someone doing that line of work. She dropped one of our experiments, and you'd have thought the world was coming to an end. I told her it was too bad, but accidents are going to happen, and fortunately, this one wouldn't hurt anyone. That's all."

"Dr. Sanford..."

I waited.

"Why is Baumgartner bugging me like this? Two days in a row now."

"Probably what a cop has to do. If he doesn't file enough paperwork, they'll think he's goofing off."

"I'm afraid he's going to louse up our plan. Money was tight enough when James was working, but—"

"Joyce, hold on. We can't let Baumgartner stampede us. He got wind of the press conference, and I stonewalled him, so there's no way we can go ahead right now. Let a little time pass, he'll move along to another investigation, and then if he gets sore when we announce, I can tell him I had to lie about the conference to protect your privacy before you were ready to handle the publicity. At that point, he's not going to reopen the case. He'd look like an idiot. But if we make the announcement tomorrow, I've got zero wiggle room."

For answer, I got a soft crying jag, then, "Okay...I guess you're right. I'm sorry."

"Don't apologize. With all you've got to deal with right now, if you weren't nervous and a little irritable, you wouldn't be human. Relax and let me handle things. If Baumgartner comes back, all you need to do is make sure you don't change anything about what you've told him. I can handle a palooka like him in my sleep."

Loud snuffle at the other end. "Thanks, Dr. Sanford."

"That's what I'm here for. Talk to you later."

◇◇◇

An hour or so after Joyce's call, I was examining my next-to-last patient for the day when Barbara knocked at the door, then pulled me into the hall. She had a bad case of the fidgets. "That police detective is out front. He wants to talk to you again."

"Fine. Tell him I have to finish up with two patients, and he can either wait or come back in half an hour."

"But he says he wants to see you right now. What should I say if he insists?"

"I don't think he'll insist. Whatever's on his mind, I can't imagine it won't wait a half-hour. People say doctors like to play God, but we're nothing compared to cops. If he does insist, though, come get me, and I'll deal with him."

She smiled. "You really are cool, Dr. Sanford. In every sense of the word."

◇◇◇

When I went out to the waiting room, I found Baumgartner stretched across one of the padded double seats, head back against the chromed armrest. "Mr. Baumgartner." I put out a hand. "Sorry to keep you waiting."

He sat up slowly. "*I'm* sorry to keep bugging you, but I've got a few more questions."

I shrugged. "I'm done for the day. Whatever you need."

Back in my office, in my desk chair, I waited until he opened his mouth to speak, then cut him off at the pass. "I've remembered something you asked about yesterday. I actually did retrieve eggs from Joyce Kennett's ovaries. Those hormones did such a good job of stimulating egg growth, there were far more ripe oocytes than we'd ever need for her insemination with the treated sperm. As I recall, I counted twelve or thirteen. So I retrieved a couple for Dr. Hearn, for her experiments."

Baumgartner made an "umph" sound, and worked his lips side to side. "Was it okay with Ms. Kennett? She doesn't seem to know you removed any eggs for experimentation."

I pretended to think for a bit, then said, "No…damn. I think you've got me there. She was already asleep when I decided to take the ova, and afterward, it didn't occur to me to mention it to her. That's how important it seemed, a couple of extra eggs, so what? My focus was on the eggs left inside, to get at least one of them fertilized."

"But how could you have done a retrieval without having the equipment ready in the room?"

"Fair question. When I saw the state of the ovaries, I told the circulating nurse to call Dr. Hearn and see if she was free to come over. She was, so I asked the nurse to bring in the retrieval equipment. By the time I was through cutting adhesions, the equipment was there, and by the time I'd retrieved the ova, Dr. Hearn was all set to take them away. But you're right, Mr. Baumgartner, I should have told Ms. Kennett afterward. I'll speak to her this evening, and explain. It was a lapse, and it shouldn't have happened. But is it a matter for police investigation?"

Baumgartner gave me a goofy little smile. "Sometimes we've got to cast a wide net. Bear with me. Aren't there usually copies of operative reports in office charts? To help doctors remember details of cases?"

"Well, yes. Of course."

"But all I saw in Ms. Kennett's chart was a short handwritten note."

"Better that than nothing. I always put a short note in the chart to at least remind me that there *was* a procedure. Frankly, our hospital's transcription department leaves a good deal to be desired. I dictate every surgery right after the case, but sometimes the dictations don't get through to the transcribers, or so they say. Or copies of the transcriptions don't get made or don't get sent to my office. My staff doesn't have time to follow up on every operation I do, and make sure we have the official dictated note. When we need to look at one and it's not there, we go to the record room and get a copy." I gave him a grin guaranteed to make his stomach churn. "As I guess you did."

Baumgartner picked a pencil off the edge of my desk, jabbed the point absent-mindedly in my direction. "Those eggs you remember now that you gave to Dr. Hearn—were they part of the experiment she dropped on the floor? You do remember that spilled experiment, don't you? The one where you had to run over to calm her down?"

"Yes, I remember it," I said. "But I can't say which experiment it was because she didn't tell me. Just said she botched one."

"But it *was* right about the time Ms. Kennett had her procedure."

I shrugged. "I think you're right, but I'm not sure. Sorry."

Baumgartner tilted back in his chair, rocked a couple of times, then came forward again. "Dr. Hearn's experimental tissue cultures were done in petri dishes, right?"

I nodded. "As far as I know."

"But what she dropped wasn't a petri dish. It was a glass tube. What would've been in a glass tube?"

"Well...*anything*, I guess. Culture medium—"

He looked as if he'd sat the wrong way on a hemorrhoid. "Come on, Dr. Sanford. We're not talking about a kid and her home chemistry set. Could there have been eggs in that tube?"

"I don't think so. Dr. Hearn always took the oocytes I gave her and put them right into a petri dish. I don't think she ever put eggs into glass tubes, but I can't say for sure."

"How about what she used to fertilize the eggs? Did sperm samples go into glass tubes?"

"Well...right. Yes, they would. Part of any sperm preparation for insemination, from ordinary washing to Density Gradient Separation, involves centrifugation, and that's done in a glass tube. You've got to separate the liquid semen from the sperm cells. All right?"

"Yep. Was that broken tube for a Density Gradient Separation?"

"Not as far as I know. All Dr. Hearn said was that she'd botched an experiment."

"Where did the sperm for those experimental runs come from?"

"I've told you. Medical students. I paid them fifty bucks a pop. But I can't show you records. No student would ever have donated if I'd kept records."

Baumgartner whistled. "Fifty bucks a pop, huh? And the money came from…?"

"My wallet."

He did a dandy Eddie Cantor impersonation, pop-eyes and open mouth. "You paid fifty dollars every time Dr. Hearn did an experiment? Out of the goodness of your heart?"

"Not to be crass, Mr. Baumgartner, but I do well in my practice, and PhD scientists don't have that kind of resource."

"Unless they have a grant, which Dr. Hearn wouldn't have had for that work, since she was doing it on the QT."

"You've got it."

"But I still have to think that was awfully generous of you. How many times did you pay a student fifty dollars? You don't have to answer, I've got the records. You attempted fifty-five retrievals, and got eggs in forty-one. That comes out to more than two thousand dollars. Which, even for a doctor with a practice as hefty as yours, is not exactly pocket change. You can understand, can't you, why I might want to know what was the quo you got for *that* quid?"

"I can only tell you if you can understand payment doesn't necessarily need to be in the coin of the realm. If I'd donated that money to the Red Cross, the American Cancer Society, or the Emerald Public Library, you wouldn't have thought even once about it. Dr. Hearn was trying to do important work in my field, but was being held back by a chairman with a medieval attitude. And by collaborating with Dr. Hearn, I could let my patients know they'd get the best possible care from a practicing doctor who was also involved firsthand in front-line University research. All right?"

Baumgartner sat and stared. I gave him about a half-minute, then spread my palms. "What's your next question?"

He pushed himself out of the chair as if he'd suddenly and unexpectedly put on a hundred pounds. "That's all for now, Doctor. Thanks for your time."

As I'd done at his first visit, I walked him out of the office, down the hall, and saw him onto the elevator. Then, I went back inside, picked up the phone, started to punch in Joyce Kennett's number, but halfway through, I lowered the receiver. Better to go see her in person. Make sure she wouldn't lose her nerve, and do or say something to blow our boat out of the water. And if Baumgartner followed me, I could tell him I was going to talk to Ms. Kennett, to make amends for having forgotten to tell her I'd retrieved a couple of her oocytes for experimentation.

Chapter Fifteen

Baumgartner

Just after six when Katie Corrigan opened her door to my knock. She looked tired. "Hard day at work?"

"Nah, not really. More booze and less sleep than I should've had last night. What's on your mind?"

"I've been wondering why it was you didn't like Laurie Mansell."

Katie seemed to take a moment to register the question, then blew a raspberry and dismissed Mansell with a wave of her hand. "Snooty little muff. She'd come here sometimes with Alma when they didn't think I'd be around. Pretending they were just good friends from the lab. Alma didn't have any trouble carrying it off, but Laurie was a riot, trying to act like a chilled-up penguin, and coming off like a cat in heat. It was fun to play along, just sit there like nothing was happening, till Laurie finally had to go home to her husband with her thighs all wet."

"Seems a little cruel to me."

"Hey, Mr. Baumgartner. You want cruel? You should've met Alma. She set the standard."

"But it was Laurie you didn't like."

Katie coughed, said nothing.

"That Labor Day weekend you went to the shore with your sweetie? What did you say was your sweetie's name? Joseph? Or Josephine?"

"Damn you." She grabbed a bookend from the table beside her, threw it against the wall. Her eyes sizzled. "Yeah, Alma *was* cruel, all right. She gave me a tumble every now and then, but nothing more than that. Said redheads turned her on sometimes, and if I wasn't a redhead, she wouldn't have any use for me at all. She liked to tease me…she liked to tease *everybody*. Once or twice before she took off, she said something that made me think she might be coming into a bundle, like not having to worry about food money any more. So I kept thinking, kept *hoping*, maybe Alma was gonna show up one day, flash a wad of money in my face, and say, 'Let's go see what it's like in Paris. Or Rio.' Stupid, *stupid*." She pounded a fist onto the arm of the sofa. "Then, when she disappeared, I figured she got her money and went off with it, probably with Mansell. So I checked in the lab. Fat lot of good it really did me, but I've got to admit, it made me feel a little better to see the little twit was still there."

"And you never did see any money? She never told you she'd gotten it?"

Katie shook her head. Copper hair flew one way, then the other. "One day, she was here, next day she wasn't. Just like that."

True enough, otherwise, that box with the ten thousand wouldn't have been in the basement with Wanego's stuff. But Katie did have a temper, and I could see her losing it, and giving Wanego a clout with a metal bookend.

She flashed me a sad grin. "I guess I'm not the first moron who lost their head over a piece of tail, am I, Mr. Baumgartner?"

"Not hardly. But I still don't get it. You had a sweetie. What did you need from a cruel woman with a tongue like a viper."

A look crossed Katie's face, wistful, longing. "Yeah, right on. Hey, Mr. Baumgartner—you ever have a viper put its tongue between your legs?"

◇◇◇

After dinner that night, I sat with Iggy in his living room. "No way to know how long this business is going to go on," I said.

"I want you to tell me if I'm in the way here. I can always get a motel room."

Iggy laughed. "Forget that, Mr. B. No skin offa my back, havin' you stay here, and besides, this's the most interesting thing I've had in my life since I went straight. You make any headway today?"

"More pieces, no more connections. But this Sanford's up to his eyeballs in everything. I think he and Dr. Hearn put their heads together to get Joyce Kennett pregnant with an in vitro baby. I'd give my eye teeth to get my hands on Hearn's log book for the secret experiments she was doing, and I'd bet anything Sanford's got it. But he's not going to hand it over to me, and I'm nowhere near having enough evidence to get a warrant. Hell, I wouldn't even know where to search. His office? His apartment?"

Iggy shrugged, palms up in front of his face.

"Number Two for Sanford. Last August, right about the time Ms. Kennett got pregnant, the lab supervisor saw Hearn spill what she said was an experiment all over the floor, and a couple of months later—when Joyce Kennett's pregnancy test would've turned positive—the supervisor vanishes, poof, and I find exactly ten thousand dollars, to the penny, in a box with her things. If she took off on her own call, she'd never have left that box behind. I think she tumbled to what Sanford and Hearn were doing, and blackmailed them. But before I tell the chief I want a warrant to look at Sanford's bank accounts, I've got to make sure I don't embarrass myself, tripping up on a loose end."

"A loose end like what?"

"Like there were other people who might not have minded seeing that lab supervisor disappear. But aside from Sanford, the only one I can see having ten thousand bucks of disposable cash would be the department chairman, who supposedly was having an affair with her. One word from her to his wife, and his rich and influential father-in-law would've had his head. I'd love to put him on the grill, but I'd feel a whole lot better if I had some hard proof of that affair with the supervisor."

"How you gonna get that?"

I grinned. "I'm going to make a phone call to Norway."

The manager of the Midnight Sun Hotel's business office spoke perfect English, just a hint of Scandinavian flavor. I identified myself as Dr. Camnitz, and repeated my story about the questionable charges by my wife during our stay the past September.

"Certainly, sir. I would be glad to check our records. Do you have the dates you were with us?"

"The conference was last September second through the fifth."

"Good. Would you like to hold on, or shall I call you back?"

"I'll hold. Thank you."

Didn't take her long. "I have your account, sir. You and Mrs. Camnitz checked in on September first, and checked out September sixth. And, let me see, there are one, two, three…four charges, two for room-service breakfasts, one from the gift shop in the lobby, and one from the lobby newsstand. You signed for the breakfasts and the magazines. The ticket from the gift shop was signed by Susanna Camnitz."

Oh, Susanna! I cleared my throat. "Can you tell me one thing, please. That item she purchased at the gift shop…"

"A one-carat Burmese pigeon-blood ruby ring. For eight thousand Kroner. Is there a problem with that?"

"Eight thous…Oh, no. Oh, my goodness, please forgive me. I'm terribly embarrassed. I'd been thinking eight thousand dollars—"

That brought a wonderful Ingrid Bergman laugh. "Yes, I can see why you might have been upset. At an exchange rate of sixteen dollars and seventy-two cents per one hundred kroner, the price of the ring in US currency was…one thousand, two hundred and eighty dollars. Quite a difference."

"Of course. Stupid of me, absolutely stupid. I'm sorry."

"Don't worry about a thing, sir." She was clearly enjoying hearing an American grovel. "You might be surprised how often this happens."

"You're very kind. Thank you."

"Not at all. Please come back and see us again."

"I certainly will. We had a wonderful stay, and my wife loves that ruby ring."

As I hung up the phone, Iggy snorted. "'Oh, my goodness, please forgive me...absolutely stupid...'"

"Laugh all you want," I said. But now, when I go in to talk to that puffed-up lard-ass, I'll be packing a howitzer instead of a popgun. And if he gets all his answers right, I'll feel a lot better about going after Sanford's bankbooks.

Chapter Sixteen

Baumgartner

Next morning, eight o'clock, Dr. Camnitz's secretary told me he didn't see people without an appointment, and she'd be glad to make one for me. "I'm a homicide detective, Ma'am, Emerald Police," I said. "I'm investigating a murder-suicide in Dr. Camnitz's department, and I'd like to see the doctor now. If he's in there, please tell him I want to talk to him. If he's not there, I need to know where he is and how I can get hold of him."

She sniffed. "He's making rounds with his residents. He'll be back at eight-thirty.

I said I'd wait.

Another sniff. "He has a meeting at nine with the dean."

"I should be done by then, but if I'm not, Dr. Camnitz will let you know to tell the dean he'll be a little late." Then I sat in a padded leather-backed chair against the opposite wall, took my notebook from my shirt pocket, and looked over the entries I'd written after my call to Oslo the night before.

Camnitz sauntered in on the stroke of eight-thirty, poster boy for precision. Full head of gray hair, every one in place. Not a wrinkle in his three-piece dark blue suit, noncommittal navy-blue tie knotted perfectly at his throat. Clear polish gleamed off fingernails trimmed just so.

"Good morning, Doctor," I said. "Bernard Baumgartner, Emerald Police. I need to talk to you. If we can get right to it, I should have you out in time for your nine o'clock meeting."

He turned a furious look onto his secretary.

"I told him you'd be busy, Dr. Camnitz. But he insisted."

Camnitz turned back. "You're that detective I saw last Friday, in the lab. What seems to be the problem?"

"The problem is that I need to talk to you about what happened in that lab last Friday." I jerked a thumb toward the door to his office.

His ruddy cheeks darkened to near-purple. "Miss Vogelsang, please hold any calls." Then, without a word to me, he stomped off. I winked at Miss Vogelsang, and followed him.

Camnitz's office was the size of our squad room and then some. A slinky, curved mahogany desk and chairs were set in the far corner. Medical books filled shelves to either side of the desk. Diplomas on the wall made it look like he'd gone to school for half a century. Two monster paintings hung behind the desk, Hippocrates on the left, and L. Gerald Camnitz, Hippo's apparent representative on earth, to the right. The room reeked of perfume.

Camnitz dropped into his chair, thud. "Yes?"

"I want to ask some questions about the disappearance of your lab supervisor, Alma Wanego."

"For heaven's sake. What does *that* have to do with what happened Friday?"

"That's what I'd like to find out. I think it's possible there were some connections between the two events? How long had Ms. Wanego worked in your department?"

Camnitz made it clear he was not in the habit of suffering fools. "Not quite three years. But—"

"Good employee?"

"Oh, yes. Excellent."

"No problems with her?"

Just a moment's hesitation. He saw me notice. "Well…I don't really know whether to call it a problem. Keep in mind, Ms.

Wanego was the supervisor, and any supervisor worth her salt is going to have to do some, you might say, unpopular things. Actually, that was why she was made supervisor. When her predecessor resigned—"

"Which was why?"

"She was pregnant, and wanted to stay at home with the baby. The person in line for promotion, Laurie Mansell, was a very nice young woman and a good tech, but frankly, in my opinion, she didn't have, well, the *backbone* for the supervisory job. And as Department Chairman, I'm the administrator of that lab, so I spoke with Dr. Hearn. We agreed that Ms. Wanego was better suited for the position."

You agreed from the beginning, or you agreed after some discussion?"

He studied my face. "What's the point, Mr. Baumgartner?"

"The truth. The facts. Did you and Dr. Hearn agree from the get-go, or did you need to persuade her?"

"Very well. The truth is and the facts are, Dr. Hearn felt Ms. Mansell had earned the opportunity, and not only she, but the other techs, might feel some resentment should we appoint Ms. Wanego. But the nature of the work in those labs is delicate and complex, and a firm hand at the helm, you might say, is necessary. So yes, we discussed the matter, and Dr. Hearn came around to my point of view."

"How did it work out."

Shrug. "I'd say quite nicely. Forgive me, but I really do think Dr. Hearn could have given you an answer from, should we say, a closer vantage point."

"But I can't ask her, can I? Let me ask you this, Doctor. If Dr. Hearn's vantage point was that much closer, why did the administrator of that delicate and complex lab overrule the person with the best read on day-to-day operations?"

His mouth and jaw locked, brows bristled. "A wise administrator keeps tabs on his staff at all levels, and never gives a completely free hand to any subordinate." Spitting the words across the table. "I'm aware that seniority has come under challenge these days from the younger segment of society, but a certain capability does accrue with age and experience. Perhaps when I was younger, I'd have made the same choice Dr. Hearn did, but I've learned not to let personal feelings influence personnel decisions. All right?"

"Fair enough. And you told me your joint decision worked out fine?"

"Absolutely. The lab ran like a well-oiled machine. Yes, Ms. Wanego did, you could say, ruffle some feathers, but everyone knew his or her job, and got it done properly and in timely fashion."

"How was her absentee record?"

"Normal. Usual. As best I can recall."

"She seems to have taken a good number of short vacations."

"Yes, she did. She felt that as supervisor, it would be a bad idea for her to be away for long stretches, so she scheduled her breaks a few days at a time, a week at most. I would guess her yearly records would show she actually was away for fewer days than she was entitled to. Mr. Baumgartner, I'm sorry, but I don't understand why you're asking me these pointless questions." He tapped his wrist. "I have an important meeting with the Dean in just a few minutes."

"I know you do. How did Ms. Mansell take it when Ms. Wanego was named supervisor?"

He shifted in his chair. "I have no idea. You really would have had to ask Dr. Hearn that."

"You mean this administrator who doesn't give a completely free hand to any subordinate has no idea how the decision he forced on the lab staff affected those employees?"

I thought that might set him off, but he shrugged. "A good administrator operates through channels. I dealt with Dr. Hearn, and it was her job, you could say, to deal with Ms. Mansell."

"Like the Army."

Smug smile. "Precisely. Now, Mr. Baumgartner, I'm sorry, but I must go.

"I understand how busy you are, Doctor, but we need to finish first. Why don't you have your secretary call the Dean's office, and tell him you'll be delayed a little longer. I'll do my best to be as brief as possible."

He slung his best harrumph at me, but he did pick up the phone and mutter instructions to the secretary. Then, he swiveled back to face me, laced his fingers across his bulging breadbasket, and said, "Could we please stop beating around the bush, and get to the point?"

What a straight man. "Sure," I said. "We can do that. I think your interest in Ms. Wanego went a long way past administrative considerations."

Every muscle in Camnitz's body contracted. He leaned over the desk toward me, aimed a sausage finger at my nose. "How dare you? That's the end of *this* conversation. I'm going to call Security and have you removed." He grabbed for the phone.

"Bad idea," I said. "This isn't a conversation, it's a police interrogation, and you're going to look foolish, trying to have University Security throw a cop out of your office. And you'll look even more foolish when your father-in-law gets wind of why you did it. Does he know about your, uh, relationship with Ms. Wanego?"

Right then, the secretary must have said something over the phone, because Camnitz snapped, "Forget it, Miss Vogelsang. Sorry," and replaced the receiver.

"Good," I said. "Much better."

He looked me over like I was a med student who'd told him his diagnosis on a case was a crock. "You have some nerve," he spluttered. "Don't you think I know there were rumors going around the lab? But that's all they were, rumors. The kind of thing small people like to bandy around about their superiors. Neither my father-in-law nor my wife would put any stock in that nasty little tittle-tattle."

"Well, who knows," I said. "Maybe your wife *won't* believe it. She must still be ecstatic over that Burmese ruby ring you bought her in Norway."

Bull's-eye. He looked like a tire on a car that had caught a nail at sixty.

"She must have loved that little jaunt to Scandinavia last Labor Day weekend. Luxury hotel, breakfasts in bed, shopping sprees while you were at the meetings. And that ring, from the hotel gift shop, 8000 kroner—why, that's over a thousand dollars, Doctor, signed for in her hand. I'll bet that was a holiday she'll remember forever. Not to mention all the other delightful brief getaways you and she have enjoyed over the past year and a half."

Long pause, then, "What is it you want?" He sounded like a frog with laryngitis.

"I want to know about the ten thousand dollars you gave Ms. Wanego right after that trip to Oslo. Was that hush money, or was there another bauble she fancied?"

He looked at his wits' end. "I never gave her ten thousand dollars. Absolutely not."

"Never gave her any money at all?"

"Well, yes. Fifty here, a hundred there. But ten thousand?" He shook his head vigorously. "Not a chance."

"She wasn't putting the screws to you, was she? Threatening to tell your wife?"

"Why would she do that? She had her supervisory position in the lab and a raise in pay, all perfectly secure as long as I was around. She had free trips all over the world, with a piece of good jewelry here and there. Let it come out about us, and we'd both lose. She was not a stupid woman, believe me."

"Doesn't sound like she was stupid, no. I'd say she was pretty clever, getting herself so nice and cozy with the big boss. What was in it for you?"

"Jesus, Baumgartner, what do you think?"

I pictured a viper's tongue. "That's all?"

He shrugged. "I'm forty-eight, my wife's forty-six." He looked me up and down. "I'm guessing you're even older than I am. Married?"

I nodded.

"Is *your* wife what she was twenty years ago?"

"None of us is what we were twenty years ago."

"You know what I mean. Women get to that age, they lose interest. Then someone like Alma Wanego comes along. Can't you understand?"

I could have told him yeah, I liked to check out merchandise in store windows, but that Irma, at fifty-one, never gave me a reason to do my shopping elsewhere, not even when she was pitching goulash at me. But it was none of his business.

Camnitz made a face that would've torn at my heart if I hadn't been so disgusted with him. "I felt as though my blood was circulating again. Christ, I had no illusions. I knew it wasn't my gray hair or my flabby muscles she was interested in. But I like to think I didn't exactly bore her in bed." His eyes fell, then he looked up at me. "I miss her."

"Maybe you do. But I still have to wonder whether she might have gotten greedy and figured she'd be better off with a big payday than with a trip, a ring, and a roll in the hay every now and then. Or did she try to hold you up because of the work Dr. Hearn and Dr. Sanford were doing behind your back? If that came out, you probably wouldn't have been chairman much longer. Most people don't keep ten K conveniently on hand, Doctor. I can check your bank and investment records."

"Go ahead, check them all you want. You won't find anything because I never took it out. I never paid Alma a cent of blackmail. I had no reason at all to suspect she wasn't satisfied with our arrangement. Yes, I did wonder about Giselle Hearn doing human work on the sly, but I had nothing concrete to proceed from. And I had no idea at all that Sanford was involved until that Kennett man went crazy."

He stopped talking, but he wasn't finished. His mouth opened, then closed.

"What?"

"I'm not sure I want to open another can of worms for myself. I don't think it relates to your case."

"Let me decide. You might do better opening the can than making me find it and open it myself."

He punched his right fist into his left palm, then looked back to me. "All right. As I said, Alma never did try anything funny, but someone else got greedy, and made a clumsy attempt to blackmail me."

I waited.

"That idiot roommate of Alma's. The Corrigan woman. About a month after Alma left, she made an appointment, came in here, sat where you're sitting, and told me she was sorry to do it, but she needed money, and she'd keep her mouth shut about Alma and me for a thousand dollars a month for two years, which she said she was sure I could afford."

Katie the Onion. Every layer peeled off smelled stronger and stronger. "Nervy," I said. "What did you tell her?"

"To get out, that's what. She obviously didn't have any information remotely resembling what you've got. She was either making a good guess, or Alma had said something to her. I told her if she was going to make accusations like that, she'd better have proof, or she'd end up in court, being sued for slander. Then she could really worry about not having money."

I checked my watch, got to my feet. "Go talk to the Dean," I said. "You're only ten minutes late."

He stood, then started toward the door. "It won't come out, will it?"

"Not if you behave yourself. Don't forget, unlike Ms. Corrigan, I do have the goods on you. If your wife's old man says one word to the mayor or the chief of police, you'll spend the rest of your career doing pelvic exams at charity clinics."

He swallowed, hard. "I understand."

Katie Corrigan never said anything to me about an affair between Camnitz and Wanego. What had made her think Camnitz was ripe for blackmail? She worked as a secretary, Psych Department, didn't she? That'd be on the main University campus, up at the other end of Emerald Boulevard.

Inside twenty minutes, I was there and parked. The first student I saw, a blond kid with hair over his eyes like an Old English Sheepdog, pointed me the way to the Psych Building.

The woman behind the reception desk in Administration was everyone's grandmother. She smiled as I approached her, but the congeniality went south in a hurry when I flashed badge and card, and told her I was looking for Katie Corrigan. Hand to throat, she asked was anything wrong.

"Routine investigation," I said. "She was a witness. I need to ask her a few questions."

"Oh, good." Grandma was relieved no end. "She's such a nice girl. I wouldn't want to see her in any trouble."

She's up to her lying mouth in trouble, I thought, but said, "Don't be concerned."

"Thank you, Officer. You had me worried there for a minute. Katie works for Dr. Smithton and Dr. Chester. When you go out of here, turn right, then go up the stairs at the end of the corridor, and turn left at the second-floor landing. She'll be three doors down on your right."

I thanked the old lady, took the stairs two at a stride, and sailed into the third office on the right. Katie glanced up from her typewriter, and let out a screech like a peacock in mating season. "Oh my God, Detective Baumgartner. You scared the hell out of me."

"Only the evil flee where no one pursueth, Katie."

She started to smile, but put a quick kibosh on it. "You look like you're mad at me, or something."

"I'm sure not happy with you right now. Where's the nearest empty classroom?"

"But I can't leave my desk till lunchtime. Please don't make me lose my job."

I pointed to the closed door on my right, then to the one on the left. "Either of your bosses in?"

She shook her head. "They're both in class."

"Good. If you're lucky, you'll be back before they are." I jerked my head toward the door. "Let's go."

Katie grabbed her fringed leather purse, sidestepped around the edge of the desk, then skittered past me and into the hall. "Classrooms are around the corner."

I followed her past the professors' offices and around the corner, into a corridor of classrooms. She opened a glass-paneled door, went inside, then stood, waiting for instructions. I shut the door, locked it, and motioned her to the front of the room. "Up there by the blackboard," I said. "Where nobody'll see us from the hall."

She trotted up to the front row, and in one quick motion, slid into a chair. I leaned over to talk into her face. "I'm going to start with the fact that any time I want, I can take you in and book you for a serious crime. Attempted blackmail will buy you a nice chunk of your life in the slammer."

She stopped breathing. One hand gripped the writing platform on the chair so hard her fingers went bloodless.

"You didn't bother to tell me you tried to shake down Dr. Camnitz for a little annuity."

No answer. Then, a very small voice. "Are you going to arrest me?"

"That depends on you. Tell me one more lie or leave out one more detail, and you can bet on it. Now. You told me your roommate hinted about a big payoff in the works, but nothing specific, no idea where the payoff was coming from. Start filling in the blanks."

Katie nodded like a robot. "Oh, I...I was *so* crazy. I told you about how I was hoping maybe Alma would cut me in, right? Well, when she disappeared, I told myself forget about it now, forget all about it. But I *couldn't* forget. And the more I thought about it, the more it got under my skin. I couldn't sleep, I was so wound up. Then I got to thinking, maybe that sugar daddy doctor of hers might figure it'd be better to kick in for me than have his wife find out he was having an affair. A thousand bucks a month for two years would get me through school, so I could get a decent job. But the bastard threw me out."

"You didn't talk to his wife, though."

Wan smile. "I was going to, but I couldn't."

"All right to blackmail someone, but not snitch?"

"That's about it."

"Okay. Now, when you say, 'that sugar daddy doctor,' who are you talking about?"

She wiped at her eyes. "Dr. Camnitz, Alma's boss. The guy she was having an affair with."

"How'd you know that? Were you and Ms. Wanego friendlier than you let on?"

"No. It was just like I said. Alma only gave me enough to keep me on a string. What happened was, a couple of nights after she got back from that last trip, I was sitting in the front room, reading, and I saw her and Mansell coming down the sidewalk. That was a little weird. They usually did their thing right at the end of the month, I don't know why. Well, I was feeling kind of mean, so I ran into the bedroom, hid myself in the closet, and waited."

"You weren't afraid they'd find you?"

"Uh-uh. I didn't think they'd be going into the closet for anything, and if they did, so what? What were they going to do to me? Anyway, they came straight through the living room and into the bedroom, and Alma was talking about Dr. Camnitz, how Norway was a blast, and how much she figured she could get for a ruby ring he'd bought her there. And then she told Mansell she was ready to spring the trap."

"You heard all that from in the closet?"

"Well, I can't say I got every single word. They were taking off their clothes and getting into it. But I know Alma said there'd been some kind of accident in the lab the month before, where Dr. Hearn had called Dr. Camnitz, and he came running over there. Then, Alma followed Dr. Hearn to Dr. Camnitz's office, and found out they were doing some kind of procedure on a patient. Alma was sure the accident had something to do with that procedure, and Dr. Camnitz and Dr. Hearn were trying to cover it up. And a few hours before Alma and Mansell came over, Alma had called Dr. Camnitz's office, pretended to be an insurance agent checking on a claim for pregnancy care, and found out the patient did have a positive pregnancy test. So with what she knew, she was sure Dr. Camnitz would pay big-time for her to keep quiet."

"That's what she said? Dr. Camnitz would pay big-time? And after the accident in the lab, it was Dr. Camnitz who Dr. Hearn called to come over? Are you absolutely certain?"

Katie looked like she was studying graffiti on the far wall. "Well…I guess I'm not a thousand percent positive, but Alma was talking about Dr. Camnitz and the Norway trip and the ruby ring when she and Mansell came into the room. After that, I think what she actually said was 'the doctor.' What other doctor could she have meant?"

I didn't answer Katie's question. She took my card, and promised she'd call my beeper if something she thought I might want to hear occurred to her. Then I drove back down to Pill Hill, hoofed it into the Anatomy Department at the Med School, and caught Charles Rapp, the janitor, as he was mopping a hallway. It took him a moment to remember me. "You're the detective."

"Right."

Rapp waggled fingers toward the wet floor. "You think you seen it all, but you never do. They're dissecting dicks and balls today, and one of the med students went green, and ran out here to pitch his cookies all over the damn place. He's gonna be a doctor? Christ Almighty, he ever saw what I did in the Pacific, he probably woulda just laid down and died." The janitor gave the mop a savage thrust. "I figure you ain't here to be social. You got more questions?"

"Yes, but no big hurry. You can get done here first."

He swished the mop around the floor, then put the business end back into the bucket, pulled the squeezer handle a couple of times, and gave the site of his work a final disgusted look. "Okay, what's up?"

"I want to get more specific about Ms. Wanego and the clogged washbasin. When exactly did that happen?"

"No trouble remembering that. First week last August, when we were havin' that goddamn awful heat wave."

"Good. Tell me all about it, every detail."

"Okay. I'm hangin' a fire extinguisher in the hall when I hear shouting inside one of the labs, swearing, the works. Then Dr. Hearn goes runnin' across the hall, into her office, slams the door shut. None a my business, I keep on workin'. I'm almost done when here comes Wanego, movin' sixteen to the dozen, and says I gotta get down to the men's room and fix the sink, it's clogged up. I tell her I'll go soon's I'm through with what I'm doing, but she says no, I got to go fix that clog *now,* right this minute, it's makin' a real mess. So I grab my toolbox, go on down in the men's room, and yeah, sure enough, there's a washbasin, water comin' over the top onto the floor. Damn fools couldn't figure out the sink was clogged till they ran enough water to make it spill over.

"So I go get the mop and pail, clean up the floor, and bail out the sink. I'm just bending over to take off the trap when this doctor charges in, bat outa hell, takes one look at me and says would I please get out of the room. I try tellin' him the sink's blocked, but *he* tells *me* it can wait ten minutes, I should come back and finish then. So I toss my wrench in my toolbox, and go back to finish up with the fire extinguisher.

"Not two minutes, Wanego's in my face again, did I fix the sink that fast? I tell her what happened and what am I supposed to do when a doctor orders me to get out of a bathroom? She wants to know what doctor told me that, and I tell her his name tag says Dr. Colin Sanford."

The creases around Rapp's eyes and mouth deepened. He snickered. "I seen him before, he'd been comin' around a lot to see Dr. Hearn. I figured they had something going, wouldn't be the first time I'd seen that stuff around here. Anyways, when I tell Wanego, she gets this funny look on her face, her mouth slams shut like a mousetrap, and off she goes, down toward the men's room. I finish up with the fire extinguisher, and then go fix the sink. Some idiot had tossed a paper towel down it. Next morning, I'm in Personnel, and poor old Miss Walker tells me they're transferrin' me to Anatomy. Which I already told you."

"That's one weird story, Mr. Rapp. What did you think when Dr. Sanford tossed you out of the men's room?"

Rapp laughed. "They don't pay me to think. What the hell was I supposed to do, ask him if he was gonna shoot some stuff in his arm or up his nose? Or if he was gonna meet Dr. Hearn for a quickie in the stall? Listen, you wouldn't believe some of the crap that goes on here. Just a few months ago, a tech in one of the Anatomy labs got canned, so who gets called in to get rid of a bunch of marijuana plants he was growin' on the window ledges…uh-oh." Rapp's voice faded. "Hey, Mr…"

I had to work hard not to laugh. "Baumgartner."

"I hope you ain't gonna tell anybody about that, 'cause it'd get me in the soup for real. They wanted the stuff outa here before the papers or the cops got ahold of the story."

I grinned. "It's our secret, Mr. Rapp."

"I guess I oughta watch my big mouth."

"That's always a good idea."

That settled it for me. Wanego had nailed Sanford trying to cover up a disaster of a lab accident by doing something that could not only get his license yanked, but also might have meant a major lawsuit, even jail time. In any case, he'd never have practiced medicine again. Ten thousand dollars would've been a bargain.

And where would that money have been when Wanego made her demand? Not likely Sanford kept five-figure sums on hand. His condo and his office were only a few blocks apart, so he likely banked right in that neighborhood. I decided to see if I could find out where.

Took me a little more than a half-hour to cover the three blocks of Hill Street between Sanford's office and his condo, and all the roads in a one-block perimeter around Hill. There were four banks, three on Hill, one on Charleston. I started with First Federal, but inside five minutes, I was out through the door, empty-handed. Next was Vancouver Mutual, where I did better. Without a warrant, no way I could have examined accounts, but the manager did tell me Sanford was a customer. First Bank of Emerald, next in line, also told me Sanford did business with them. The last bank, Western Savings, had no record of dealing with the good doctor.

Eleven-thirty. I went into a coffee shop, dawdled over my cup for twenty minutes, got my thoughts in line, then hoofed over to Sanford's office. New York Sally told me the doctor was running a little late, I should have a seat, and she'd make sure he knew I was waiting for him.

◇◇◇

The woman in the chair next to me must've been a stunner before she went to seed, but the smile in her eyes could still make a man take notice. "Is your wife in with the doctor?" she asked.

"Huh…oh, yeah. She was a little nervous, so I came in with her."

"That's nice of you. To take a day off from work like that." She motioned with her hands for me to relax. "Well, you don't have to worry, and I'm sure your wife doesn't either. Dr. Sanford's the best."

Even if he says so himself.

"And nice? I first starting coming to him six years ago. I was forty, and pregnant with my fourth, and what with all the stuff you hear about birth defects, my husband and I were really nervous. Dr. Sanford didn't have time to finish talking to us right then, so he told us to come back at five o'clock, and then he sat with us for almost an hour, didn't charge us extra, and told us everything we wanted to know. He gave me that amniocentesis test, it was brand new then, and Dr. Sanford was the only doctor in Emerald who was good enough to do it. And the minute he had the results, he called me. *He* called me, not the nurse. How many doctors would have done that?"

"Not many."

"You can say that again. Now, I've got these tumors on my uterus, and he's told me all about them, made sure I knew they weren't cancerous, and he can fix me up with a hysterectomy from down below, so I won't have any scar. He says he's had special training, and no one else in Emerald, not even anyone at the University, can do it exactly the way he does. I wouldn't go anywhere else...well, look how I'm going on." She patted my hand. "Anyway, your wife couldn't be in better hands."

"Thank you," I said. "I feel a lot better now."

Chapter Seventeen

Sanford

When Barbara came in to tell me Baumgartner was back to take up another lunch hour, I forced a smile. "Tell him as soon as I'm done with the morning patients." She forced a smile of her own, and ducked out the door.

This was past being a minor annoyance. Joyce was clearly on edge, and I'll admit, I was feeling antsy, myself. Rumors were coming out of England, thicker and faster every month, and if Baumgartner dragged it out long enough, Steptoe and Edwards might sneak under the wire and scoop me.

It didn't take me long to get through Ms. Chapman's list of questions about her fibroid tumors. A couple of minutes after she left, Barbara showed Baumgartner in. Quick handshake, then he dropped into the chair across the desk, gave me a long study, then said, "The insemination procedure you did on Mrs. Kennett, the one with the Density-Gradient sperm? That was in your office, here, right?"

"Yes."

"Who was in the room?"

"Besides Joyce and me? My nurse and Dr. Hearn."

"Which nurse?"

Now, what was he after? "I'm pretty sure it was Ruth Ellen Marcus."

"Would you please ask her to come in here for a few minutes."

"She's in the lunch room, and I really don't like—."

"I know. But I'd appreciate it if you'd make an exception this one time."

I didn't like the idea of leaving Baumgartner alone in my office, but no choice. I pulled Ruth Ellen out of the lunch room, and hustled her back.

Baumgartner's greeting to her was honey butter on a biscuit. Big smile, an apology for interrupting her lunch, and a promise to take as little of her time as possible. "Ms. Marcus, you helped Dr. Sanford do an unusual procedure on Mrs. Kennett last August. Do you remember that procedure?"

Ruth Ellen glanced my way.

Baumgartner raised a finger. "Over here, Ms. Marcus. No cheating on this exam."

She giggled.

"Do you remember the procedure?"

Ruth Ellen nodded. "Oh, yes, sir. Very well."

Baumgartner smiled again. "Good. Tell me about it."

Ruth Ellen returned the smile. "Well, sir, Dr. Sanford told me he wanted me to help because I was the senior nurse in the clinic, and it was a very important procedure. He said Dr. Hearn had developed some kind of treatment to make the uterus more receptive to an embryo. Kind of like a 'baby glue.'"

I coughed. Baumgartner flashed me a silent warning, then turned back to Ruth Ellen. "Go ahead, Ms. Marcus. What about that baby glue? How did Dr. Sanford use it?"

"Well…while Dr. Sanford and I got Ms. Kennett up in stirrups, Dr. Hearn took this little plastic dish out of an incubator she'd wheeled over, looked in the dish through her microscope, and said, 'It's a go.' Then Dr. Sanford put in a vaginal speculum, did a sterile prep, checked Ms. Kennett's cervix, and passed an insemination catheter into the uterus. He said that was a practice run, and it went fine, and now he was ready. Dr. Hearn gave him another catheter attached to a small syringe. He put that catheter up inside Ms. Kennett's uterus, and pushed the syringe. It was over so fast I couldn't believe it."

"What was in the syringe and the catheter?"

Ruth Ellen shrugged. "I guess...well, I really don't know, exactly. Whatever the treatment was to...you know, the ba..." She giggled, then started to cry.

"Baby glue?" Again, Baumgartner smiled.

She wiped a hankie over her eyes. "Yes. I'm sorry. I know it sounds silly, but that's what I remember."

"No need to be sorry, Ms. Marcus. You were a big help, thank you. Go on back and finish your lunch."

We watched her sail out of the room and push the door shut behind her. Baumgartner looked around at me. "Baby glue."

Not a question, but I took it as one. "I don't remember word-for-word what I told her about the procedure, but it was along the lines of we'd been trying to get better quality sperm that would swim faster and stick to the egg better. She must've gotten 'baby glue' into her head."

Baumgartner shot me a heavy dose of skepticism. "You injected the treated sperm up into the uterus. I thought artificial inseminations were done in the vagina."

"The turkey-baster technique, you mean."

He grudged me a smile.

"If I'd been doing the usual kind of artificial insemination, you'd be right," I said. "But for intrauterine insemination, where you're trying to give the sperm that much of a head start, you have to use a micro-syringe with a tiny amount of fluid, a small fraction of a c.c. More might make the uterus cramp and push the sperm back into the vagina."

Baumgartner scratched at his forehead, sucked his cheeks in, blew them out. "Aren't testicles outside of the body because body temperature is too high for them to make sperm?"

"Yes. So?"

"So what did you need the incubator for? Why didn't Dr. Hearn just bring over the syringe in some kind of a sterile wrap?"

"Because the temperature in the testicles isn't nearly all the way down to room temperature. It's in between room and body temperature, so that's where Dr. Hearn had set the incubator."

Baumgartner took a pen out of his pocket, fiddled with it for a few seconds. "Dr. Sanford, wasn't Dr. Hearn playing Edwards to your Steptoe? Looking at embryos in that plastic dish, before she loaded them into the syringe for you to inject? She and you were doing in vitro fertilization, weren't you?"

Careful. Buy a little time. "You've been doing your homework, Mr. Baumgartner. You get extra credit for all that voluntary reading." Then, before he could say anything, I added, "Sorry, shouldn't have said that. I can see where your research gave you that idea, but the problem is, a lot of clinical procedures are similar. From appearances, I guess we could've been doing IVF, but we weren't. Even if we had been, though, what of it? It may be controversial, but as far as I know, there's nothing illegal about it."

"No, Doctor, it's not illegal. But murder is, and so is blackmail."

"Wait a minute. Blackmail? Where's blackmail coming from?"

"I was hoping you could tell me that."

"I don't have a clue. Are you trying to say I was blackmailing someone? For what?"

He rocked back in his chair, then came forward again. "Try this. Shortly before Alma Wanego vanished, she received ten thousand dollars, cash."

"Wanego…that's the lab supervisor you mentioned yesterday. Lucky her."

"Maybe not so lucky. No one's seen her since September tenth of last year. But the money didn't disappear with her. Now, here's where we get specific. I know you have accounts at Vancouver Mutual and First Bank of Emerald, and if I need to, I'll get a warrant to examine those accounts. What I think is I'll find is that you withdrew ten thousand dollars early last September, maybe part from each bank, so you wouldn't trigger an IRS review of a five-figure withdrawal. Do you want to save us a little time, or do I need to go through the motions?"

I shrugged. "Do what you need to do. You might find some withdrawals around that time."

"And that would be a mere coincidence?"

"Absolutely."

"All right. If you coincidentally took ten thousand dollars out of your accounts last September, what was it for?"

"Probably to make a bet on a horse race."

"Oh. Right. And the horse had to be dragged over the finish line."

"Something like that."

"And you made the bet through a bookie, and didn't keep any paper."

"Would you have?"

Baumgartner looked as if he was having trouble keeping a straight face. "Dr. Sanford, please. Is that really the best you can do? You don't strike me as the kind of man who'd blow ten grand on a horse race."

I laughed. "When you practice medicine, you learn in a hurry that people never stop surprising you. Isn't it the same in police work? Fact is, I make a lot of fair-sized withdrawals *and* deposits because I like to play the horses, and most of the time, I win. Ms. Wanego may have had ten thousand dollars, but that doesn't mean I gave it to her. I'm not a lawyer, but it sounds circumstantial as hell."

I thought he was going to read me the riot act, but no. "Dr. Sanford, I can prove that right before Ms. Wanego disappeared, she called your office, found that Ms. Kennett's pregnancy test had turned positive, and then told someone she was looking at a big payday. Good enough for you?"

Too good, I thought. "Not to offend you, Mr. Baumgartner, but this 'someone' of yours who Ms. Wanego talked to? Is she for real?"

"Count on it. In my business, bluffs are dangerous, because guys like you will call them. Now, why don't you quit with the shuffle-off-to-Buffalo bit. Don't make me go through getting a warrant and examining your bank records, so I can check the numbers on the bills Ms. Wanego received against the ones you got from the bank. We both know they'll correspond. Just tell me why you paid her that money. Save both of us at least one more meeting."

I leaned all the way back in my chair, arms behind my head. "All right, Mr. Baumgartner. Let's try a little hypothetical. Suppose Ms. Wanego came to me and said she'd seen the accident, that it got her attention, and made her wonder what was going on in the lab that Dr. Hearn had to call me over urgently. Suppose she also wondered what might happen if Dr. Camnitz heard about the incident. He'd certainly look into it, and if he found out Dr. Hearn was working on human oocytes, she'd lose her job. Ms. Wanego might've said she could use a little money, and for, say, ten thousand dollars, she could manage to keep her mouth shut. Now, if she *had* said that to me, I probably would've felt obligated to protect Dr. Hearn's job. The work was her idea, of course, but we were in it together, and as a PhD, her income was nothing to write home about. But I would've made sure Ms. Wanego knew it would be a one-time payment, that my sense of obligation could go only so far, and that if she ever did anything to cause Dr. Hearn to lose her job, she could count on my reporting her to the police for blackmailing me. Again, this is just a hypothetical. I didn't know Ms. Wanego."

"But you did hear she suddenly vanished from the lab. Do you happen to remember how you found that out, and when?"

"I'm not really sure, but I think it was some time in early fall. Dr. Hearn mentioned it in passing. She said I should go easy on giving her oocytes for a while because her lab supervisor had left without notice and she'd have to take time to get the replacement up to speed. I think if you check my operative records, you'll see my retrievals did fall off by a fair amount around then."

From Baumgartner's face, you'd have thought I'd just said it was a nice day. "It still bothers me that Ms. Kennett's conception was right in there with the accident," he said, very quietly.

"And I've already told you, there was no connection between the experimental accident and the Density Gradient Separation."

"If it really was just a Density Gradient Separation."

Keep moving. Throw him off balance. "I think you need to accept the ten thousand dollars as a coincidence."

"I'll decide what I need to do, thanks." He sucked at his lip, looked out the window. Then he turned back abruptly. "I sure wish I could take a look in that missing log book of Dr. Hearn's."

Straight out of left field. Guess he figured two could play a game. Underestimate this guy, I'd be the biggest damn fool in Emerald. I paused, just for a moment, then said, "If wishes were horses, beggars would ride."

He laughed, actually laughed, then pulled himself to his feet. "Be seeing you."

Weird, I thought, but all right. I checked my watch. Time to get a sandwich and coffee before my first afternoon appointment.

After the office closed for the day, I took the elevator down to the skybridge, cut across to the hospital as if I were going to see a patient, then took another elevator to ground level, and went outside. No way Baumgartner could have followed me through that route without having me see him. No sign of him all the way to the parking garage under my apartment building, or along the road to Sunset Bluff. When I turned the corner and parked in front of Joyce Kennett's house, no car was behind me.

Now that Baumgartner had straight-out accused me of doing IVF, I wanted to be make doubly sure Joyce stayed strictly on our page. Touchy situations are better handled face-to-face than over the phone. Whenever I had bad news for a patient, one of the nurses called her and got her right into the office. Start discussing cancer or birth defects by telephone, the discussion spirals out of control in a hurry.

When I rang Joyce's bell, I expected Mrs. Enright to answer, but it was Joyce who came to the door, Robbie up on her shoulder. She patted his back. Her skin was drawn tight over her cheekbones, eyes reddened, eyelids at half-staff.

"Bad night?"

"He hardly stopped crying."

Robbie let out a monster of a belch. Joyce responded with a wan smile. I laughed. "That should help."

"Yeah." She sat on the couch, swung Robbie down so his head was in the crook of her arm, then picked up the bottle, and worked it between his lips. Then she looked back to me. "What's going on?"

"That detective, Baumgartner, paid me another visit. He's managed to figure out we were doing IVF, but I don't see any way he can prove it. I thought you and I ought to touch base, though. We can't have him blow the whistle before we're ready."

To the background of quick sucking noises, she said, "I think we'd better schedule that press conference."

"But it's not even a week—"

"Dr. Sanford, I'm exhausted. My mother needs to go back home in a few days, and then I'm on my own. If money were coming in, I could hire a nanny. I can deal with the publicity better than this waiting, on top of giving full baby care."

"I know how you're feeling," I said, like someone negotiating a path through a mine field. "But we need to be careful. If we go ahead now, with the cops still investigating what happened to James and Dr. Hearn, that could give us some pretty bad press. It might make people hesitate before they throw money at you. There could even be attempts to legislate restrictions on the procedure. It could set the work back years. Decades."

"I don't see it that way," Joyce snapped. "If those doctors in England beat us out, there goes my money and Robbie's. Bad press, good press—I think *any* press we get will give me *more* coverage, not less. I want to go ahead now." She took the empty bottle from the baby's mouth, slung him up to her shoulder again, patted his back.

"I understand," I said. "I really do. In my business, I go through stretches where I think I'm never going to see my bed again. But you're forgetting something. Even if *you* can handle negative publicity, Robbie would be another story. Starting off in life under a cloud of ugly tabloid articles could haunt him as long as he lives."

She pounded the baby's back harder. Fortunately, he produced another pair of burps. As she laid his head into the crook of her arm, he gave a satisfied little sigh, then closed his eyes.

She was on the point of losing it. I talked fast. "I want to go ahead, too, believe me. But we've got to think of Robbie. It can't be long till Baumgartner gets something new and more interesting to investigate. Once he closes this case, we'll be home free."

She looked out the window, then turned her head back. Eyes icy, mutinous. "You practically tied yourself in knots, persuading James and me to do this, and it worked. I'm grateful...I really am. But what finally decided me to look past the risks of being Number One was having you tell us it would not only give us a baby, it'd also make us rich. With James' problems, that sounded like the best insurance policy I could buy, and if I miss out cashing in that policy...Dr. Sanford, I'll give you till next Monday. By then, if you aren't ready to make an announcement, I'll call the papers and do it myself."

"I can't promise—"

"This is not negotiable. Say no, say maybe, and I'll pick up the phone right now."

To win a war, sometimes you need to concede a battle. "All right. I'm guessing a week will be long enough."

"It better be. Otherwise, Robbie and I will take our chances, and you can either be on the bus, or under it."

I felt as if a bus had already had a go at me. My neck and shoulders were one massive spasm. Time for a good workout. Hit the treadmill, pump a little iron, toss a few at the punching bag, and I'd be back in the pink.

Chapter Eighteen

Baumgartner

After dinner that evening, I sat Iggy down in his living room, and gave him a Reader's Digest update. The little guy was all ears. "Well, I guess you don't never know," he muttered. "Doc Sanford, pullin' a fast one? My mother goes to him, and so does a lady-friend of mine. To hear them talk, you'd think he was God."

"To hear *him* talk, you'd think the same thing. And slippery? He talks in slug trails. You should've heard him, playing games with me, dancing, dodging, having himself a ball. Giving me goddamn *hypotheticals*. But he's right at the middle of everything going on in this case. All I need to pin him to the wall is that missing log book from the lab."

"And you think you know where it is, huh?"

"Yeah, I do. That wise guy, bragging about how much he learns about people from his medical work, and isn't it the same in my line? Well, one thing *I've* learned is that when I tell someone I wish I could look at a log book, and his eyes glance off to the left for a fraction of a second, he's telling me that's where the log is."

A lopsided grin flickered at the left corner of Iggy's mouth. "So now you're gonna ask me to help you get into that doc's office so you can find the log book. Right?"

"Sounds like you're volunteering. But think about it first. So far, if any shit hits the fan, I can probably talk you into a safe corner, but do this, and you're in as deep as I am."

"I don't need to do no thinking. Tonight?"

"You have anything else planned?"

◇◇◇

We played a couple hours of gin, then set off for the hospital. At that hour, no trouble finding a spot in the parking garage. I knew we couldn't go through the lobby of the Puget Community Doctors' Tower, then up the elevator to the twelfth floor, because even if the guard on duty didn't stop us, he'd sure as hell notice us and remember us. He might watch the elevator and see where we got off; he might even come up and look around. But no one was going to think anything about two men, one carrying a doctor's bag, the other, a little plastic bag, walking into the lobby of the busy Washington Public University Medical Center, and into an elevator. I only had to hope there was no guard watching the fifth-story skybridge connecting the hospital with the Doctors' Tower offices. There wasn't.

Once in the Tower, we took the elevator to Twelve, then went into a men's room and changed into the green scrub suits I'd liberated from the Surgical Unit dressing room after I'd left Sanford's office. Now, Iggy and I could be two doctors, consulting about a case.

At the door labeled in gold letters, DR. COLIN SANFORD, SPECIALIST IN WOMEN'S HEALTH CARE, Dr. Iggy opened his leather bag, took out a tool that looked like something a dentist might put into your mouth, worked it inside the lock, twisted it one way, then the other, then jiggled it. Nothing. I began to get nervous. The one point where it'd be tough to explain to a guard would be while we were picking the lock to an office.

Iggy muttered, "Wait a minute," then pulled a flashlight from the bag, directed the beam to the lock, and said, "Why'm I makin' things difficult?" He shook the leather bag so the tools settled to one end, reached in, and came out with a ring of keys, sorted through them, selected one, slipped it into the lock, and turned it. The door opened.

Iggy grinned. "After you, Doctor."

I took the flashlight, and led him through the waiting area, then back down the corridor to Sanford's office. Once inside, I flipped the light switch and pointed at the two chairs opposite the desk. "Sit in one of those."

He gave me a funny look, but did as I said. I settled into Sanford's chair, leaned back then straightened. "Tell me, 'I sure wish I could take a look in that missing log book.'"

He chuckled. "Okay. I'm gettin' it. I sure wish I could take a look in that missing log book."

I flashed a glance leftward, just my eyes moving, then came back to Iggy. "Where's the log?"

We both stared at the fake-woodgrain metal file cabinet. "Start at the top?" Iggy asked.

"What're we waiting for?"

The top drawer was all professional business records, nothing useful to me. The next drawer was crammed with personal material, some of which were banking records. In the folder labeled Vancouver Mutual Bank, I found a withdrawal slip for fifty-eight hundred dollars; in the First Bank of Emerald folder was a slip for forty-two hundred. Ten K, on the nose. I pulled the withdrawal slips from the folders. "Let's make copies of these before we go."

While Iggy put the reports on the desk, I opened the third drawer. It was about half-full of charts, all from patients who'd told the doctor they were leaving his care. In each case, Sanford had written in great detail how he'd tried to convince the women that his experience and results with whatever was wrong with them were more than the equal of any doctor on earth. One patient with cancer had died a year after her defection, and Sanford's note made it sound like he blamed himself for her death because he'd failed to keep her in his care. But none of the charts had anything to do with in vitro fertilization.

The bottom drawer blew me away. It was full of newspapers and magazines, all having to do with horses and horse racing. *Thoroughbred Times. Horseman and Fair World. Chicago Barn to Wire. At the Races. Hoosier Hoofprints. Getting Down.* "Son of a bitch," I growled.

Iggy looked over my shoulder. "Huh?"

"I waved a copy of the *Daily Racing* Form in his face. "The bastard really does bet on horses."

"So what? So do a lot of people."

"A lot of people haven't just tried to make me believe they took ten grand out of the bank to bet on a horse." I started to laugh. "I've never seen anything like this guy."

I tossed the newspaper back in the drawer, kicked it shut, then checked my watch. "Christ, we've been here an hour and a half." I looked back to Sanford's chair. "This is where his eyes went. If that log's not in this cabinet, how about under it?"

"That'd sure put it outa the way."

I leaned against the cabinet. "Take the flashlight and get down there. I'll tip the cabinet back."

Iggy stretched full-length on the floor, turned on the light. "Okay, Mr. B. Just make real sure you don't drop that thing, okay? Else I ain't gonna be opening locks for you or anybody else for a while."

Lord, it was heavy. I leaned into it. From somewhere near my feet, I heard, "Well, hey, hey. Lookit what we got here."

I set the cabinet down, then grabbed the eight-and-a-half-by-eleven-inch book Iggy held up to me. Gray fabric cover with red trim. As I lifted it, two loose pages fluttered to the carpet. Iggy snatched them up, and slapped them into my free hand. "Something?"

"Oh, yes, something. Chart records, Joyce Kennett." I scanned the pages. "It's about how she left his care, went to the U, and then he called her back to offer her 'a new infertility technique.' Right after that, there's an office visit, where he tells her and her husband about this new technique, and then comes a record of the procedure here in the office that got Ms. Kennett pregnant."

I dropped the pages onto the desk, on top of the bank statements, picked up the gray book, and settled into Sanford's chair. "Let's see here…"

The log started with a short note saying these were experiments to establish the conditions under which human oocytes could be reliably fertilized in vitro, then the embryos cultured successfully to where they could be implanted in a uterus. Even with my book smarts from my library time, I had to skip over a lot of stuff. I had no idea how compulsive a lab scientist needs to be. The procedure for every egg Dr. Hearn tried to fertilize and culture was put down in excruciating detail.

The forty-first patient was JK. Sanford had retrieved five mature oocytes, and fertilization was successful in three of them, but there was, in fact, a little hitch. Good old compulsive Dr. Hearn. She documented that she'd dropped Mr. K's initial sperm sample, but received a second one promptly, and processed it for fertilization. By August 9, 1976, the embryos looked normal, and then came the entry I'd been waiting for. "Aug. 9, 3:45pm. Embryos taken in incubator to Dr. Sanford's office, examined microscopically. All appeared normal. All three embryos loaded into catheter with attached 1 c.c. syringe, and injected by Dr. Sanford into Patient JK's uterus."

Iggy, who'd been reading over my shoulder, whispered, "Holy catfish. There it is."

"In black and white. Hearn dropped the sperm sample, got a second one, and went on to fertilize Ms. Kennett's eggs. But before Mr. Kennett shot Hearn, the new supervisor heard him yell, 'What do you mean, second sample?' And it was right around the time of the lab accident that Sanford threw Rapp, the janitor, out of the lab men's room."

Iggy looked queasy. "Hey, one thing for a guy to get cozy with somebody else's wife, but this is Rosemary's Baby stuff. What did Doc Sanford have to say when you asked him why he threw the janitor out of the can?"

"He didn't say anything because I didn't tell him I knew. The janitor's story is a little powder I've been keeping dry, but that's about to change. If Alma Wanego really did get the goods on Sanford, he'd have had every reason to get her out of the way, and for that matter, so would've Hearn. She'd gambled everything on this, money, reputation, her job, her whole future. I didn't learn much from her mother right after the murder, but I think I'll go talk to her again in the morning."

Iggy started to scoop up the log, the chart pages, and the bank records. "I can put 'em in my bag."

"No." I held out my hand.

"What, you're gonna leave 'em here?"

"Not that I really want to. But I don't want Sanford to find them missing before I have him dead to rights. Also, better if Sanford's lawyer can't claim I got my hands on them illegally. Once I have everything nailed down, I'll bring my boy in, and get a warrant to search his home and office."

Iggy looked doubtful. "What if he gets nervous and shit-cans them?"

"He won't. Without this stuff, he'll never get credit for that IVF baby. Let's go make some copies. Sanford's got a Xerox machine back in a little room behind the reception desk. I'm sure he'd want his guests to feel welcome to use his facilities."

◇◇◇

Turned out the doctor wasn't so accommodating. The copy machine wouldn't start. I checked the plug; it was connected. Then I noticed the little key slot on the front of the machine. "They must turn the thing off at night, damn. Is this something you can crack?"

Iggy scratched at his head. "I ain't never had a call on one… lemme go get my bag." But before he'd taken two steps, we heard, "Hey. Anybody here?"

I looked at Iggy, did a quick mental calculation, then pulled open a door to the right of the copy machine. Coat closet. I slipped the chart pages under my arm, slammed the log book into Iggy's hands, motioned him inside the closet, shut the door behind him, and walked out of the workroom. Across the desk, a skinny guy in a blue Security uniform gave me the fish eye. He had to be on the shady side of sixty, stooped, and unarmed. I could've had him down and out in nothing flat, but that wasn't the way to go. I flashed him a grin. What's up?"

He pointed at the light fixture above his head. "Just checking. There ain't usually lights on this time of night, and my last time through, it was dark in here. You a doctor?"

I nodded. "Dr. Colin Sanford. My office. I've got a patient in labor, and I need to copy some pages from her chart to take over there." I waved Sanford's notes toward him.

He wasn't convinced. "Can you show me some ID?"

Was I glad I'd thought of the scrubs. I ran my hands up and down the front of my green suit. "My wallet's in my locker, over on the Labor Floor."

"Yeah…yeah…" He clicked his tongue against the roof of his mouth.

If he decided to call the Labor Floor to check me out, I'd have to get rough with him, but I really didn't want to do that, especially with Iggy's prints and mine all over the office. I pictured Sanford, talking to me that afternoon, then tried to put the same snotty arrogance onto my face and into my voice. "Listen," I said. "I'm glad you're doing your job, but I have to do mine, too. I've got a patient in labor, she's pretty sick, and if she doesn't get taken care of, she and her baby could both die. Now, are you going to let me finish what I came here to do, or do I need to ignore you, and then file a complaint?"

Just what the doctor ordered. "Yeah, okay, go on," he muttered. "Sorry to bother you, Doctor."

As he went out into the hall, I walked back to the workroom, opened the closet door, put my finger to my lips. Then I tiptoed out to the reception desk, and checked the waiting room, to be sure the guard hadn't sneaked in again and crouched behind a chair. All clear. I ran back to the copy room, where Iggy was wiping a handkerchief over his face. "Whew. Damn hot in there."

"It wasn't much cooler where I was. Listen, we better not stay here long enough for that guard to find out Dr. Sanford doesn't have a patient in labor. Guess we'll have to take the originals after all, and hope Sanford doesn't decide to peek under the cabinet."

We hustled down the hall to Sanford's office, where I dropped the chart pages, bank records, and log into Iggy's bag. "I'll go out and scope the hall," I said. "You get changed, then go back the way we came in. Take the elevator to five, turn right, across to the Washington Pub Building, then take that elevator to the lobby, and go straight out to the car. I'll meet you there. Don't forget to bring my clothes."

"Got it."

◇ ◇ ◇

All the way down the hall, I looked left and right, making sure every door was closed tight, and no eyes were peeping out from behind blinds in any of the windows. But I saw nothing, and once in the elevator, I was home free. No problem going through the hospital lobby, and outside. I was just another doctor, too busy and important to change out of my scrubs before I went off to my car in the parking garage.

Chapter Nineteen

Baumgartner

Next morning, I detoured from the direct route to Mrs. Hearn's, and drove out to Sunset Bluff. When Ms. Kennett opened the door, the baby cradled in her left arm, she did not look pleased to see me. "You again?"

"The original bad penny. I've uncovered some new information, and I need to talk to you. I won't take long, I promise."

She led me into the living room, where she lowered herself into a rocker. "Nice, quiet baby," I said.

She rolled her eyes. "You should've been here last night. He didn't stop howling. My mother said she was sure it was colic, that I'd done the exact same thing. She took him about two o'clock." Ms. Kennett pointed toward the back of the house. "Now she's taking a nap."

"She must be a big help," I said.

"Well, yeah. But she has to leave the day after tomorrow."

"I guess that's not going to make it any easier."

"There's no choice. My father hasn't been well." She pushed hair back out of her eyes, settled the baby, then sat up straight. "Okay, Mr. Baumgartner, you didn't come here to make small talk. You said you have some new information?"

"That's right. Ms. Kennett, I've got firm evidence now that there was in fact an accident in the lab during your procedure.

Your husband's sperm sample was dropped, and he supposedly gave a second one."

She was shaking her head before I'd finished. "No one ever said anything to me about needing a second sample."

"Your husband didn't mention it? Or Dr. Sanford?"

Through tight lips. "Isn't 'No one ever said anything to me' clear?"

"Clear enough. You've told me the procedure Dr. Sanford and Dr. Hearn performed on you was an insemination with treated sperm. Is that right?"

"Mr. Baumgartner, what *are* you driving at? First, you want me to practically sign in blood that I never heard anything about a second sperm sample, and now you ask me about something we've been through several times. What else could that procedure have been?"

"In vitro fertilization. Is your son the first IVF baby in the world?"

She pulled the baby in closer to her. "You are irritating me to my limit."

"I'm sorry to do that, but I still need you to answer me."

"No. He's not an IVF baby. Is *that* clear enough for you?"

"Clear, yes. Truthful, I'm less sure. I still think you're holding a medical bombshell there, and if you are, I can't help wondering why you and Dr. Sanford haven't already gone public."

"Maybe because there's nothing to go public about. Is it even remotely possible you could be wrong? Or doesn't that ever happen?"

I felt bad. I really did. But now was the time to push. If she didn't crack, she might at least pressure Sanford out of his cave. "Yes, it happens. But this time, it's *not* possible. I can prove there was a second sperm sample, and that Dr. Sanford performed an in vitro fertilization procedure on you. And the murder, suicide, and unexplained disappearance I'm looking into all seem to be tied right in with what you and Dr. Sanford were up to."

The words were barely out when Ms. Kennett hauled herself out of the rocker, set the baby onto the sofa, slid a pillow between him and the edge, and jabbed a finger into my face. "What we were 'up to?' You slimeball, I don't care if you're a cop or a prosecutor or Jesus Christ. We were 'up to' getting a baby for me, we didn't do anything illegal, and I've got every right to the privacy of my medical condition." She wheeled around to redirect her finger toward the door. "Now get yourself and your questions out of my house. I'm through talking to you. If you bother me again, I'm going to call my lawyer."

I got up, took a step toward the door, then turned around. "It really would be a shame, after all you've been through, for somebody to scoop you and Dr. Sanford. The first IVF baby's going to get all the press. No one's going to give a thought to Number Two."

As I hit the front porch, the door slammed behind me, and I heard a lock turn. I felt like a jerk. Who was the guy that said a policeman's lot is not a happy one?

Chapter Twenty

Sanford

The instant I saw Barbara's face around the corner of the exam-room door, I knew I had trouble. She motioned me to come out. I inclined my head toward Mrs. Wadlin, lying on the table, gripping Ruth Ellen's hand, then held up an index finger to Barbara, wait a minute. She shook her head, no.

You hire people whose judgment you can trust. I excused myself, helped Mrs. Wadlin sit up, then followed Barbara into the hall. "Ms. Kennett," she said.

"With a problem."

"She insisted she had to talk to you immediately. I'm sorry."

"Don't be. I'll take it in my office."

Joyce didn't even say hello, just opened fire with both barrels. "Detective Baumgartner was here again. He said he knew we were doing IVF."

"Joyce, listen, please? He can't possibly know anything about your procedure. There's no record in any chart. He's blowing smoke."

"He also went back to that accident in the lab, and said it was connected with my procedure. You told me the accident was on an experiment, and had nothing to do with me."

"That's because it *was* an experiment, and it *did* have nothing to do with you."

I heard her mutter something, but couldn't make it out. Then she said, "One other thing. Baumgartner told me he knew about some second sperm sample in my procedure. You never said anything about that. I don't see any way James could've given a second sample. When we first came to you, and you wanted a routine sperm sample to make sure he was fertile, I had to go in the room with him and help him get it, and then I did the same before I went to the operating suite for the egg recovery. And besides…oh, *damn*. When we'd go to bed, he was one and done, every time. He simply could not have given—"

"There was no second sperm sample, Joyce. Period."

No answer.

"Joyce, there *was* no second sample. That cop is desperate. His captain is probably pushing him to make an arrest, so he's inventing stories, trying to get you upset."

"Well, he's doing a goddamn good job."

"That's the point. Don't let him. We've talked about this, and we've got to hold firm until the police go away. We can't have them turning this into a media circus that will ruin everything."

"What will ruin everything is if another doctor beats us out. That's what Baumgartner said before he left."

"Sure he did. He's trying to get us to do something foolish, And we'll *be* foolish if we let him send us into a panic."

I heard a whoosh in the receiver, air being forced across the mouthpiece. "Dr. Sanford, I can't see why you're so insistent about waiting. What can the police do to us if we go ahead now?"

"Turn up the heat. And then, there's the press." They'll have people talking all over the world about the police investigation of a murder-suicide involved in the first reported IVF success."

"And according to Baumgartner, some kind of suspicious disappearance. What the hell is that all about?"

Like in surgery, when you think you've got all the arteries tied off, but whoops, there goes another one, spurt, spurt, spurt. "Baumgartner told me about that, too. A lab worker quit and left town right about the time you got pregnant. Apparently, nobody thought anything of it then, but now he's trying to tie it into his case. He's so far out on a limb, he can't possibly hold on much longer. There's nothing of any substance there. Please trust my judgment on this, Joyce. We agreed to wait a week."

More silence. Then a clipped. "Okay. But you'd better be right."

"I'm sure I am. What're the odds that Steptoe and Edwards, or anyone else, are going to announce a success within the next week?"

"More than zero," she shouted. Then I heard a click.

After I hung up, I took a moment to pace the room. New mothers aren't nearly the most stable creatures in the world, and this particular one had a lot more than just the new baby working to unsettle her mind. I picked up the phone on my desk, and started to dial Sally, to ask her to get me the Emerald Police Department. But then I hung up. Better to do it myself.

It took going through a receptionist, a desk sergeant, and a secretary, but finally I heard, "Dr. Sanford, this is Chief Melville Richmond. What can I do for you?"

"We've got a problem," I said. "One of my patients had a baby last week, her husband committed suicide, and one of your officers has been awfully rough with her. He's got her on the edge of a nervous breakdown."

Chapter Twenty-one

Baumgartner

Elsa Hearn was a lot better put together than when I'd called on her a week earlier. She greeted me at her door by saying she hoped she hadn't sounded reluctant when I'd called to ask if I could come by."

"Don't worry," I said. "I think that's a natural reaction when a cop says he wants to talk to you. I don't take it personally."

Like her daughter, Mrs. Hearn was a large woman, but not fat. In fact, she was quite attractive. White hair, gathered round and round, pinned up atop her head, a fair complexion, and blue eyes that I thought could deliver spring warmth or a January freeze, depending on the circumstances. Right then, she was doing June, though I couldn't miss the fatigue lines spreading out from the corners of her eyes. "I suppose I really shouldn't have been surprised," she said. "It's quite reasonable, isn't it, that you'd want to check back with me. Have you found out any more about…Giselle."

"I've got some thoughts," I said. "I'm hoping you might be able to help."

"I certainly will, if I can. Please, come in.

We sat in the living room of a large farm house built some fifty years before. The furniture looked to be from the same era, comfortable upholstered chairs, a sofa with carved round mahogany tables at each end. There was an orderliness to the room, everything in its proper place. A mahogany grand piano sat below a picture window to my left. On the wall to my right, I saw a photograph of a younger Mrs. Hearn, standing between a stout, smiling man whose head came up just past her shoulders, and a very serious girl just at the point of becoming a teenager.

She saw me looking. "Now, I'm the only one left," she said. "It's not supposed to happen that way."

"No, it's not. I'm sorry."

"It's as if someone somewhere placed a horribly wrong order that's not subject to correction." She cleared her throat, then worked her body upright in her chair. "Well, then. What can I do for you, Mr. Baumgartner?"

Feeble smile, but give her credit. "Do you know the name, Alma Wanego?"

Her forehead crinkled, eyebrows approached each other in the middle. She shook her head. "No…no, I'm quite sure I've never heard that name. I'm sorry."

"Don't worry about it. She was the supervisor in your daughter's lab. About eight months ago, she disappeared, from one day to the—"

"Oh, for heaven's sake. Yes, of course, I do remember that. Giselle said it was the oddest thing. One day, the woman was there, the next day, she was gone. Giselle was irritated, but not altogether displeased. She said Miss Wanego was not an easy person to work with. She never did show up again, so Giselle appointed a new supervisor, someone who got along much better with people, and that was that. Do you think there was some connection between that and…?"

"Some things suggest that possibility."

Sly smile. "And you can't be specific. That's all right, Mr. Baumgartner, I understand. Go ahead, ask me whatever you'd like."

"Tell me about Giselle. Start from when she was a girl."

"Well, I'd be glad to, but what possible connection could there be—"

"You'd be surprised, Mrs. Hearn. Sometimes, the smallest thing makes a critical connection."

"All right. Giselle was born in Emerald, in 1933. My late husband was a tool and die maker, and after Pearl Harbor, his company was conscripted into the war effort. Not that Michael was unpatriotic, but he was terribly individualistic, and he couldn't put up with the government agents and their regulations. He also thought it would be a bad idea to bring up a young girl in Emerald, with all the sailors around…oh, he was very old-fashioned, Mr. Baumgartner. Which sometimes made me want to *shake* him, but I have to admit, in some ways it was charming. So we bought this working farm from an older couple who were delighted that Michael was going to hire some help and keep it running. The children took to it as well, Randolph and Giselle—they were eleven and eight when we moved in. They loved the farm animals, and seemed to enjoy the chores, at least most of the time."

Mrs. Hearn pointed out the back window, to a thick stand of tall trees. "Giselle was always a bookworm. In the summer, she'd take two or three books back there, find a spot and read the whole day long. At one point, Michael mentioned cutting down the trees to get more farming space, but the fit Giselle threw made him change his mind."

"Sounds like your daughter didn't have a lot of friends."

"Not ever. Even back in Emerald, when all the other girls were out playing jump rope, she'd sit for hours, reading. Some of the neighbor women brought their daughters to meet her, and sometimes she'd visit with one or the other, but not often. She lived in her head. Not that there was anything, you know, the matter with her. She simply preferred books to people."

I smiled. "Sometimes I feel the same way."

"Randolph was more outgoing. He got into groups at school, 4-H, the football team. He always had a friend or two around. He went to Washington State, then to Indiana University, and became a veterinarian. He met a girl out there, so that's where he's stayed."

"Not entirely to your satisfaction."

"Well, of course not. I was so glad to have Giselle as close as she was."

"I understand she had been married."

Mrs. Hearn nodded. "Yes…my, that was seventeen years ago, in 1960, while she was in Chicago, in graduate school. Her husband's name was Patrick Carver. I met him only a few times, but he seemed like a nice young man. He was quite gregarious, and I hoped he might be able to, oh, get Giselle out of her shell. But it didn't work that way. The way I heard it, Patrick was always out with friends, playing ball, going to theaters and concerts, but to Giselle, that was all a waste of time. So after a few years, she and Patrick grew apart. No hard feelings on either side, and fortunately, they'd not started a family yet. Patrick was interested, but Giselle didn't want the distraction of a baby. In the end, they separated, then divorced. It's common these days, isn't it, Mr. Baumgartner? Perhaps it's better than feeling as though you need to hang on forever, as people did in my generation."

"Do you know where Mr. Carver is now?"

She shook her head. "Giselle said after the divorce, he got a good job in New York City. But they didn't keep in touch, at least as far as I know."

"Since her divorce, did your daughter have any other relationships? Any men friends?"

"Not to my knowledge, but then, Giselle never did talk much about herself. I will say, though, over the past year and a half, she seemed more animated. She told me she'd begun a collaborative project with a Dr. Sanford. He took human eggs from patients at surgery, then she did experiments on them, studying what might go wrong at fertilization. She said it was a great opportunity. To hear her talk about it, her relationship with Dr. Sanford was purely professional, but I'll admit, I did wonder. Late one night last September, I was awakened by noises, and thought I might have a burglar. I tiptoed out of my room, and looked down over the banister, and there was Giselle with a man."

Mrs. Hearn smiled knowingly. "Giselle was as surprised to see me as I was to see her. I'd gone on a cruise, and she'd thought I wouldn't be back until the following week. She introduced the man as Dr. Sanford, and explained that they'd had some major success in their work, and had driven up to the Gold Bar Restaurant, a fancy place a few miles up the road. They didn't seem inebriated, but Giselle said they'd had a few drinks, so they thought they'd come by here, make some coffee, and sit around for a couple of hours."

A smile even more knowing than the first. "They both were a bit disheveled, and, I thought, nervous. I hoped perhaps since I'd caught them in pre-flagrante delicto, they were going to tell me they'd decided to get married. But they didn't. I made a pot of coffee, we sat and drank it and talked for a little more than an hour, then they left. And I never met Dr. Sanford again."

"You said this was late at night? How late?"

"Between twelve-thirty and a quarter to one. I remember looking at the clock when the noise downstairs woke me."

"Do you know how late the Gold Bar stays open?"

"That would depend on the day of the week. I remember it was a Friday night, because I'd gotten home from the cruise the day before, and that was a Thursday. On Friday and Saturday, The Gold Bar is open till two in the morning."

I could hardly keep my butt in my seat. Wanego had been at work on Friday, September 10, then never showed up over the weekend, or on the following Monday. And here were Hearn and Sanford, sneaking around the old family farm, thinking Mother was still away on her cruise. Maybe they really were going to celebrate with a roll in the hay, but one reason for the celebration might have been that they'd gotten rid of a nasty fly who'd settled in their ointment. Or, given that Wanego had vanished just after the Kennett pregnancy had been confirmed, it could've been a double celebration. "Would you mind if I look around?"

She shrugged. "Not at all. Please go right ahead. Any way I can be of help."

About halfway back to Emerald, my beeper shrieked. I snatched it off my belt, and barked my name into it. A woman's voice came through a cloud of static. "Detective Baumgartner, this is Roxanne McClure."

Richmond's secretary. I thought I heard alarm bells in her voice. "What's up, Roxanne?"

"Chief Richmond wants you to come in. He needs to talk to you."

No question on the alarm bells. "When?"

"Now, Mr. Baumgartner. He said to tell you whatever you're doing, please drop it, and come right in."

◇◇◇

As she ushered me along the hallway into the chief's office, Roxanne looked like the priest at the side of a man on his way to the execution chamber. She was back out, door shut before I was two steps inside.

The chief's face could've been carved on Mt. Rushmore. He motioned toward one of the chairs opposite his desk, then grabbed a pencil and banged out the rhythm to God knows what tune on his desk blotter. I sat, waited. Finally, he said, "I had a phone call a little while ago, a very disturbing phone call. From Dr. Colin Sanford. He claims you've got Ms. Kennett on the edge of a nervous breakdown."

"I'm sorry about that, Mel, but the truth is, she's earned it. For that matter, so has he."

Richmond started to say something, caught himself, sighed. "Bernie, didn't I tell you I wanted this investigation done quietly? Now I've got a doctor out there, one of the biggest names in the local medical community, complaining that you're browbeating his patient, a woman whose husband killed a lab scientist and then himself less than a week ago. Do you have any idea what will hit the fan if that doctor decides to talk to reporters? Or tries to go over my head?"

"Mel, listen to me. Please? I'm not surprised Sanford's trying to muscle you." I held up a thumb and forefinger, nearly touching. "I've got the case this close to cracked, and he knows it. He and Hearn were working in secret, doing some very questionable fertility work on Ms. Kennett. A supervisor in Hearn's lab caught on, started blackmailing Sanford, and guess what. She disappeared last September, right at the time the Kennett pregnancy was confirmed."

All the time I talked, Richmond's face got redder. His blood pressure must have been off the charts. "And what ever came out of *that* investigation?"

"There *was* no investigation. No one reported the woman missing. But I've been—"

"God damn it to hell, Bernie." Mel was out of his chair, leaning across the desk, shooting a fine spray in my face to punctuate the G, the d, and the B. "Now, *you* listen to *me*. I asked you to tie the ends together on this case, nice and quiet. A schizo goes off the deep end, shoots a lab doctor, and then himself—how much more open and shut does it have to be? So what do you do? Get yourself all worked up about some esoteric research stuff, and go poking around after a lab supervisor who probably had it up to here with her job, her boss, the rain in this part of the country, whatever, and decided she needed to go off some place and 'find herself.' And now you're turning the screws to a new mother who also happens to be a new widow."

"She's no innocent little flower. And as for Sanford...Mel, I'll have this whole business tied up no later than tomorrow. When you called, I was on my way back from talking to Hearn's mother, and—"

I braced, thinking he was about to fly across the desk and fling his hands around my throat. For a guy twenty-two years on a desk job, he could still move. "And nothing, Bernie. It's over. What you're going to do is forget about this case. I'll close it myself, take care of all the papers personally. As of this minute, you're on two-weeks leave. Go take your wife on a nice trip."

I felt something shift inside my head, shudder, and settle into a new position. Words came out of me that I never, ever, thought I'd say to Mel Richmond. "Take my wife on a nice trip—because you don't have the balls to tell Bancroft and the mayor where to stick your job, then go tell the paperboys exactly why you're quitting. Christ, Mel, how do you sleep at night? Or look in your shaving mirror in the morning? If somebody like Horace Bancroft could take away my job, I wouldn't want it."

Richmond sank back into his chair. He looked like he needed every drop of gas in his tank to wave his hand. "We go back a long way, Bernie."

"Which is why—"

"Which is why I'm going to ignore your insubordination. I respect you, Bernie. I really do. I should've known you couldn't handle a quick, quiet wrap-up, my mistake. By now, Olson would've had this mess signed, sealed, and delivered, which, believe me, is no compliment to him, or a knock on you. Now, please. Don't make this any worse. Take your leave, cool off, then come on back, and we'll figure it never happened. Okay, Bernie?" He smiled, held out his hand. "I'm sorry I shouted at you before. I was upset."

He was upset? All the way to Iggy's, those three words ran through my head, like a hippie's mantra. To save Mel Richmond's stinking job, I should go take my wife on a nice trip. No way. I was going to finish this case on my own, and I was going to finish it right. If the price of keeping *my* job was to let Sanford walk, I didn't want my job.

Good there were no customers at Iggy's. The little guy was reading a newspaper behind the counter, but when he looked up and saw me, he dropped the paper to the floor. "What, Mr. B?"

I gave him the quick version of my meeting with the chief. "I'm working privately now," I said. "You've been great, a huge help, but I don't want you to get caught keeping bad company. Give me the stuff you're holding, and I'll go find a room in a motel with a safe."

He set his mouth, shook his head. "That ain't the way I do things, Mr. B. I don't jump ships. I told you before, if you're in, I'm in. Something in particular you want me to do, just say it."

I started to object, but I didn't get a word out. "I'm serious, Mr. B."

Deep breath. "Okay, Iggy, I hear you, and I appreciate it. Nothing right now, but I may have something big for later."

"All you gotta do is ask. Easy as that."

"Thanks, Ig," I muttered. "I'll check in with you dinnertime."

I drove to Pill Hill, left the car in the Med Center Garage, and made a flying stop at Puget Community's Medical Records Department, where I flashed my badge, and a few minutes later, walked out with a copy of the newborn chart for Baby Robert Jackson Kennett. A couple of minutes paging through it on a bench in a hallway told me I was going to need help, so I crossed over to the Doctors' Tower, and took the elevator to the third floor, the low-rent district. No surgeons here, no OBGYNs. This was pediatrician and family doctor territory.

Halfway down the hall was Dr. Milton Edgerton's office. I went in, and up to the reception counter, then held out my badge to the receptionist. "My name's Bernie Baumgartner," I said. "I'm a patient of Dr. Edgerton's, but I'm here on police business. I need to ask him a question."

The receptionist gave me the look she probably used to get five-year-old patients to sit down and shut up. "Dr. Edgerton's having a terrible morning, all kinds of emergencies." She reached for a pad. "If you'll tell me your question, I'll pass it along to Doctor, and he'll call you as soon as he has a moment."

"I'm sorry, but I really need that moment now. I promise, it won't take more than a couple of minutes."

She sniffed, then picked up the phone, and dialed a two-digit extension. "Dr. Edgerton, there's a policeman out here who's one of your patients. He says he's got to see you urgently, on police business." She looked back to me. "What's your name again?"

"Baumgartner."

"Baumgartner…all right, Doctor. I'll tell him."

She hung up the phone, then motioned me across the room. "Please have a seat. The doctor will be out as soon as he can."

I thanked her. She pretended not to hear.

I'd gotten through only two pages of a six-month-old *Sports Illustrated* when Doc Edgerton came through the door. Good-looking man, over six feet, slim, wavy white hair with a nice trimmed mustache to match. He wore a white jacket over a green scrub suit, bloodstains on the legs, and a smear of God knows what on the front of his jacket. He extended a hand, which I shook, then released as quickly as I could. "Sorry to bother you, Doc, but I need some help."

He grinned. "Police business, eh? Something interesting, I hope."

"It is to me." I pulled the chart copy out of my pocket, and put it into his hand. "Look at these blood types. The woman's A positive, and her husband's B positive. And the baby here is O negative. Any reason to think the husband's not the father?"

Edgerton laughed. "Well, there's always a reason to think that. There was a study not long ago of a fishing village in England where blood tests showed that fully one-third of the children could not have been fathered by the mother's husband. But in this case, no. You can't prove this man wasn't the father."

"Even with the A's, B's, and O's all different like that?"

He snatched a glimpse at his watch. "Here's how it works. In the ABO blood groups, A and B are dominant over O, so a Type A mother can have two A genes, or one A gene and one O. Same with the husband there—he could have two B genes, or one B and one O. And if the baby got an O-gene from each parent, he'd type out as O. It works the same way with the Rh system. The father and the mother could be Rh positive, with one positive Rh gene and one negative, and the baby could have gotten the two negative genes, making him Rh-negative. You see?

"Yeah, I do. You explain things well." I folded the page back into my pocket. "Not what I wanted to hear, but knowing it, I'm still better off than before I talked to you."

"There are more detailed blood tests that might show up discrepancies. If that helps."

"I'll keep it in mind. Thanks, Doc."

◇◇◇

It was three-thirty. Sanford would be in the middle of his after-noon office hours. I was hungry, hadn't eaten since breakfast, so I took the elevator to the lobby, but pulled up halfway to the coffee shop. A block down from the Medical Center and around the corner was Maxie's KayCee Barbecue. Sold. I hustled out through the revolving door, crossed the street, and started along the sidewalk, but right as I was about to turn the corner onto Williams Street, I heard a loud pop, and felt a giant bee sting on the left side of my ass.

I pulled my gun from the holster, and staggered a step to dive around the side of the building. Good thing I'd gotten Richmond to requisition the piece, good thing he hadn't thought to take it back. I edged a look around the marble cornerstone. No one on my side of the street. On the other sidewalk, three women strolled in my direction. I hobbled across the street, motioned the women to come over. They looked away and upped their pace along the sidewalk. My rear end hurt like hell, but I forced myself into their path. "Did you hear a gunshot just a minute ago?"

They could have been grandmother, mother, and teenage daughter, three generations of beetle-brows. "Yeah," the teenager chirped. "I did hear a shot." She pointed across the street. "See that alley there? After I heard it, I saw somebody duck back in there and take off."

"Somebody like who?"

"I ain't got no idea, I didn't see him but a second. I couldn't tell you if he was short or tall or fat or thin, or how old, or what color, or nothing."

I looked at the other two women. "Either of you see any more than that?"

They both shook their heads.

The girl was practically jumping up and down. "You want, I'll go find a cop for you."

Just what I'd need, having to explain to Mel why I wasn't at a travel agent's, making reservations for a nice trip. I shook my head. "Thanks."

I crossed the street, and peered down the alley. Nothing. No point chasing down there. If the guy was waiting around the far corner, I'd be a pigeon all the way down that narrow corridor. I thought about hightailing it back to the Med Center, and seeing whether Sanford was out of his office or maybe had just come back from a little break, but I wasn't in shape to hightail anywhere. Not with my ass throbbing the way it was. First consideration, get the bullet out.

But how? If I went back to the hospital ER, they'd report the case, and next thing, I'd be in Richmond's office. Have to be inventive. I limped along the sidewalk, around the corner, into Maxie's.

No man has ever been better named than Maxie Gross. Just about my height, weighing in at an easy three-fifty, he was the best ad around for his food. Maxie and I had a little history, going back to when he used to run as many numbers cards as platters of ribs over his counter. But Maxie always took care of people in his neighborhood, widows and orphans, down-and-outers. Nobody on Williams Street went hungry if Maxie could help it. So one time I told him what a shame it'd be if a sting that was going down in a few days, or another one some time in the future, would set a bunch of people to dumpster-diving, begging in the streets, or grabbing stuff that wasn't rightfully theirs. The next time I went in for a plate of ribs, Maxie let me know that any insistence on paying would be taken as a serious insult.

Fortunately, at a quarter to four, the restaurant was empty, save for a couple of men at a table in the back. Maxie waddled up from the counter, and started to give me the big hello, but then looked down to my legs. "Hey, Mr. Baumgartner, you're limping. You hurt or something?"

"Somebody took a shot at me," I said. "Can we go in the back?"

"You don't want to go to the hospital?"

"No."

Maxie knew when to stop asking questions. He loosed a phlegmy cough into his hand, then led me behind the counter, through the kitchen, and into his office. After he closed the door, I turned my back to him, undid my belt, and slid my pants and shorts down to my ankles. Maxie whistled. I snatched a peek at him over my shoulder. He could've been Fats Waller, bugeyed to the limit.

"What's it look like?" I asked.

"Like a kindergarten kid's finger painting. Red and blue and purple, and a little black around the edges."

"Can you see the bullet?"

He grunted to squat, then struggled back upright, and pushed a messy pile of papers from the front to the back of his desk. "Go lay on your stomach there."

I climbed up, slowly stretched to the limit. Maxie pushed this way on my butt, then the other. He wiggled his fingers. Pain shot down the back of my left leg. "Yeah," Maxie grunted. "Right in the middle of your bun here, feels like a little bump. Not too far under the skin." He coughed again.

I looked around. "Maxie, you ought to lay off the smokes."

"You sound like my doctor. I just got a little cold, that's all." Another cough.

"You think you can get that slug out?"

All the red juice drained out of the big man's cheeks. "You're kidding, Mr. Baumgartner, right? All I ever done in my life is work in a restaurant, and you want *me* to dig a slug outa your ass?"

" I want even less to go to a hospital and have to explain how it happened. You've got clean knives, right?"

"They ain't sterile."

"Got a lighter? Some alcohol?"

Maxie pulled a silver cigarette lighter from his pocket. "Only alcohol I got is in the booze."

"I guess that'll have to do."

"But what the hell am I gonna use to pull the thing out?" He held up a hand before I could say a word. "Hold on, lemme think…" A huge grin broke through the barrier. "I got it. Be right back." He started for the door. "Don't go nowhere, okay."

Not three minutes, he trucked in, clutching a bottle of Jack Daniels in his right hand, another brown bottle tucked into his left armpit. "Peroxide," he said. "And some JD, unopened." He put the bottles on the desk, then pulled a knife from his pocket, and waved it in my face. "Paring knife, ain't never been used. I can make a li'l cut…" He pulled a flat red leather container out of his back pocket. "Then pull out that mother with something from in here."

"What, you keep a surgical kit in your restaurant?"

"Not exactly." He ran a zipper around three sides of the pouch, opened it, held it to my face. "Bonnie, one of the waitresses, she spends more time fixing up her face and her hair than looking after customers." He plucked a small pair of tweezers free of its holding loop. "Looks like this was made for the job." He tapped the peroxide bottle. "This's Bonnie's, too. You know, 'Her blonde comes out of a bottle, her blonde comes out of a bottle.'"

I groaned. "Let's get it done."

Maxie set the case next to the bottles, then took a handkerchief from his pocket, opened the Jack Daniels, dripped some onto the cloth, swabbed the knife, and set it on the edge of the desk. Carefully, he picked up the tweezers, dipped the business ends into the whiskey bottle, then flicked his lighter open and held first the knife, then the tweezers, up to the flame. Pale blue shimmered off the tweezers. Maxie laughed.

"What the hell's so funny?"

"Just thinking about doing this at a table. Specialty of the house today, Tweezers Flambe." He snapped the lighter shut. "Okay. Ready…oh wait a minute."

He set down the tweezers and the knife, then walked around the desk, opened the top drawer, pulled out a small drinking glass, filled it with whiskey. "Here. Anesthetic."

I shook my head. "I've got a visit I need to make after you're done, and it won't be good if I show up stinking of JD."

He shrugged. "Suit yourself." Then he looked at the glass, threw back his head, downed the whiskey in a gulp, and let out a long "Aaaaah. It shouldn't go to waste."

"God forbid."

I stretched out flat on my stomach. Maxie poured peroxide onto the handkerchief, wiped it over my rear end. "Burns," I said.

"Yeah, well, it'll kill the germs. Okay, here we go."

I picked up a pencil from his desk, bit on it, hard.

Maxie grunted. "I'm down on top of the slug, ain't deep at all. Put your hand on your ass over here and pull sideways. That'll open up the cut so I see better."

"Yeah, be good if you can see," I muttered around the pencil.

I felt Maxie slide the tweezers into the crevice, then work them down slowly, around the bullet. My fingers went icy and slippery from sweat; my stomach thought it was on open water during a hurricane. Another cough; the tweezers sent little electrical charges down my leg. "Keep pullin' your cheek sideways," Maxie muttered. "Here goes."

You want to talk about pain? This was blinding. I felt the tweezers fly up and out of the hole. I made a sound, something like 'bulurp,' and swallowed hard.

"Got it," Maxie shouted. "You okay, Mr. B.?"

"Fine and dandy." Cold sweat poured into my eyes, down my cheeks, past my ears. "How's it look?"

A moment of silence, then, "Pretty good, considering. It's oozing a little blood, and the skin's kinda burned around where the bullet went in. Maybe I ought to clean it out." Maxie set down the tweezers, opened the peroxide bottle, and poured.

I wasn't ready for that. It felt like he'd lowered the flame from his cigarette lighter into the hole. I threw a hand over my mouth, wiggled around on the table, flung my legs every which way. Maxie whistled. "Looks like a Pink Lady in there."

"Push the sides together," I groaned. "Squeeze that shit out."

Slowly, the agony tapered off. "Maxie, what the hell *is* that stuff." I grabbed the bottle away from him, read the label. "Jesus Christ. 'Madame Louise's 20 Volume Peroxide. Best hair lightener available…not for medical use.' This stuff is twice as strong as drugstore peroxide."

Another shrug. "So what's the big deal? It'll kill twice as many germs."

I started to sit up, but Maxie grabbed my hand. "Hey, wait a minute. You got this open hole in your butt, about an inch, inch and a half. We better close it up." He looked around the room, then waddled back to the other side of his desk, and returned holding a roll of masking tape. "It ain't sterile or nothing," he said. "But it'll hold the sides together. Better'n walking around with pieces of fat hanging out."

I rolled back onto my stomach and let Maxie tape me up. "Bet no doctor's ever thought of taking out a bullet this way," he said.

"Bullet…" I reached for the tweezers, grabbed the little slug, scratched it with my thumbnail. "Copper-washed lead, a twenty-two short." I closed my eyes. "That alley where the guy shot me from was about thirty, thirty-five yards away. He must've been aiming for my heart."

Maxie shook his head. "Lucky for you he didn't know shit from shoe polish about guns. Twenty-two from thirty-five yards? I'm surprised he didn't hit you in the foot. Probably a kid being a wiseass or joining a gang."

"Maybe," I said, but I didn't really think so. I slipped the bullet into my shirt pocket. "When I find out who fired this sucker, he's gonna have it in *his* ass and then some." I pulled up my shorts, then my pants. Then I pulled out my wallet, took out a fifty, pressed it into Maxie's hand.

He pushed the money away.

"Relax," I said. It's for your waitress, Blondie, Bonnie, who-ever. Somehow, I don't think she'll want to use those tweezers again."

He gave my hand a hard shove. "What she don't know won't hurt her. I'll give her a Jack Daniels on the house."

Chapter Twenty-two

Baumgartner

Next morning, my rear end was sore and more than a little stiff, but nothing I couldn't handle. I stopped by Bergstrom's, picked up a pair of pants that wasn't air-conditioned in the left rear, sat for an hour with a newspaper over coffee and a donut, and got to Sanford's office about a quarter to twelve. Sally gave me the big New York greeting. "Mr. Baumgartner—hey, maybe Dr. Sanford ought to put you on the payroll, you're here so much. He's on his last patient now. Soon's he's done, I'll let him know you're waiting."

His last patient ever, I thought. I thanked her, and went off to sit in a padded chair.

When I walked into Sanford's office, he wasn't his usual jaunty self. He probably figured I was there on account of his call to Richmond, and he was letting me know he wasn't about to lie down and roll over. "We'll have to keep this one short, Mr. Baumgartner. There's a new man in town who thinks he's an expert in laparoscopy, and he's going to give a talk to the hospital staff over lunch. By the time I'm done with him, he'll be lucky to get any referrals at all."

"You'll go to your meeting when we're finished," I said. "And not before."

He drew a purse string around his mouth.

I slid carefully onto the chair opposite him. "Start with an easy question. "Where were you between three-thirty and four yesterday?"

"Yesterday?"

"Yes, yesterday. Thursday, May fifth, three-thirty to four PM, in the afternoon."

"Spare me the sarcasm."

"Spare *me* the stupid games. Especially if you want to get to your meeting before it's over."

"I was here. In my office. Seeing patients from two o'clock till five, straight through."

"You didn't leave the office at all? Not even to go to the bathroom?"

"We have our own bathrooms right here. But for the record, no, I didn't use the bathroom from lunchtime till the end of office hours. Can I ask why you want to know where I was yesterday afternoon?"

"No. Now, I'm taking it as established fact that you and and Dr. Hearn were doing IVF on the Kennetts, and the sample Dr. Hearn dropped was Mr. Kennett's sperm. You told me it came from a medical student, for an experiment, but that was a lie. Dr. Hearn was going to use that sample to fertilize Ms. Kennett's eggs for IVF, wasn't she?"

Sanford's smug smile made a comeback. "Think whatever you want," he said. "The only procedure Dr. Hearn did on James' sperm, on the one sample she had, was Density Gradient Separation."

"You're sure? There really was only one sample?"

"Yes."

"You're on shaky ground, Doctor. I've told you, I've got a witness who'll testify that you came running over there right after Dr. Hearn dropped the sample, and then you and she went off in a hurry to the supplies room. And here's something else. I know that when you left the supplies room, you went straight to the men's room, found a janitor fixing a clogged sink, and threw him out. Why'd you do that? How much privacy do you need to take a leak?"

No smug smile now.

"Dr. Sanford, be careful what you say. Tell me lies, I promise, they're going to come back to haunt you.

He ran his tongue over his lips. I raised a finger. "Careful."

"All right. I did have to get a second sample from James Kennett, or we'd have had to cancel the procedure. Infertile couples are fragile under the best of conditions, and I thought Joyce was on the razor's edge. She'd fixed all her hopes on that Density Gradient Procedure. So after Giselle called me, I got hold of James and told him his sample was inadequate, that we'd need a second one quickly, and best not to say anything to Joyce."

He paused, clicked his tongue. "Try to understand, Mr. Baumgartner. Most men don't find it easy to go into a public bathroom and masturbate, but to produce a second sample within a short period of time is even tougher. A janitor there, cursing and clanking pipes, would've been a real problem. So when I went into the men's room, yes, I did have a collection vessel in my pocket. I'd left James waiting around the corner while I made sure the coast was clear. I had no idea how long the janitor was going to fuss around with the sink pipe, so I asked him to leave. Can you see why I didn't tell you this before? I didn't want it to get back to Joyce, and I still don't. I hope you'll have the decency not to tell her."

I ignored the request. "But Ms. Wanego noticed the accident, thought something was fishy, and found out who your patient was. Then, when she found out Ms. Kennett was pregnant, she wanted ten thousand dollars to keep her mouth shut. If the accident didn't amount to anything in the end, why didn't you tell her to get lost? Ten thousand dollars can't be chump change, no matter how well off you are."

He leaned back in his chair, arms behind his head. "Look, we've talked about this before, the last time you were here, in fact. I told you then, and I'll tell you again, I did not pay any blackmail to that supervisor. Now, unless you can prove I did, can we move along?"

I'd thought about checking the numbers of the bills in Wanego's little wooden box against bank records for Sanford's withdrawals. But for that, I'd have needed a warrant, and I was in no position to get one. Didn't matter, though. The plan I had in process would be a whole lot more conclusive. Airtight-conclusive. "Last time I was here, you gave me a hypothetical," I said. "Let's take it further. If Ms. Wanego actually had tried to blackmail you, would you have discussed the situation with Dr. Hearn?"

He looked at his watch. "Mr. Baumgartner, I—"

"It's your hypothetical. Your game. Play it."

He shook his head. "All right. Yes, I guess I would have talked to Giselle, if only because I wouldn't have wanted the supervisor to try for a double dip, and blindside her."

"And what would have come out of that conversation?"

"I guess we'd have decided to see whether the supervisor would stick to her word."

"And if she didn't?"

"We'd have had to figure out how to deal with it."

"No ideas right then?"

"Not from me. But Giselle had a close daily association with Ms. Wanego. She might've had an ace in the hole."

"What might that ace in the hole have been?"

"I wouldn't know."

"You wouldn't have asked her? Doctor, I give you credit for having a good set of smarts. How about you return the favor?"

"Credit where credit's due? All right. Yes, I suppose I might have asked if she had anything in mind, but even if she did, if she hadn't wanted to tell me, I wouldn't have gotten anywhere. When Giselle planted her feet on something, you couldn't move her off it with a winch. So I'd have told myself to wait and see what develops. One step at a time."

"I wonder what would happen if I took you downtown," I said. "Hooked you up to a polygraph while we discuss your hypotheticals. I'll bet that reading would look like an earthquake."

He didn't flinch. "I'll tell you what would happen. You'd be out of a job. I called the chief of police yesterday, and filed a complaint about the way you were harassing Joyce Kennett. I told him I wasn't going to sit still for it. He assured me he'd have a talk with you, and that if I had any further problems, I should let him know." He pushed back from his desk and walked around to face me. "Mr. Baumgartner, you've put my poor patient through hell, not that things haven't been bad enough for her. I'm not going to let you persecute her even more over a lab accident that in the end had no effect on her care."

"It would've had a big effect if that second sample didn't really come from her husband."

He rested a hand on his desk, an inch away from a hefty letter-opener. "Even if you're right, that would be a civil, not a criminal, matter. And in any case, it's a nasty accusation."

"Nasty wouldn't be even close to the right word if that was the way it went. And if Mr. Kennett found out about it—say, if Dr. Hearn told him how glad she was that that second sample had worked—I wonder if he'd have been upset enough to pull out a gun and start shooting. You told Dr. Hearn the sample came from Mr. Kennett, didn't you? But I don't think it did."

The hand came off the desk, formed a fist, punched the other palm a couple of times. "All you've done since you walked in here has been to throw maybes and what-ifs at me. You said Dr. Hearn and I were doing in vitro fertilization on the Kennetts. If you've got proof of that, go ahead, I'm listening. Otherwise, I'm on my way to my meeting. Take me downtown, if you'd like. We'll see who comes out the worse for it."

"The proof is in Dr. Hearn's log," I said, very quietly, and damn if he didn't glance for a split second at the file cabinet. "Right on, Doctor. You sure it's still where you hid it?"

For the first time, I saw Sanford at a loss. I almost laughed, watching him freeze to the floor, trying not to turn and take a hard look at the cabinet. "Check it out," I said. "See if you've still got it."

He looked like a yokel, trying to read a shell game. "You're a decent bluffer, Baumgartner. But no go. I don't have any idea where that log is."

I got up, walked to the door. "I'll wait outside."

I didn't have to wait long. Less than a minute later, the door slammed open and Sanford burst through. He looked like someone had painted his cheeks and lips with library paste. "You broke in here and stole them. If you didn't have a warrant—"

I strolled back inside; he stomped after me. "Stole 'them?'" I said. "Did you hide something else with the log? I didn't say I broke into your office, and I didn't say I stole anything. I didn't say I had the log. All I said was that the log proves you were doing IVF."

"How would you know if you didn't read it?"

"I didn't say I read it. I only said what it proves. But if you really don't have it any more, I guess there's no way you can prove to the world you won your race. All that hard work for nothing. What a shame."

This was where I was going to give him a quid pro quo he wouldn't be able to resist. But he moved like a snake, shot out a hand, and grabbed my shirt. Pure reflex, I shoved him off, and swung my left forearm toward his chin. A bolt of pain flew from my bullet wound down the outside of my leg, and I flinched. Before I could react, Sanford had delivered a fist to my bread-basket. I doubled over, straightened, and launched a left to his jaw, but when I tried to follow it with a right, he made a move the likes of which I'd never seen, and planted a right cross on the side of my head. Lights flashed on and off. I took a couple of steps back to regroup, then moved forward, both fists ready. Sanford ducked, grabbed at my left arm, twisted, and I was on my back. If I'd thought the punch had hurt, the pain as my can whacked onto the floor made that seem like nothing.

My ego hurt even worse than my ass. A doctor, five inches shorter than me and forty pounds lighter, had made me into chopped liver. I thought about reaching inside my jacket for my gun, but figured Sanford might kick out my teeth before I could work the piece out of the holster. He stood over me, a look on his face like he'd just woken from a dream. He hadn't followed up the judo move, and I felt pretty sure the fight was over if I wanted it to be. Which I did. Not that I wouldn't have minded a chance to even matters, but that wasn't why I was there.

I worked my way up off the floor, forced myself to stand straight, then took a few seconds to clear my head. "Now, you've really got problems," I said. "Assault on a police officer."

"Damn you." Not much more than a whisper, then a thoroughly disgusted look as he lowered himself onto the edge of his desk. He pulled a handkerchief from his pocket, and dabbed at the little stream of blood at the corner of his mouth. "Well, I've only got myself to blame, letting a bozo like you work me up like that. All right, go ahead. Take me in, and let's see what happens."

"You mean what happens when you tell the chief I stole your…Dr. Hearn's log? Forget it. I'm not going to take you in, and I'm not going to say anything about what you did. Frankly, I'd be embarrassed."

All the slump went out of him. His jaw set. He was winning again. He thought.

I smiled. "Where'd a little fucker like you learn to fight like that?" I asked. "Big brother give you lessons?"

Surprise, his eyes went watery, and when he started to talk, his first words were quavery. "I learned to fight like that because I *am* a little fucker. In grade school, guys like you used me for a punching bag till I got sick and tired of it. Remember Aldo Ferrigno, the old welterweight? He used to come by the Boys' Club a couple of blocks from where I lived, and give boxing lessons. The first time I clocked one of the guys who was always after me in school took care of that problem. And I've been doing judo since I was in college. It's come in handy more times than you'd think. You underestimated me, didn't you?"

"Hard to deny it."

"All my life, that's how it's been. Whether I'm in an operating room or a bar, people underestimate me. They think a little guy like me is a sure pushover. Their mistake."

I nodded. "I should've known, no matter how mad you were, you wouldn't have started something with a guy half a foot taller than you if all you had in your pocket was a few lessons in the manly art from a big brother."

I wasn't just making conversation. Sure enough, his eyes filled again. "What?" I asked.

He raised his head just enough to meet my eyes. "I did have a brother, but he died when I was four. Accident. My fault."

"What happened?"

"I was four, he was five. My father had the cover off a wall socket that wasn't working right. I was sore—you know how it is with kids. I wanted to go to the Fourth of July parade, not sit and wait for my father to fix a lousy socket. I went into the living room to sulk, but that didn't make me feel any better, so I decided to play a tune on my mother's music box. Major no-no, but I didn't care. When I reached up to the shelf and pulled on the handle to wind it, the way I'd seen my mother do, the damn thing toppled and came crashing down on me. My father ran in, and while he was gone, Victor stuck a metal screwdriver into the socket. He was off-the-charts brilliant, five years old. My parents already had a private tutor for him." Sanford shook his head. "My mother never got over it."

They named him Victor, I thought, and gave Number Two a name like Colin. How unintentional *was* that broken music box? "I'm sorry," I said.

"Thanks."

I took a deep breath. "All right. Let's get back to business. I've got a lead in Alma Wanego's disappearance, but I need help to follow it up. Here's the deal. Later tonight, you give me that help, and then you've seen the last of me. How does that sound?"

"Damn good. But what exactly do I have to do?"

"Come along with me."

"And?"

"You'll see."

"You've got to tell me more than that."

"No, I don't. You can play ball and help me close this case, or else I'll have to take the long way around Robin Hood's little red barn, and you'll end up spending a whole lot more time in my company. And if you get me taken off the case, I'll make sure every news reporter in this city has the information I've got. Think about the field day they'll have with that. Ms. Kennett will find out about the second sample, and then you'll be lucky to hold onto your license to practice, never mind that no woman in her right mind will set foot inside your office again. Gossip's harder to deal with than truth. You know that."

"And you don't care about your job?" He squinted at me. "You're *not* bluffing, are you?"

"Nope. I care about my job, but only up to a certain point."

I had him. It was all over his face. "What've you got to lose, Sanford? If you really had nothing to do with Ms. Wanego's disappearance, why should you say no?"

"Suppose you're wrong? What happens if I do what you say, but it doesn't work out, and you can't close the case?"

Time to play *my* hole card. "You help me follow this lead, you're off the hook, win, lose, or draw. You and Ms. Kennett never see my face again. I forget everything I've heard about the second sample. And besides, you never know. Maybe the Good Deed Fairy is so pleased, she gets your missing log book back to you. That's a hypothetical, of course."

He didn't want to laugh. "Baumgartner, you are a bastard. Anyone else ever tell you that?"

"Start with my wife."

He gave me a long look.

"I think we've got a deal," I said, ignoring the complaints from my leg muscles and the pounding from my left hindquarter. "Give me a pencil and a piece of paper."

He reached to the desk, then handed me the pencil and a little pad. I scribbled Iggy's address and phone number, then passed the pad back to him. "Can you get over there by six?"

He nodded. "Office hours are done by five. Do I need to get coverage for my patients?"

"Definitely."

"And you won't give me any idea where we're going?"

I shook my head. "Trust me, Doctor."

◇◇◇

All the way to my car, I felt restless, feverish. I couldn't stop thinking about that business with Sanford and his brother. Why should remembering an accident that happened nearly forty years earlier turn an arrogant, cocksure doctor into a teary-eyed little boy? Didn't add up. But in police work, when something doesn't add up, you go find yourself a better calculator.

A ten-minute drive from Pill Hill, and I was in front of the Emerald City Hall. I parked in a Police Only space out front, then worked my way up the twenty-seven marble stairs to the door. By the time I pulled the handle, my shirt was sticking to the skin on my back. First heat wave of the year, temperature in the mideighties, with ninety percent humidity for good measure. I mopped my handkerchief over my face, went inside, and took the elevator to the sixth floor, Department of Vital Statistics.

A young Mexican woman with a stupendous swirl of black hair and teeth like a movie star flashed those pearls from behind her barred counter window. "What can I do for you, sir?"

"I need a death certificate."

"Oh, sure." She took a form from a pile at her side, and pushed it toward me, underneath the bars. "You can fill this out here, or you can take it home and mail it in. We'll send you a copy in two to three weeks."

"I need it now," I said, and held up the badge.

"Oh, police. This is for a case you're investigating?"

"Right." I put the billfold back into my pocket.

"Is it a murder…oh, I guess you can't really tell me, can you?"

"Right again. Here, I'll fill out the form for you."

No trouble filling in name and age. Victor Sanford, five years old. Date of death, Fourth of July…I did a little quick math. Victor had been five, a year older than Sanford, who'd been born in 1935. So, July 4, 1939. I hesitated before I signed my name and the reason for my request, but I didn't see any way around it. Besides, this was City Hall. That form would get filed and shoved into a cabinet, never again to see the light of day. I slid the paper back to the clerk, and pointed to the row of tan vinyl chairs against the opposite wall. "I'll wait over there while you get it for me."

"Yes, sir." She picked up her phone.

A minute later, a walking beanpole with a pair of black-rimmed glasses hanging on a cord around her neck came out from the back, and marched up to my chair. "You're with the police, and you need a death certificate?"

"That's right, ma'am."

"May I see your identification, please?"

I opened my billfold to show her the badge and ID.

She slipped the dark-rimmed cheaters onto her nose, and studied my credentials. "Bernard Baumgartner…detective, Emerald police. Very well." Off with the glasses, on with a grudging, tight-lipped smile. "I'll have it out for you just as soon as I can, Mr. Baumgartner."

"I appreciate that, ma'am."

Less than fifteen minutes, she was back with the certificate. I thanked her, then scanned the paper, folded it, and slipped it into my shirt pocket. Now that I had it, I'd have to think about what to do with it.

But right then, all I felt like was taking a nap. The fight with Sanford had really taken it out of me. My left shoulder was sore, the side of my chest felt tight, my right temple was tender to the touch, and my rear end throbbed. Soon as I got back to Iggy's, I hit the couch.

I slept for three hours, and when I woke up, I felt logy. I stumbled into the bathroom and washed my face with cold water, which seemed to help some. By the time Iggy came back from work, I was in the living room, reading the paper. Iggy gave me the twice-over, then whistled. "Looks like you was in the wrong place at the wrong time, Mr. B."

"Wait'll you see the other guy." Then I told him about Sanford, and what I had in mind for the evening. "I'd appreciate it if you'd come along. I might need a witness, and if things get rough, I wouldn't mind another pair of fists on my side."

"You want we should take my car?"

"If you don't mind. That way, I can have both my hands free the whole time."

"No sweat. Then, I guess I oughta go out now, before our boy shows up, and put the equipment in the trunk."

"Good thinking. I should've thought of that myself."

Sanford rang the doorbell right at six. I let him in. Iggy, in his chair, looked up from the paper, like for all the world he didn't have a clue. Sanford sported a nice little swelling at the right corner of his mouth, which I'll admit gave me a bit of satisfaction. "Iggy," I said, "I want you to meet Dr. Colin Sanford. Dr. Sanford, my friend, Irwin McKeesport. He's going to come along with us later. Let's get some dinner, then we can take off."

Iggy laid down the newspaper. "Okay by me. Whatever."

Sanford didn't say a word. He was too busy trying to figure what was up.

We dallied over our eats at Grandma's Oven, a small formica-table, vinyl-booth comfort food joint a couple of blocks from Iggy's. By the time we got back to the house, it was a quarter past eight, deepening twilight. "I'm going to make a pit stop," I said. "There's a fair ride ahead of us." When I came out, Iggy went in, and when he reappeared, zipping up, I asked Sanford if he wanted a turn. He shook his head. "I'm fine."

"Good. Let's get moving."

In the garage, Iggy got into the car behind the steering wheel. I motioned Sanford to the front passenger seat, climbed in the back, ran my hand absent-mindedly over the little bulge inside my jacket.

Half an hour up the Interstate, I told Iggy to get off at Holcomb County Road, then directed him to the west. We'd gone about a mile when Sanford half turned. "Baumgartner, where in hell are you taking me?"

"You'll see. We're almost there."

He looked at the lock button on the door. "If you're thinking about getting me out of your way, you'd better think again," he said. "If I don't show up for work tomorrow, my office staff'll call the cops and tell them how you've been living in my office. Then, you'll have to explain why you look like you've been through a war, especially after they see the note I left with someone that says I was going off I-didn't-know-where with you tonight."

"Relax," I said, and tapped Iggy's shoulder. "Go right here, kill the lights, go slow."

I turned back to Sanford. "You've got a good imagination, but you can only help me if you're alive. Another couple of hours, we'll have this wrapped up, and you won't ever have to think about me again." If you can do that from behind bars, I added silently.

The house at the end of the dirt road had one light on, probably the living room. I told Iggy to stop. "From here, we walk," I said. "No lights, no talk."

We got out of the car. Iggy opened the trunk. I gave him a shovel, took the other one myself, picked up the lantern with my free hand, and started leading my troops through the farmland, our feet squishing in the wet field. "My shoes are going to be ruined," Sanford groused.

"Shut up and keep walking," I hissed. "You'll be able to afford all the shoes you want after the Good Deed Fairy takes care of you."

We gave the farmhouse a wide berth, then cut back to walk toward the grove of trees. Once there, I turned on the lantern, directed the beam toward the ground,. "Single file," I whispered.

We snaked through the trees till we came to a small clear area under a couple of giant maples. Sanford, directly behind me, stepped to the left, lurched, but caught himself before he fell.

"Right," I said, and tapped at the dirt with my shovel. "Ground's sunken in there, isn't it. Let's start digging."

Sanford reached for Iggy's shovel, but I wasn't about to give him anything that might become a weapon. "Iggy and I have calluses on our hands," I said. "You hold the light for us."

Every shovelful I lifted sent a message straight to my ass. I ignored them. Get this close to nailing down a case, I could handle a little pain. After five minutes of gritting my teeth, I felt something solid at the end of my shovel. I reached down. "Over here," I called to Sanford.

I watched for any sign he might be thinking about swinging the lantern, but he did no more than squat over the hole and hold out the light. A piece of fabric came into view. Sanford zeroed in on it. Iggy and I set to clearing the area, first with shovels held short, then with our hands.

Iggy whistled. "This the lady who disappeared, Mr. B?"

Gently, I lifted the left arm. Bones showed through decomposing flesh. I slid my fingers over the corpse's hand. "Light here." I glanced back toward Sanford. "From this ruby ring, I'd say yes."

His face told me nothing. "What's a ruby ring got to do with… is this the woman you've been looking for? The lab supervisor?"

"One and the same."

"Where the hell are we?"

"Dr. Hearn's mother's farm."

That got his attention. "Giselle's…oh, no." The lantern shook in his hand, cast a weird, trembly glow over the grave. "That's why…I didn't know the first thing about this, I swear."

"You've never been up here before? As close as you and Dr. Hearn were?"

"We never socialized. No."

"Never? Or hardly ever?"

"Baumgartner, you could drive a man nuts. No, I've never been here, not ever, not once. Never in my life. Got it?"

I sighed. "I need to let Mrs. Hearn know what we've found."

Sanford stood up, stretched, brushed off his hands. "All right, go tell her. I'll wait in the car."

"No," I said. "We're all going."

Sanford started to object, then threw his hands in the air. "I've done what you wanted. I don't understand why, but I did it."

"We've still got a little more to do."

"I can't see any reason why I should go in there. That poor woman doesn't need a committee to give her more bad news."

"Come on, Sanford. She's old, and with all the people you've had to give bad news, I figured you could help with her. It's part of the deal."

"But that's it? No more after that?"

"That's it."

He swept up the lantern, started to walk away from the grave. I told him to wait. "Don't you think we ought to cover her up so the animals can't get to her."

"Sorry. You're right."

◇◇◇

Mrs. Hearn gave us a very hard eye as we stood under the porch light. Not that I could blame her. Imagine finding three sweaty men with filthy-dirty shoes, two of them with faces straight out of *Ring Magazine,* on your doorstep late at night. "I'm sorry to bother you this late, Mrs. Hearn," I said. "But I need to talk to you. May we come in?"

She hesitated long enough for me to add, "We'll take off our shoes."

Embarrassed chuckle. "Well, of course, Mr. Baumgartner. I was surprised, that's all. Please, do come in."

We stood in the vestibule, light from a crystal chandelier showing off our war wounds a lot more clearly than they must have looked under the dim bulb on the porch. I took care to get myself between Sanford and the door. "Mrs. Hearn, this is my associate, Irwin McKeesport."

Iggy tipped his cap.

I readied myself to intercept Sanford and hold him long enough for Iggy to help me. No breakables anywhere I could see. "And you've already met Dr. Colin Sanford."

Now, Mrs. Hearn looked even more confused than when she'd opened the door to us. "I beg your pardon?"

"Dr. Sanford," I said, gripping his shoulder. "You told me you'd met Dr. Sanford. Unexpectedly, one night last September."

"Well, yes…" She peered into Sanford's face, trying, I think, to imagine him in fully-restored condition. "But this isn't Dr. Sanford."

My turn to be confused. "This isn't the man who came out here with your daughter that night? When she thought you were still away on your cruise?"

"No. That man was a good ten years older than this one, and heavier. Taller. With a lot of wavy gray hair, and a distinguished-looking mustache."

Sanford and I locked eyes. I'm not sure who said, "Camnitz," first. I nudged him, and whispered, "Later." Then I turned back to Mrs. Hearn. "We've found the body of that missing lab supervisor. She's back in that grove of trees where you said your daughter liked to sit and read."

It took a few seconds to sink in. The old woman put a hand to her mouth, and I thought she was about to hit the deck. Sanford grabbed one arm, I caught the other, and we helped her into the living room, into an armchair. Sanford knelt at her side. Before I could say anything, he took her hand between his. "Mrs. Hearn, I'm so sorry," he said. "Things aren't always the way they seem. I know there's a good explanation for this."

Mrs. Hearn snuffled, pulled a tissue from her pocket, wiped her eyes, then blew her nose. "You're very kind, Doctor." She tried to smile, couldn't quite manage it. "We go to such extremes to lengthen our stays on earth, don't we? Proper diet, good exercise, mammograms. But I don't have words to tell you how much I wish I'd gone off on my long journey a month ago. I don't know how I'm going to face people when all this comes out. What can I possibly say?" Then, she really started to cry.

We hung around till Mrs. Hearn was better settled. I told her that other policemen would come by and remove Ms. Wanego's body, but in the meanwhile, I'd be grateful if she'd not speak to anyone about the situation.

"Who would I speak to?" So softly, I could barely hear the words.

◇◇◇

The instant we closed the car doors, Sanford took off on me. Iggy gawked as the good doctor angled himself between the two front seats to call me every name in and out of the book. "Start the car," I called past him to Iggy.

Sanford was past furious. "Bastard! You were trying to trap me."

"So? That's what cops have to do sometimes to catch a bad guy."

"It didn't mean a goddamn thing when you said we had a deal."

"With all the lies you've fed me this week, you'd be the last person on earth who's got a right to complain." I shifted, to put more weight on my healthy buttock. "But I didn't lie to you. We *did* have a deal. Even if I'd collared you, I'd have gone through with my part. Think about the press you'd have gotten, standing there in an orange suit and cuffs, presenting the first IVF baby in the world. But cool it. You're coming out like a rose. Mrs. Hearn will take one look at Camnitz, and that'll be that. Then you can go ahead with your announcement. Go make history. Satisfied?"

Iggy snickered.

Sanford ignored him. "How did you know where to find the body?"

"Mrs. Hearn told me that grove of trees was her daughter's favorite place to go and read when she was a girl. When I saw the depression in the ground, just the right size and the dirt still not packed tight, I knew that had to be it."

Sanford shook his head. "I can't believe you thought I'd gone up there with Giselle and buried that body."

"Give me a break. What *should* I have thought when Mrs. Hearn told me you and her daughter showed up here unexpectedly in the middle of the night, looking nervous as hell, and right about the time Wanego vanished?"

No answer. Then, Sanford said, very quietly, "Now what?"

"Back to Iggy's, then you can head on home. I'm going to have a talk with Camnitz."

"You've got his address?"

"Personnel records."

"How about Mrs. Hearn?"

"Damn it, Sanford, I'll take care of it all. But I've got to do some thinking first. Thanks to you, I'll be lucky to keep my job. That phone call you made to the chief? He took me off the case, said he'd tie it up and write the report himself. He put me on two-weeks' leave."

The stretch of streetlights along the freeway lit up Sanford's face, a strobe show of confusion wrestling with disbelief. "You've been working the case on your own since yesterday...but now that you've solved it, why would the chief put your balls in a sling?"

"Richmond's got skin like wet cigarette paper. Starting tomorrow, I'm dead meat in that department."

Sanford grunted. "Then why in hell did you—"

"You're a smart boy, figure it out for yourself."

"I'm going with you to Camnitz's," he said.

"Hell you are. That's the last thing I need."

"Maybe it's the first thing. Don't you want a witness, Mr. Insubordinate Cop?"

"God damn it, Sanford. If I wanted a witness, I wouldn't bring somebody Camnitz knows. Besides, let two or three people march in on him at eleven o'clock at night, and he'll head straight for his phone to call his lawyer. *That's* the last thing I need. He thinks I'm a schmuck flatfoot, but I'll nail him cold before he knows what hit him. I appreciate both you guys' help, but now, go on home, the two of you. I'll check in with you later."

Chapter Twenty-three

Baumgartner

Schmuck cops don't live in neighborhoods like Camnitz's, a tony district on a bluff in northernmost Emerald, overlooking Puget Sound. I followed the winding road lined with ancient maple trees framing palatial residences till I came to Cliffedge Avenue, then turned right. The rich smell of seaweed at low tide came in through my open car window. I wondered whether the owners of the land-side houses dreamed of the day they might double their mortgages, move across the street, and brag about their unobstructed views of shipping traffic going up and down Puget Sound.

Camnitz's place was on the water side, Number 1525 Cliffedge. I parked in front, then sat for a few minutes to catch my breath. My left butt pounded like a jungle drum, and the cheek felt twice the size of its mate. Every time I had to hit the brake, a wave of pain shot up my back and down into my crotch. I told myself I wouldn't have to hang on much longer. Another couple of hours, I'd have this business wrapped.

I climbed out of the car as carefully as I could. No lights on in the house. One second-story window was open. I walked up to the door, pushed the button three times, then drew in close to the wall, under the overhang, where Camnitz couldn't see me from above and decide to ignore me.

Not thirty seconds later, I heard a roar. "Who's down there?"

"Baumgartner," I shouted back.

"*Baumgartner?*" Do you know what time it is?"

"Six minutes after eleven. Come down and open the door. I need to talk to you."

"You can jolly well wait till morning. I'll see you in my office."

"This isn't a social call, Doctor. If you aren't down here in one minute flat, I'm going to call in reinforcements, and then you can explain to your neighbors why the street in front of your house was full of lights and sirens at midnight. I'm starting to count. Now."

It took him seventeen seconds to open the door. He looked like a comic book character in his red and white striped pajamas. His hair was all over the place, and his flamboyant PJs didn't do much to disguise his ample midsection. "What in the name of anything holy is so important that you have to ring my bell at this hour?" he bellowed.

"I'll come in and tell you about it." I stepped past him onto the slate vestibule. "I hope I didn't disturb your wife."

"Hmmph. Nice to know you have *some* consideration. No, my wife takes sleeping pills. She wouldn't hear the end of the world."

I pointed toward the living room. "Can we sit down?"

He humphed again, then said, "Would my study suit you?"

He led me down the hall, past walls covered with paintings that looked like they'd been done by kindergarteners, all in thousand-dollar frames. I thought I might sink into the carpet up to my ankles.

Camnitz's study fit the profile and then some. More Emperor's-Clothing artwork on two walls, the others taken up by in-built bookcases. State-of-the-art stereo system in the recess adjacent to the huge glass-covered mahogany desk. Camnitz shuffled behind the desk, started toward the chair, but detoured to open the window. "Hot as hell in here," he muttered, then sank into his chair, and motioned me to sit opposite him.

My butt said a nice thank-you for the thick padding on the chair.

Camnitz tilted his head back, adjusted his glasses, all the better to look down his snoot at his unwelcome visitor. "Let's get this over with, Mr. Baumgartner. What is it that couldn't wait until morning?"

You don't rush your moves in a chess game. "Well, Doctor, it starts with what we talked about in your office. You were in a certain relationship—"

"Shh." Finger to lips, he glanced toward the door. "I don't want my wife to hear this."

"But she's asleep, you said. Wouldn't hear the end of the world."

He frowned. "Are you here to blackmail me?"

"No. That's the one thing you don't have to worry about."

"Well, come on, man. Get to the point."

"I'm getting there," I said. "You and Ms. Wanego had a nice trip to Norway. Then, a few days after you got back, she disappeared—"

"One thing had nothing to do with the other. I have no idea why she left or where she went."

"No, the trip and the disappearance weren't related. But you do know why Ms. Wanego left. You also know where she went."

He'd been twitchy all along; now he steepled his fingers to try to cover a tremor that was getting worse by the moment. "I said I have no idea, and I don't."

"Yes, you do. Was Ms. Wanego turning up the heat on you? Tightening the screws more than you could hold still for? What I'd really like to know is how, after you killed her, you got Dr. Hearn to help you bury the body in that grove of trees, out on Mrs. Hearn's mother's farm."

He looked like one of those old-time circus clowns, calcimined face, blazing nose, red-striped pajamas. "Right," I said. "Too bad for you that Dr. Hearn was so wrapped up in her work, she forgot when her mother was coming back from her cruise. Dr. Hearn introduced you as Dr. Sanford, but Mom's going to take one look at you in a lineup, and point straight at you. What'll you have to say then?"

He cleared his throat, swallowed air, worked his tongue around his mouth. Finally, he managed, "Does this really have to come out?"

"Well, no, of course not. This is just a party game, Pin the Murder on the Killer, and now that we've done that, let's go have some ice cream and cake."

"I can make it worth your while," Camnitz said. "I'll give you more than you'd make in five years of work. No, ten years." He gave me what he thought would pass for a chummy smile. "How does that sound?"

"Tempting. But I've come this far, and I'm not going to spend the rest of my life wondering what really went down with the three of you." I wiped my face on my sleeve. "Tell me the story. The real story."

He looked twenty years older than when we'd walked into the room. His shoulders slumped, loose skin below his cheeks. "I had nothing to do with Alma's death," he said. "Giselle Hearn came into my office late one afternoon. She said she'd tried to talk to Alma about her behavior as lab supervisor, but it didn't go well. The talking became yelling, and then things, you might say, got out of hand. They started to fight, and…well, Giselle was a big woman. She said Alma suddenly went limp, and Giselle realized she'd strangled her. She wanted my help getting rid of the body."

"And out of the goodness of your heart, you helped the person who murdered your mistress to bury her. Dr. Camnitz, please."

"Giselle told me she knew about Alma and me, and if I didn't help her, she'd tell my wife."

"So what? She didn't have any proof, did she? Would your wife really have believed Dr. Hearn, once you'd turned her in for murder and attempted blackmail?"

Even with the open window, the room was a blast furnace. My head felt light. "Look, I don't have all night. You've swung and missed, Strike One and Strike Two. Here comes the next pitch. One more swing, and that's the old ball game."

He held out his hands like a street beggar. "It was an accident. It really was. I shouldn't ever have made Alma the supervisor of that lab. I knew there'd be trouble, but she insisted, and I thought I could handle it. Earlier that day, Giselle made an appointment to see me. She told my secretary it was urgent, but she was in the middle of an experiment, and couldn't come by till after five. I said all right, I'd stay."

He shook his head. "When she came in, she was in a rage, absolutely frothing at the mouth. She said the situation in the lab had become impossible, that her whole staff was going to quit, and if I didn't fire Alma, she'd tell my wife about how every time I was at a medical meeting lately, Alma was gone, too. Giselle insisted on getting it settled right then, once and for all, and stormed out.

"When she sailed back in with Alma, I asked Alma if she couldn't be a little more patient with the lab staff, but it was like tossing a can of gas onto a fire. She told me it was Giselle or her, and I could decide which one of them would talk to my wife. 'Use your head, Gerry,' she said. 'Tell that cow she's got till morning to get her stuff out of the lab. If she does say anything to your wife, I'll deny it. Look in the mirror. Do you really think your wife would believe I'd have an affair with you?'"

Camnitz looked like a little boy, his mother took away the cookie he'd pinched out of the jar. "The next thing I knew, Giselle ran over and gave Alma a smack in the face that knocked her across my desk. I tried to pull Alma away, and then both Giselle and I were tugging at her. She was screaming like a siren on an ambulance, and when I put my hands over her mouth, she bit me. Giselle had her arms around Alma's neck, and then, just like that, Alma went limp. Giselle had broken her neck. It was an accident."

No, it wasn't, I thought. It was Hearn's hypothetical ace in the hole.

Now that he'd gotten started, Camnitz babbled right along. "When we realized what had happened, Giselle said she knew where we could get rid of the body. So I called my wife, told her I was supervising the residents on a difficult case, and wasn't sure when I'd get home. Giselle and I waited till late in the evening, then I went over to the hospital, got a wheelchair, and we pushed Alma out to my car in the parking garage. No one was around. We put Alma into the trunk, drove up to Giselle's mother's place, got shovels out of the garden shed, and buried the body. Afterward, we went into the house to have a drink, but Giselle was a week off on when her mother was coming back from a cruise, and she caught us. Giselle introduced me as Sanford, and made up a cock and bull story about a celebration over a lab success. That's the truth. You've got to believe me."

"Actually, I do." My mouth was so dry, I could hardly say the words.

Camnitz seemed to relax. "You *can* see, can't you? It was an accident. I didn't mean to kill her. I would never have killed her."

"You loved her."

He didn't hear the sarcasm. "Well, yes. I really did. She was such a strong woman, she made *me* feel strong. Made me feel like I could take on any problem."

I sighed. "She can't help you with this one."

Message received. He looked like a beagle who'd gotten an unprovoked kick from its owner. "Mr. Baumgartner...I told you, I'd make it worth your while, didn't I? Alma's death was an accident, and it wasn't even me who broke her neck. What's the point of ruining my life?"

"I'm going to break into tears." I stood, wobbled a bit, recovered. "Let's go."

"Where?"

"Down to the station. Some other people would love to hear your story and put it on tape."

"You want me to go like this? In my pajamas and bathrobe?"

"They'll give you their own brand. You'll feel right at home. Come on, Camnitz. Up."

As he got to his feet, he whipped a hand into the pocket of his robe, and came out with a small handgun. "No," he said, like a two-year-old. "We're not going anywhere."

I couldn't take my eyes off that gun. Son of a bitch. I rubbed my pounding ass.

"Why couldn't you have been reasonable?" he whined. "We both could've have come out of this all right." He leveled the gun.

I tried to figure what to do. This time, he stood just across a desk from me, not thirty yards down the street, and I didn't see any way to get at him before he could pull the trigger. If I made a move toward my gun, he'd shoot before I was halfway there. Bad game, trying to dodge a bullet, but I thought maybe a little rapid motion might get him nervous enough that he'd panic and shoot wildly. I dodged to the right.

He swung his arm around. "Stand still," he growled. If I hadn't been so damn scared, I'd have laughed.

Then, as I ducked left, I saw motion behind Camnitz. The partly-opened window flew all the way up, and a man jumped up on the sill and into the room, behind Camnitz. "Am I breaking up an important meeting?" Sanford asked.

Camnitz didn't know whether to spit, shit, fish, or cut bait. As he gawked at Sanford, I made a move toward him, but the desk was in the way, and he turned the gun back on me.

"The man's got a problem," I said to Sanford. "There's somebody on both sides of him. He may shoot one of us, but no way he's fast enough to get us both. The second guy is going to nail him."

Sanford pointed at me. "Shoot *him*," he said. "Kill me, what's going to happen to my patients?" He took a step toward Camnitz.

I moved around the edge of the desk. "No, shoot *him*. Kill me, who's going to protect the citizens of Emerald from scum like you?"

"We'd better watch out," Sanford said. "If his hands are as fast as his mouth, he could reload and get the two of us before we knew what hit us."

Camnitz's eyes flicked right, left, right, again. His hand wavered. Sanford was about five steps away from him. I was a little closer, but the corner of the desk was in my way. Grab for my gun now? No, Sanford and I had a good thing going. Push too hard, Camnitz might decide it'd be worth taking one of us along, most likely, I guessed, me. But who knew what his feelings were toward Sanford? One of the first things I learned from Mel Richmond was that it's dangerous to expect a cornered rat to think like a philosophy professor.

Camnitz's jaw tightened. His body stiffened. No choice now. I nodded toward Sanford. We both sprang. If we'd been a little closer, it would've been perfect, but Camnitz had just enough time to whip the gun up against his right temple. I had my hand on his elbow when he pulled the trigger. Maybe he was bluffing, hoping we'd back off and give him more wiggle room, but it was a bad move to bluff off the hand he was holding.

For a moment, Sanford and I stood over him, then we each went for a carotid. Neither of us found one. Sanford looked at the left side of the corpse's head, then up at me. "Where'd the bullet go?"

"A twenty-two short doesn't have much oomph," I said. "Which is why it's probably the best weapon for what he just did. The bullet bounces off the inside of the skull, then goes ricocheting around inside. All that's left in there now is a bowl of raspberry Jell-O."

It was New Orleans on Labor Day in that room. I perched carefully on the edge of the desk and shook my head back and forth, trying to clear the fog. "Sanford, what the hell were you doing out there?"

"You're not the only one who thought Camnitz owed him."

"But I told you not to—"

"I came anyway. After you dropped me off, I looked up Camnitz's address in the County Medical Directory, then drove right on over. You still had to take Iggy home, so I actually beat you here. I parked a couple of houses down, and waited for you. When you went inside, I watched to see where a light went on, then ran around outside and ducked under the sill to listen. Figured I could be a witness, if you needed one. But then I saw I'd better do a little more than that."

"The way you came through that window…oh. Judo."

"Couple of yards off the ground? Piece of cake."

"Why didn't you stay out there? You could've watched him shoot me, then turned him in, and you'd have been home free. Nothing to stop you calling the newsies in the morning."

He started to laugh. "Do that, and the hypothetical Good Deed Fairy would never give me Giselle's log."

I felt weary like never before. "I should've figured."

He gave me a long, hard squint. "Baumgartner?"

It seemed to take all my effort to say, "What?"

"You look like hell. You've looked like hell all evening. I thought you were just in a snit about this case, but..." He put a hand to my forehead. "Jesus, you're burning up. You must have a hundred-three, at least." He fingered my pulse. "One-thirty-two."

"I think I've got an infection," I said.

"Fair bet. Any idea where?"

"I *know* where." I waved a hand toward Camnitz. "I had a meeting with that gun yesterday afternoon. I must've made him nervous enough that he snuck up behind me down the block from the hospital, took a shot, then ducked into an alley. He nailed me in the butt. I didn't want to go to an ER and have to answer questions that'd put me on the carpet in front of the chief to explain...damn it, Sanford, I had a friend dig out the bullet for me. Now, it hurts like hell, and it's getting worse every minute."

"Let's see."

I hesitated, then got to my feet and dropped my pants and boxers. Sanford whistled. "What the hell—*masking tape?*"

"It's all we had to hold the edges together."

"And keep the crud inside. Hold on."

He pulled, and I thought I'd die. I wished I'd die. My body was just one big holding tank for pain. As it began to ease off, I heard Sanford say, "...probably a strep. Looks as bad as I guess it feels."

"Strep, huh? The guy who got the bullet out was coughing all over me. But he cleaned it out with peroxide, double-strength peroxide, in fact. Like they use for hair coloring."

"Double-strength...Baumgartner, that was one of the worst things you could've done. Double-strength peroxide damages tissue, and then you closed it all off, which kept the dead material in there. Like spreading a banquet for bacteria and inviting them to bring all their friends and neighbors. Listen, this is serious. You've got red streaks over your buttock and down your leg, and they're spreading practically while I watch them. We need to get you to a hospital."

"I can't do that. I've got this mess here to deal with. And besides, how would I explain—"

"You wait much longer, you're not going to have to explain anything, because you'll be dead. Let that infection get into your bloodstream, you're a goner. You need big-time antibiotics and drainage. Pull up your pants. I'll get you down to Puget Community, and start treatment."

"You? Start treatment? You're an OBGYN."

"So what? I'll have you admitted to the House Service on Male Medicine as a pelvic infection. I treat pelvic infections all the time, and a lot of them are strep. I can tell the resident you're a friend who's in a little bit of an embarrassing situation. Then, when he takes your history, you say you were walking down the street yesterday, and some kid shot you in the backside and ran away. You figured the bullet wasn't far in, you could get it out yourself."

"And he's going to believe that?"

"Of course not. Before he talks to you, he'll know I'm taking charge of your care to keep it quiet. No resident would ever screw over one of my patients."

Sanford pulled a handkerchief, carefully wiped the armrests of my chair and the edge of the desk where I'd settled down. "Come on, would you. Get your pants on, and let's go."

I glanced over at Camnitz, on the floor. "And just leave him lying there?" I winced as my trousers came up over my rear end. "Fat fuck!"

"Sure, leave him there. What's anyone going to think when they find a corpulent copulant in his pajamas in his study, a gun next to his hand, and a hole in his head?"

I started to laugh, coughed, damn near choked. Sanford pulled at my arm. "Can we please get out of here before I have to resuscitate you?" He yanked me toward the door.

"What about Wanego's body? Up at Mrs. Hearn's."

"Leave that to me. Did you see the way Mrs. Hearn looked at me when I was talking to her there, before we left? Like the mother of a patient who wasn't going to make it. I've been there once or twice."

I didn't remember how Mrs. Hearn had looked at Sanford, but I guessed I really hadn't been tuned in. "Can't you just give me a shot of penicillin?"

He tugged at my arm. "Come *on*, man. That'd be like trying to kill a tiger with a water pistol. If you can manage to drive your car a few blocks, I'll follow you, leave my car there, and take you to the hospital. Once you're settled in, with penicillin running, I'll go get Iggy to drive me back for my car. And then, I'll take care of Wanego's body."

"How?"

"Trust me. I'm a—"

"Shove it."

◇◇◇

On the way to the hospital, I began to drift in and out. I was in one of those between-states when I asked Sanford what he really knew about Hearn, Camnitz, and Wanego. "Get off the hypothetical crap," I said. "You must have talked more to Dr. Hearn about the blackmail than you told me. You *must* have."

"Sure we talked. We both knew that woman would be back for more, and Giselle said she thought she knew what to do about it. Afterward, she told me it was like taking candy from a baby. She went to Camnitz, told him she wasn't going to put up with Wanego any more, that he had to get rid of her, and if he didn't, Giselle would resign, and then tell Mrs. Camnitz *and* the dean all the reasons why. So Camnitz cut a deal with Wanego. He gave her a year's pay out of his pocket, she took off, and that was that."

"And you believed it," I said, not quite a question.

"That's what Giselle told me." Sanford's voice was very quiet; I had to strain to hear him. "My God, she must've orchestrated the whole thing, got Wanego so worked up, it'd look like an accident when Giselle broke her neck. No more blackmail, no more lab techs quitting on her. Can you believe that?"

"After thirty years on the force, yes. But am I also supposed to believe you never knew the first thing about it till now?"

He glanced toward me, then had to spin the steering wheel to keep from going off into the ditch at the side of the road. "I've done a lot of stuff, Baumgartner, but I don't think I have in me what it takes to kill someone. Not even you."

I held off for a moment, then said, "Well, I guess I don't have any right to pull your chain. I should've been all over Camnitz, especially after I found out about him and Wanego. But by then, I'd decided it was you, and all I wanted was to nail your snotty nose to the wall."

"Let it go. No hard feelings. Listen, one other thing."

"What now?"

"You don't want to have the hospital crew find a police badge and ID, and a gun on you. Give 'em here." He held out one hand. "I'll get them back to you when you can look after them."

Nothing left in my tank, not even fumes. I shucked out of the holster, dropped it onto the seat beside me, then pulled out my wallet and passed the badge and ID to Sanford. He dropped them into his shirt pocket. "Never know when they might come in handy," he said, then quickly added, "Just kidding."

I closed my eyes.

Chapter Twenty-four

Baumgartner

I woke out of the weirdest damn dream, where I was staggering down a dusty country road on a hot day, carrying an old man on my back. He kept shouting, "Go on, boy, faster. This rate, you ain't never gonna get there." Then, he'd hit me with a horsewhip. I tried telling him I was going fast as I could, but the words wouldn't come out. Sweat ran off me in rivers, down my face, all over my body. When I opened my eyes, I was sitting straight up in bed. You could've wrung out my hospital gown.

Outside the window of my room, the sun was high. I shivered, then grabbed up the little handset, dangling on a cord from the top of the bedrail, and pushed the Call Nurse button.

She was there almost before I set down the device. Skinny little thing, not more than twenty-five, brown eyes magnified like in a cartoon, behind granny glasses a quarter-inch thick. One of those silly white upside-down-cupcake hats pinned to her black hair completed the image. "Well, Mr. Baumgartner. How are you feeling?"

"Like I got caught under a steamroller," I said, and held out a fold of my gown. "And then got soaked with a fire hose."

She pinched the gown, and those dark eyes got even bigger. "Oh, my, that's wonderful. Your fever must have broken." She plucked a thermometer off the night table, and pushed me onto my side. "That's it, please hold still now, that's right."

I shivered again. "Can't you please get me a dry gown."

"Certainly. Absolutely. As soon as I see…hold on a minute while I take a look…oh, your wound looks wonderful. All those awful red streaks are gone. There's a little redness and swelling around the bullet hole, but that's all."

"Good," I muttered, then felt the thermometer slide out.

"Oh, and look at this. Ninety-eight-point-two. Dr. Sanford's going to be so pleased."

"Well, I guess I'm pleased, too. But I'd be really pleased if you'd get me out of this damn wet gown before I either drown or freeze to death."

She giggled, showing two rows of uneven teeth. "I'll do better than that. I'll give you a nice sponge bath, and clean up your wound, and re-dress it. We want you looking your best when Dr. Sanford comes to see you. I'll be right back."

"I won't go anywhere," I mumbled, then shucked out of the gown, and pulled the sheet up to my neck.

Inside an hour, my wound and I were nice and presentable for Dr. Sanford, and I'd had a decent breakfast, eggs, bacon, toast and coffee. I still had to favor my left buttock, but the pain was nothing like the last time I was aware of it. I asked Nurse Chipper when I might expect the arrival of The Doctor; she said she didn't know exactly, but she was sure it would be as soon as he could. "He's always so solicitous of all his patients, but the night nurse said she'd never seen him more concerned than he was about you. He's a wonder, the way he keeps going, day and night, year after year. He's the most dedicated doctor I've ever seen. You're so lucky to be his friend."

I bit down hard, then managed, "I don't know what I've done to deserve it."

◇◇◇

When I heard the door open, I expected to see Sanford come sailing in, a team of adoring nurses riding his wake. But it wasn't my heroic doctor; it was my wife. Irma stopped when she saw I'd spotted her, then walked up to my bedside like she was navigating a river bank studded with alligators. She took my hand. "You're better."

"Better than what?"

"Better than you looked when I was in here last night."

"You were here…when? I don't remember—"

"I'm sure you don't." The real Irma came blasting through the fragile layer of concern. "First, you were out of your mind, thrashing around, yelling, and then you were laying so still I thought you could be dead."

"How did you know I was here?"

"Card in your wallet. I'm your next-of-kin, remember?"

"Oh."

"Right. I really did think you were going to die. You had a fever up to a hundred and five, and the bedsheet had more color than you did. But that doctor-friend of yours told me you were going to be fine, that he'd gotten your treatment started in time, and I should go get some rest and come back in the morning. That's one ballsy pal you've got, Bernie. Where'd you pick him up. He doesn't seem like your type."

"We were working on a case together."

"I should've known. Was that the same case—"

"That bought me a goulash bath? Yes. It's over now, but before it was done, I managed to get shot in the ass, and it got infected."

Her whole attitude changed. She dropped my hand; her nostrils flared. I thought of a bull in a ring, about to charge the matador. "Bernie, damn you. Don't lie to me. It doesn't matter. I was going to wait till you were out of the hospital to tell you—"

"You're going to leave me. For Henry Streator."

That stopped the bull in her tracks. "How the hell did you know? Henry promised he'd stay away from you and let me handle it."

"I haven't seen Henry in days. You told me. The way you walked up to me from the door there, the look on your face, the way you've been talking to me. Like you're an old friend, someone I've known for years, and meet a couple times a week over coffee and donuts. You're not coming across like a wife whose husband was half-dead last night."

She smacked her hands to her hips, then blew out another chestful of vexation. "You're good, Bernie. You can tell at a glance what makes anybody in the world tick, but you don't have a clue about yourself."

"I know what makes me tick, Irma. So do you."

"But you don't want to do a damn thing about it."

And live the life you've got in mind for me? "No. I'm sorry, but I don't."

She moved a step away from the bedside. "Well, okay, then. I've had it, Bernie. Henry's not exactly a blazing lover, but he's a nice guy, and he *talks* to me. He's been lonely since his wife died, he's up for retirement, and he's been wanting to see Egypt since he was a little kid and saw pictures of the mummies and the pyramids. Damn it, Bernie, I want a life. Can you understand that?"

"Yes, I understand." Sounding like somebody was playing a recording through my mouth. "I'll miss you, I really will. But I wish you the best." I paused, swallowed. "Henry, too."

She was crying now. "Maybe your married girl friend'll be better for you."

"My what? Irma, I don't have any girl friend, married or not."

The Hungarian temper roared back, front and center. "I *told* you, Bernie, don't lie to me. Not now." She pointed toward my crotch. "You didn't get shot in the ass on that case, or any other one. A mad husband plugged you, going out a window. I heard a couple of nurses talking last night, while everyone was running around, trying to get you back to life. I'm not about to fault you, but listening to you try to feed me bullshit really pisses me off."

If I'd been watching this scene in a movie, I'd have been laughing and crying at the same time. Sanford, that dog. He *said* he was going to tell the resident he was covering for me in an embarrassing situation. Lie down with dogs, get up with fleas—but it was either lie down with that particular dog or never get up at all. If the strep hadn't nailed me, Richmond would've.

So what was I supposed to say to Irma? Could any words out of my mouth stop her from leaving? Try to give her the facts, she'd probably launch a bedpan at my head. It didn't take a genius to see it hadn't been easy for her, dropping that adios on me. Why I should make it harder?

"Okay, Irma," I said. "I'm sorry. I was embarrassed."

She made a disgusted face. "Bernie, Bernie…" She bent over, kissed my forehead, then turned away and headed for the door. "I'll be out of the house by the time you're home. And oh yeah. Your gun's in your shirt drawer."

"All right. Thanks."

"I never would've used it. You know that, don't you, Bernie."

"Sure."

I was going to tell her, stay in the house, I'd find another place, but she was already at the door. "Good luck, Irma," I called after her.

◇◇◇

She couldn't have been halfway to the elevator when Sanford charged into the room and up to my bed. He ran eye tape over me, then said, "You look pretty good. How're you feeling?"

"Better, but still a way to go. You sound like you're surprised. What were you expecting?"

He jerked a thumb behind him. "Your wife went past me like a tornado. I said hello to her, but she didn't even look my way. I couldn't believe you'd gotten worse, but—"

"No small thing like that. She's leaving me."

"And she thought right now was a good time to tell you?"

"Tact never was Irma's strong point. To be fair, though, she was going to wait till I was back on my feet, but she heard a couple of nurses gabbing about how I caught a bullet, going through a bedroom window."

Will wonders never cease? Sanford actually looked embarrassed. "Shit," he mumbled, then looked me square in the eye. "I'm sorry, Baumgartner. I really am."

"I appreciate that. But no harm done. Today, next week, it doesn't matter. She hung in for a lot of years, hoping one day I'd retire and we could sail off into the sunset, but now she knows that's not in the cards, and she found somebody else to take her on a trip to Egypt."

Sanford looked lost for words. Finally, he managed, "How long were you married?"

"Twenty-four years."

"Twenty-four...whew. I didn't even make it to two."

"But you know what, Sanford? It's ironic as hell. She finally packs up and takes off because I won't quit the force, and now that's exactly what I'm going to do. Soon as I'm out of here, I'm applying for a private investigator's license—which according to Irma would be more of the same, just with a different label."

Sanford looked like a kid about to sneak up behind a cop and give him a hotfoot. "My guess is that she'd be right."

"Mine too. So, tell me, Doc. How much longer do I have to wait before I can go tell the chief to take a hike?"

"Few days, probably. You're pretty pale, and right now, if you weren't propped up on those pillows, you'd fall over. Let's see, vital signs..." He plucked the clipboard off the foot of the bed. "Pulse 86. Blood pressure 132/80. Temp 98.2. "Penicillin's good stuff."

I gave him the eye. "You look like you've had a full night's sleep."

"Not close. Just an hour or so, but I'm used to it. Some nights, I don't get any."

"You must be on your lunch break."

He checked his watch. "Actually I'm not. I canceled all my appointments for today. I'm still sorting out last night's business."

"You're still sorting out...what's there to sort out? What in hell are you up to now?"

"Relax, Baumgartner. You'll have your fever up to a hundred-five again. Everything's under control. After Iggy and I straightened out the cars, I went back to Mrs. Hearn's, and had a talk with her. Remember what she said after we told her we found the body? That she had no idea how she was going to face people, or what she could say to them when it came out what Giselle had done?"

I cleared my throat, poured water from the bedside pitcher into a glass, drank. "Yeah. So?"

"So I apologized for not getting back to her till three in the morning, then told her there was no need for anything about Giselle to become public knowledge. I said Camnitz and I had been close-working colleagues—"

"Oh, Lord. When was the last time you told anyone the truth?"

"Listen, would you. I told her Camnitz and I were sitting in my office about five-thirty yesterday, working on arrangements to keep Giselle's lab running. He seemed distracted, said he'd been having bad dreams. Then, while we were talking about Giselle, he broke down. He said he'd been having an affair with Wanego, and she was after him to divorce his wife. Said if he didn't, she'd pay the wife a visit herself. He snapped, strangled her, hid the body in a closet. He knew Mrs. Hearn lived on a farm out in the middle of nowhere, so he ran down to Giselle's office, told her what he'd done, said it was an accident, and persuaded her to help him get rid of the body by promising to take all restrictions off her human embryo research.

"I told him he had to call the police, but he said he wanted to talk it over with his family and call his lawyer, then turn himself in. We started to argue. Finally, he ran out, all in a lather.

"So I told Mrs. Hearn, of course I called you right away. You said political pressure had gotten the case closed, but you didn't like it. You even thought you knew where the body was, and you asked me to go up to Mrs. Hearn's with you, and check that out. If you were right, and we did find the body, then you'd walk me past Mrs. Hearn to confirm I wasn't the person she said Giselle brought up there last September. Then you'd pick up Camnitz, take him in, and let the chips fall where they may.

"But on the way back to town, it came apart. You hadn't been feeling well all day—when I said that, Mrs. Hearn told me yes, she'd thought you looked terrible—and before we got back to Emerald, you became delirious, then passed out. I got you to my hospital, found you had a serious streptococcal infection, and admitted you for treatment. After I had your care under-way, I was going to call in the cops, but I thought about Mrs. Hearn…and you…"

How thick can you smear grease? "Sanford…"

"I told Mrs. Hearn I felt responsible for what was going to happen to her and you, that instead of letting Camnitz run out of our meeting, I should've told him I'd go along with his plan if he'd tell the police he'd driven out to Mrs. Hearn's alone to bury the body. That would've spared Mrs. Hearn any embar-rassment, and also wouldn't have left you hanging out to dry. So I told her that after I got you in the hospital, I went to find Camnitz, make sure he did turn himself in, and see whether he'd be decent enough to say he'd acted on his own. But when I got to his street, it was chaos. He'd killed himself. Which, I told Mrs. Hearn, cleared the way to not involve Giselle, and also to get you off the hook. She was a little reluctant at first, but she finally decided she didn't want you to get into trouble."

A water hammer started to pound over my left temple. "And she believed…sure she did. Coming from you? Definitely."

"I called the local cops, and when they came by, I told them about my meeting with Camnitz, what he said, and that I checked in with you afterward. But when you told me the case was closed, it bothered me enough that I finally went up to Mrs. Hearn's, found the body, talked to her, and called them. All the while I was telling my story, Mrs. Hearn sat, nodding her head. I got a little heat for not calling the police before I went out on my own to look for the body, and I apologized for that. I said Camnitz had been acting odd lately, and before I called in the police on him, I thought I ought to make sure he hadn't gone over the edge and was having delusions."

Sanford put on an embarrassed, little boy grin that must have left the Holcomb County cops bought, sold, and packaged. "I said if I were a cop, I'd probably have thought like a cop, but a doctor's going to think like a doctor."

"And that's that?"

"Pretty much. When I'm done here, I've got to go down and make a formal statement to the Emerald Police, but I can't imagine they're going to put me under any kind of pressure. Can you?"

"No. They'll want to slam down the lid and seal it tight. But what actually happened with Camnitz's body?"

"Turn on your TV. The Holcomb County cops called Emerald, the Emerald cops went to Camnitz's house, found the body, and labeled it an obvious suicide. Especially after what I'd told them."

I scratched at the stubble on my chin. "Two levels of lies with just enough truth mixed in to keep the whole crazy concoction from caving in. I don't know how you do it."

"Loosen up, Baumgartner. What's the sense in making the rest of a poor old woman's life miserable? And do you really want to try explaining to your chief why you and a couple of civilians went off in the middle of the night to dig up a body, and then you and one of the civvies ended up in a fatal face-off with a murderer? Much better my way. Everyone gets what they deserve. Including you."

He pulled something out of his shirt pocket, and tossed it onto my lap. Two somethings. My badge and ID. Then he took a cloth sack out of the pocket of his white coat, and tossed it into my lap. "Your firearm and holster, Officer."

I gathered up the badge and ID, stuffed them into the sack with the gun, then slipped the sack under the sheet. "You are some piece of work, Sanford. Trying to figure out what *you* deserve could be a lifetime job."

"Your call. Yours and the Good Deed Fairy's."

Manipulation by the master? Was he really concerned for Mrs. Hearn and me? Or was that simply a piece of his overall game plan? But any way I tried to cut it, I kept coming up against the fact that I owed him my life two times over.

I studied him from the corners of my eyes. He was so pumped, he couldn't stand in one place. "You really do want to go ahead and make that announcement?"

"Why shouldn't I?"

"Given that you've got no shame whatsoever, I guess no reason. But don't you ever think about the cost of your glory? Four people dead, and how many other lives ruined?"

"Who's going to mourn Wanego? And Camnitz, that pious hypocrite? In the end, he got himself off easy. As for James and Joyce Kennett, and Giselle, yes, believe it or not, I feel terrible about all of them. But what am I supposed to do, walk around in torn clothes with a face full of ashes the rest of my life? If people stopped to consider all the possible consequences of their actions, the human race would end in one generation. I can't bring Giselle back to life, but I'm going to make her immortal. Everyone's going to know Giselle Hearn conceived the world's first IVF baby."

"I'm sure. It'll make your story even better. 'The dedicated, heroic…' no, check that. 'The martyred scientist.'"

He nodded extravagantly. "You know, you're right. That's perfect. 'Dr. Giselle Hearn, the martyred scientist, who was so devoted to her work…' That's exactly the way I'm going to put it."

I couldn't take any more. "All right, Sanford, go ahead. Set up your press conference. I'll get on the horn to the GD Fairy, and tell her to give Iggy the log and your chart notes. You can pick them up at his shop. Give me a paper, I'll write you the address."

He pumped on my hand. The plastic IV tubing quivered. Then he pulled a notebook from his shirt pocket, opened it onto my lap, put a pen between my fingers.

When I finished writing, he slid the notebook and pen back into his pocket. "Thanks, Baumgartner. I'll be back to check on you, and if there are any problems…" He patted the beeper on his left hip. "They'll get me for you."

"Not so fast. I'm also sitting on a little bit of money, ten thousand dollars. I can't turn it in to the police now, can I? And if I try to stretch far enough to keep it myself, I'll break. If

I could give it to its rightful owner, I would, but I don't know who that is. Once upon a time, I'd have sworn it was you, but no. You bet on a horse."

He walked slowly back to the bedside. "Last night, on the way over here, when you asked me about what Giselle and I said to each other about dealing with Wanego, did I say anything about horses?"

"Hmmm. Yeah, we did talk about that, didn't we? But I guess I was pretty delirious, and I can't remember just what you said. So, since I can't find the rightful owner, I'll tell you what I'd like to do. I'd like to give that money to a certain young woman so she can go back to school and get her degree. She was one of the people I interviewed, and I needed to squeeze her a little harder than I feel good about. Maybe that'll make it up."

He worked a chuckle into a full-throated belly laugh, wiped at his eyes, then shot me a double thumbs-up. "I'd have never believed it, Baumgartner, not from you. I like that. Go for it." He stepped away from the bed.

"One more thing."

He turned back. "What?"

I was going to ask him again about the second sample, but then I told myself, forget it. He'd feed me one of two answers: either insist the sample really did come from James Kennett, or tell me if questions ever arose as to the kid's paternity, he'd figure how to handle them. He was the Lion of the Puget Community Hospital Surgery Unit. In an emergency, everyone prayed Dr. Sanford would be available.

While I was thinking, he bent over me. "You look like you're about to give me a bad biopsy report."

"Not quite. I'm going to tell Iggy to give you something else along with the log and the chart entries. I may be making a mistake, but I guess if you're not going to worry about the consequences of your actions, I won't worry about mine."

"Fair enough."

I reached for the phone on the night table, but stopped, halfway there. "Sanford?"

"What now?"

"Just wanted to say thank you."

"Don't mention it. All in a night's work." He waved a sloppy salute in my direction, then took off toward the door.

"Good luck, Sanford," I called after him.

Chapter Twenty-five

Sanford

My statement to the Emerald Police took less than an hour. I told Chief Richmond and Detective Olson what I'd told the Holcomb County cops the night before, including the same explanation and apology for handling the matter the way I did. The chief told me it would be best if I didn't speak to the press or anyone else, publicly or privately, about the case. His PR staff would handle it; he hoped I'd understand. I assured him I did.

The tires of my car squealed against the curb in front of Iggy's Lock Shop. As I came through the doorway, Iggy aimed an index finger in my direction, then reached under the counter. "Got your stuff, Doc. Hey, sounds like Mr. B had one foot in that hole out by Mrs. Hearn's place. He says, hadn't been for you, he'd be under six feet of dirt by now."

I couldn't take my eyes off that gray-covered log on the counter. "My patients don't go out of the hospital feet first, Iggy. Not if I've got anything to say about it." I picked up the log. My heart went thump against my ribs.

He gave me a close study. "You don't really come across like a doctor."

"What do I come across like?"

Shrug. "I guess a regular kinda guy. Somebody I could sit down with over a beer or a dinner, and talk to. Like Mr. B."

I laughed. "I can think of worse shoes to have to wear." I glanced at the chart pages. "Yep, all here…but there's something else…oh, right. Baumgartner said…"

"Doc. You okay?" Iggy sounded like he was talking through a tube.

"Yeah, sure. Why?"

"The look on your face. Hey, go have a seat over there, I'll get you a glass of water. You want I should call 911?"

While he was talking, the entry bell rang. A hefty woman in her fifties stormed in, waving a door lock. "Wouldja lookit what they did to my lock," she shouted. "Damn kids, after drugs. You got something they can't get through?"

Iggy could've been watching a ping-pong match. I waved him off. "I'm okay. Just a little surprise." I started for the door. "Take care of your customer. I'll catch up with you later."

◇◇◇

The ride to my parents' house should've taken twenty minutes; I was at the front door inside fifteen. I let myself in with my key, then followed voices into the kitchen, where my mother and father sat over the remains of lunch. They both jumped as I came through the doorway. "Colin, for heaven's sake," my father said. "Don't you have patients?"

I shook my head. "No patients and no patience," I barked.

Dad gave a twist to his hearing aid. "Sorry, Colin, I didn't quite get what you said."

I slammed a sheet of paper down in front of him. "Maybe this'll clear things up for you. Then you can explain it to me."

My father needed just a quick peek. He lowered his head into his hands.

"Death certificate, Victor Franklin Sanford," I said. "July 4, 1939. Cause of death, electrocution. Other conditions, *mongoloid idiocy*."

My mother batted lashes at me. "Well, what of it?" Bland as olive oil, but I'd known her too long. No missing the tautness in that short string of words.

"What of it? Wasn't he supposed to be a genius child, the marvel of the universe? Didn't you have some kind of tutor for him because he was already making Einstein look like a moron?"

She was up in a flash, caught me with an open hand to the cheek. "Don't you dare talk like that about your brother. If you hadn't misbehaved, he'd be alive today, and the whole world would know his name."

I looked to my father. He motioned me to calm down or sit down, or both, I couldn't tell. And didn't care. I jabbed a finger at the death certificate. "Are you people crazy? He had Down Syndrome. 'Mongoloid idiocy.' He'd never—"

My mother had me by the shirt sleeve, tugging, screaming. "Dr. Ehrenstein had been treating mongoloid children for twenty-five years. I took Victor to his office five days a week for injections of the vitamins and minerals he needed, and electrical brain treatments with the doctor's machine. I was scrupulous with his diet and medicines. The doctor told me Victor was coming along beautifully, and by the time he graduated from high school, he'd be first in his class."

She shook my arm savagely. I tried to pull out of her grip, couldn't. "But you! Always getting in the way, clinging to me, trying to get me away from Victor. You weren't even supposed to have been *born*. They told me women don't ovulate while they're breast-feeding." She pointed with her free hand at my father. "*He* even said it. Well, I guess I must have ovulated, because inside half a year, there you were, making me throw up five and six times a day. Inconsiderate from the moment you were conceived, impossible from the day you were born. Jealous of every minute of attention I gave your brother. And spiteful? Daddy brought me that music box all the way from France when he came home from the war."

Her eyes narrowed, and a corner of her mouth curled upward in a way that gave me chills. "You broke it on purpose, didn't you?

To get your father away from the electrical outlet. You weren't going to be happy till you'd destroyed my two most precious possessions." She flung my arm down as if it were contaminated, then marched out, into the living room.

Up to then, my father had sat silent, looking miserable. Now, he got up, and followed my mother. I took a step after him, but he motioned me back to the kitchen.

A few minutes later, he was back, looking twenty years older than when I'd come into the room. He plopped into his chair, and gazed at me, hollow-eyed. I started to speak, but he held up a hand. "The pediatrician told us there was nothing to be done for Victor, which I knew, of course. But your mother wouldn't accept it. She consulted doctor after doctor, and they all told her the same thing. The last straw was finding herself pregnant again. If doctors didn't even know when a woman could or couldn't get pregnant, why should she believe what they said about Victor?

"Then, somebody told her about a German professor up on Seneca Road who claimed congenital mental deficiencies were caused by nutritional imbalances, and the kids could be cured if they got treatment early enough. She took Victor to see him, then dragged me along to the second visit. The man was one of those charming charlatans who can talk their way around anything and anyone. According to him, doctors didn't want to take the time and trouble necessary to cure those children, but he'd made it the mission of his life, and his results proved how right he was.

"Afterward, I tried to talk some reason to your mother, but it was useless. What could be the harm in trying? What could we lose? I thought, all right, she'll see soon enough it's not helping. But that never happened. The man was very persuasive, and as your mother kept pointing out to me, he had a wall full of diplomas from impressive-sounding German and French academies. He gave Victor periodic tests that he claimed were showing progressive subclinical improvement. Obvious balderdash, but your mother told me I was talking like all the other doctors who called the professor a quack, because they were jealous of his success.

"Finally, I gave up. I suppose I might have insisted she stop, but I couldn't bring myself to take away her hope without giving her anything to take its place. Sooner or later, I thought the truth would force itself on her, but then…"

"But then, he stuck a metal screwdriver into an electric outlet, and you blamed *me*."

"I never blamed you. Do you ever remember me blaming you?"

I wanted to pull him out of the chair and shake him. "You just sat there while *she* blamed me. All those years, you never said a word. You didn't even say anything today. You just sat there with your head in your hands."

"Colin, for heaven's sake. You're forty-two years old, and a doctor, a very skillful and successful one. You don't need me to defend you from a poor woman who's never recovered from a terrible blow to her mind."

"How about when I was four? Or five, or six, or seven? How could you *do* that to me? It wasn't me who didn't bother to throw the circuit breaker, and then left that screwdriver sitting in front of the live outlet. To hell with that 'poor woman,' and to hell with you, you sorry excuse for a father. You've got a banana for a backbone."

As I stormed out of the room, my father's words sailed after me. "You're no one to criticize, Colin. You've never been where I have."

◇◇◇

I drove like a madman to a little strip mall a few blocks from Joyce Kennett's place, parked, walked into a coffee shop, ordered a large black drip, then sat and sipped at it while I paged through Giselle Hearn's log and Joyce's chart notes. I'd left Victor's death certificate on my parents' kitchen table, but it didn't matter. The entries had burned themselves into my mind for the duration. I damned Baumgartner up, down, and sideways, which didn't do me a bit of good. Not his fault I was here.

I turned the log pages to Patient JK's entry, and saw myself peering through Giselle's microscope at three tiny balls of cells, shimmering in culture medium. Which one became Robbie, squeezing out of his mother, into my care? A tear surprised me by plopping onto the paper, smearing the ink.

If I scooped Dr. Edwards, he'd probably want to look at my records, and there would be that second sperm sample, spelled out on the log page—after I'd told Joyce over and over there was no second sample, period. My plan had been to persuade Giselle to copy the entire log into another book after our press conference, but leave out the reference to the second sample. That way, by the time anyone wanted to check our data, we'd have no problem. But if I copied the log myself, how did I know Edwards wouldn't have a handwriting expert check it out? Wasn't that what I'd do if the situation were reversed? And what if Edwards insisted on definitive blood testing? Could I get past that? I wouldn't bet against myself.

But the real question wasn't whether *I* could handle the situation. As worked up as Joyce had been for the past week, what effect would all that commotion have on her? If results from a battery of blood tests came out any way other than strictly kosher, I could easily see her going off the deep end.

And then, never mind Edwards. What might Joyce do to Robbie?

I'd known when Giselle called me, frantic over the dropped sample, that any reasonable doctor would've eaten a plate of crow, called off the procedure, talked to the couple, and offered to reschedule it for a month later. So why didn't I do that? Because in that month, Edwards and Steptoe might have beaten me out. The Kennetts might have gotten sore and walked, maybe talked to reporters, even filed a lawsuit. But would that crow have tasted uglier than what was heaped on my plate right now?

I starting crying, softly at first, but then it smashed through. I wept like the chief mourner at an Irish wake, loud honks, one right on the heels of the last. The intensity of emotion astonished me. Tears streamed down my face, onto the log page. I'd never cried before, at least not that I could remember. Not even when my mother dragged me into the hall, stood me over Victor's body, shook me till my head rattled, and smacked my face with her open hand, first on one cheek, then the other. The fact I was sitting in a public place meant nothing. I was beyond reasoning, in terra incognita, not a landmark in sight.

I don't know how long I went on, but finally, the fountain ran dry, and I managed to get hold of myself. I wiped my sleeve across my face, then took out my handkerchief and mopped. A few tables away, a couple of working men didn't even try not to gawk at me.

I looked down to JK's log page, the entries still legible in the damp smear of ink. They'd stand up fine to professional scrutiny—except for that second sample, which was not going to go away. It might as well be written in red ink.

"I'm sorry, Giselle," I mumbled, then tore the page out of the log, and systematically reduced it to confetti. Next, I ripped away the rest of the pages, put them together with the chart entries, shredded the lot. I gathered up the tiny pieces of paper, slammed them into a trash can, and trudged into the john to wash my face. I was in for some heavy thinking before my next stop. How far could I stretch truth before it got so thin, Joyce would see right through it?

At least Baumgartner knows I won the race.

When Joyce opened the door, her face lit the hall. A gut cramp nearly doubled me over. "I saw on the TV, the case is closed," she said, all bubbly.

I looked around. "Your mother's gone?"

"Last night. I took her to the airport. My father isn't doing well."

"I'm sorry."

"Thanks. He'll perk up once she's back."

I looked around. "Robbie?"

"Sleeping, back in his room." Knowing smile. "The police said they acted on an anonymous tip to go up to Mrs. Hearn's and find that lab supervisor's body there. You couldn't have been Dr. Anonymous, could you?"

"Me? I'm a doctor, not a detective. Or, for that matter, a stool pigeon."

We walked into the living room. "Well, I guess it doesn't matter," Joyce said. "But I've got to admit, it does tickle me. For all the work that awful Detective Baumgartner did, he was never even mentioned."

"Win some, lose some," I said.

She made a wry face. "You don't seem as happy as I thought you'd be. You're not nervous, are you?"

"In a way, yes."

"Ah." She waved off any concern that might have been burdening my mind. "You're the last person I'd have thought would be nervous about anything. When are you going to schedule the press conference?"

Show time. "We need to talk about that."

"Any time you want is fine with me."

She was not making this easy. "Joyce, there's not going to be a press conference. Let me—"

"There's not going to be a...Dr. Sanford, what are you saying?"

"That the game's over, and we've lost. Baumgartner's got the goods on me. Robbie's not an IVF baby."

One lie.

I thought she might faint, scream, or take a swing at me, but all she did was say, "I think you'd better explain." Calm. Way too calm.

"That's why I'm here. Start with that accident in the lab...yes there *was* an accident in the lab. Dr. Hearn was getting ready to fertilize your eggs, and she dropped the culture dish."

Two lies.

Now, Joyce screamed.

I talked faster. "Dr. Hearn called me over, we talked about the situation, and made what we thought was the best decision. I didn't think you could handle what really happened, thought you'd do better dealing with a failed embryo transfer than a lab accident. So she froze the sperm sample."

Three lies.

"Froze it?" A high-pitched tremolo, barely this side of hysterical. "Dr. *Sanford*."

"That wasn't a problem. Dr. Hearn had the technology in hand. Inside a year or two, you're going to see sperm banks all over the world. I persuaded her to keep the log going as if we'd succeeded with IVF. Three days later, she thawed the sperm, and ran it through a Density Gradient Separation."

Four lies.

"Then, when you thought I was transferring embryos, I was really inseminating you with Density Gradient-enhanced sperm."

Five lies.

"I wouldn't have bet a nickel on that Density Gradient procedure working, you were so long past the egg recovery. But you had so many preovulatory follicles, your eggs must have ovulated over a longer time period than usual.

"The problem was, lab scientists are so damn compulsive. It was beyond Dr. Hearn to do any procedure and not record it. Baumgartner found a file folder yesterday with her supplemental notes documenting the accident and the Density Gradient Separation, and that was that. He told me he'll keep quiet out of regard for you and Robbie, but if I try to claim credit for an IVF success, he'll release the notes."

Six lies.

She sank down to the arm of the sofa. "And if James hadn't... I've been wondering and wondering, what could have made him snap, and shoot her? Did she tell him the truth, about that accident, and what the two of you did?"

"I have no idea. Really. That's something no one's ever going to know."

Seven lies.

"You son of a bitch! You *bastard*! All these months, it's been one thick slice of baloney after another. Why should I believe you now?"

"What can I say? You can believe me or not."

"Thanks a bunch. What I ought to do is sue you."

"And bring all that ugly publicity down on you and Robbie? Besides, what would you sue me for? I pointed toward the back of the house. "You wanted a baby, the procedure failed, I did a different procedure, and you got your baby."

Up on her feet, arms pumping, fists tight. "Right. Now, here I am, me and my baby. With no husband, no job, no interviews, no money for anything. We can go ahead and starve, who cares?"

"I do. And I've got an idea."

"Oh, wonderful. The latest, greatest con job."

I thought she might spit on me. "Wait, let me tell you—"

"Crap. You are the living end. Hang on a minute while I go check on Robbie."

I lowered myself into an armchair, ran through my pitch. If Joyce decided to call the newspapers or the County Medical Society, I might as well take off for Brazil. I was halfway through my second practice go-round when she came back in, walked straight up to me, pulled a handgun out of the pocket of her apron, and aimed it square at my face. I started out of the chair, but she sent me back with one word: "Don't."

I eased away from her. "Joyce, I'm sorry about this, but I'm going to make it right. Let me tell you—"

"Shut up. Make one move and I'll shoot you." She gripped the gun with both hands, her right index finger on the trigger. The way her hands shook wrung all the moisture out of my mouth and throat. "I missed Baumgartner, but there's no way I'll miss you from this distance."

"What? *You* shot Baumgartner?"

"I shot *at* Baumgartner, but he was halfway down the street, and I missed. I thought if I could get rid of him, that would take care of the problem. This was the smallest gun James had, so I thought it would be the easiest to use. I asked my mother to stay with Robbie while I went to an appointment at the hospital. With all the time Baumgartner was spending on Pill Hill, I thought I'd spot him there, and after two hours on a bench in the plaza, I did. He came out of the lobby, and I followed him down the street. Right before he came to the corner, I took a shot. I'd never fired a gun in my life. He started to turn around, so I ran down an alley, up the next street, and then went on home. I guess it's lucky I didn't hit him. He was only doing his job, going after crooks like you."

"Joyce, put down the gun. Your hand's shaking."

She firmed her grip and her aim.

I thought about jumping out of the chair and trying to hit her low, knock her over, but she looked as if nothing more than a sneeze from me might set off her trigger finger. I made my voice as calm as I could, no small task. "Joyce, listen to me, please. You're making a terrible mistake."

"I made my terrible mistake a year ago, trusting you. Go ahead, talk. Let's hear your great idea. It better be good. But if you tell me you were only thinking of James and me, I promise, I will kill you."

"I wanted that IVF to work as much as you did," I said. "And let's be honest. Neither one of us took James' feelings into account, not ever. For that matter, we never thought about the baby, either. Too late now to fix things for James, but we've still got a chance to do right by Robbie."

She narrowed her eyes, waggled the gun.

"Here's the deal," I said. "The first day of every month, from this month on, I will give you a check for five thousand dollars. And that's just the beginning. I'll also set up a trust for you and Robbie, and rewrite my will in Robbie's favor, so if I drop off the end of the earth, you'll both still be all right. All together, you'll get more than you'd have gotten from IVF publicity. You'll never have to work again. On the other hand, if you shoot me, you go to jail, and your mother finds herself bringing up a newborn baby. Along with having to look after your father."

She was shaking all over. "You think I'm going to trust you again? After everything that's happened?"

"I can't blame you for feeling that way. But I don't think you've got a better choice. Do you?" Without waiting for an answer, I said, "I'm going to get my wallet and write you the first check, the one for May. All right?"

She was crying now. Not taking my eyes off her, I reached slowly into my pocket, pulled out my wallet, took a check from the rear compartment, and held it up to Joyce. Then, I took a pen from my shirt pocket, leaned on the wallet, and started to write.

Joyce let out a sound, more shriek than howl, lowered the gun, staggered to the sofa, collapsed onto it. The gun fell to the floor.

When I finished writing the check, I took it to her, pressed it into her hand. She wailed even louder.

Then I heard another cry, higher-pitched, thinner, from back in the house. Robbie. His mother must have wakened him, but no sign she'd heard him. I turned, ran, followed the sound. The baby lay face-down in his crib, legs kicking, red-cheeked, howling. I swept him up, put him to my shoulder, patted his back. "It's all right," I whispered. Little feet banged against my stomach. I patted until he loosed a monster burp, and lowered his head onto my shoulder. His whole body relaxed.

I ran my fingers along the midline separation between his parietal bones, touched the fontanelles at either end. Standard obstetrical landmarks I'd palpated during thousands of deliveries. But this time was different. My eyes watered over. I hoped I wasn't going to lose it again.

I carried Robbie back into the living room, swept up the gun, then lowered myself to the sofa, just out of Joyce's reach. She stopped crying, looked ready to explode. "Are you going to shoot *me*?"

"Of course not." I slipped the weapon onto the floor near my foot, barrel pointing toward the door. Then I transferred Robbie into the crook of my arm and rocked him gently as I spoke. "But while we're talking, I'll feel better on this side of the gun."

She started to reach for Robbie, but her hands shook so fiercely, she lowered them. "Need a drink of water?" I asked.

She shook her head, wiped at her eyes. "Go ahead and say your piece, then get out of here. Send your checks by mail."

"That isn't what I've got in mind. I'm not going to let this kid grow up with no father, wondering why his mother gets a check in the mail every month from some doctor in town. Sooner or later, he's going to ask questions. I want you to let me be his uncle who takes him to the zoo, buys him ice-cream cones, comes to his birthday parties. Is there when he needs me."

Joyce spluttered, an engine that couldn't quite get started. Finally, the ignition caught. "'Uncle Colin...'" She looked like a stroke in the making. "My God, you are beyond preposterous. What *ever* would make you think I'd agree to that."

I leaned forward, passed Robbie off to her, then picked up the pistol. "This." I unloaded the little weapon, slipped gun and bullet into my pocket. "I've got some news for you. You didn't miss Detective Baumgartner. When they dug the bullet out of his rear end, he made very sure to keep it safe, so one day he could match it to the gun that shot it. But I'll hide your little cannon away where no one, Baumgartner included, will ever find it. Oh, and before I leave, you're going to give me any other guns and ammunition James had, and I'll make them disappear too."

She glared at me, eyes hot, dry. "I can't believe how selfish you are."

"Selfish? You and Robbie will never have to worry about money again, and your son will have a man in his life who cares about him. He'll have financial *and* moral support. Where am I being selfish?"

"Moral support?" You have the morals of a mongoose."

"Maybe so, but it's nice to have a mongoose around when there are snakes and rats everywhere."

She stroked Robbie's head. I waited, but she didn't say anything. Didn't even look up at me.

"You'll see, Joyce." I kept my voice low, soothing. "This'll work out for everyone, especially Robbie."

Picture someone who's been put on a rack, given a couple of stretches, then released. "How am I going to explain all this to my parents?"

"Easy. Tell the truth. Dr. Sanford, who has no family of his own, felt terrible about what happened to James, and volunteered to be Robbie's Uncle Colin." I choked off a gulp.

At the catch in my voice, she gave me a hard look, then a harder smile. "There's one condition."

I waited.

"What are the names of those doctors in England you've been racing against?"

"Edwards and Steptoe. Robert Edwards and Patrick Steptoe."

"Okay. When they announce their first IVF baby, that night you are going to take me out for dinner to the fanciest restaurant in Emerald. We'll order the best champagne in the house, and toast the winners till I can't see straight. Deal, Uncle Colin?" Biting off those final two words.

I nodded. "Deal."

Chapter Twenty-six

Sunday, July 4, 1982

Sanford

As angry as he was with me a few minutes ago, my father's face lights when the nurse brings Robbie into the bedroom. Kid's a natural, climbs right up on the bed, gives the old man a kiss, says he's very glad to meet him. He tells Dad about his dog, Pucci; his friends, Buster and Charlene; his T-ball team; his kindergarten; and how he's going to first grade in September. Chatters away as if he'd known his grandfather all his life. He does exaggerate his batting and reading abilities a bit, but I'm not about to say anything.

Dad asks him whether he wants to go to medical school, like his father and grandfather. No hesitation. "Sure. I'm going to be a great operator like Daddy. He operates on ladies to get their babies out safe when they're having trouble being born."

Dad looks at me over Robbie's head, raises his eyebrows. I grin and shrug. Dad rolls his eyes.

After about an hour, the nurse comes in to ask Dad how he's feeling. "Fine," he says. "Wonderful, in fact. But I'd like to talk to Colin. Why don't you take Robbie down to the kitchen, and give him a glass of milk and some of those cookies Mrs. Rollins left."

He watches them go out and around the corner, then turns my way. "I can't believe how gray your hair's gone, Colin. You're grayer than I am."

"I've been where you never went, Dad."

"You have, have you? Then please tell me something. It's been five years since you were last in this house. Your mother died without knowing she was a grandmother. So why, out of nowhere, do you show up today with your five-year-old son? *Why*?"

"I wanted you to see him. And I wanted him to see you."

He can still project the definitive exasperated father. "Colin… oh, very well. So be it. I'm glad you came, and I won't pretend otherwise. But I can't understand—"

"His mother and I aren't married."

"What? You're saying you didn't tell me I have a grandson until I'm on my deathbed because you didn't marry his mother?"

"That's part of it. She and I barely speak. Dad, it's a strange situation."

He studies me hard. Weak as he is, his gaze is riveting, a face I've never seen on him. "Is there something you want to tell me?"

"No. Let's say it was one of those things that never should have happened, but it did."

"Was she one of your patients?"

What began in my mind as a firm 'No' comes out as "Yes."

Dad glances away, purses his lips, then looks back at me. "I remember one evening, years ago…the last time you ever came here for dinner. The husband of one of your patients who'd had some sort of fertility procedure killed the embryologist who'd performed it, then himself. It was in all the papers and all over TV. When I asked you about the procedure, you said you couldn't tell us anything right then, but we'd be the first to know, and we'd be impressed."

Uh-oh.

He edges himself up on his pillows. "I've never stopped wondering…an impressive fertility procedure, some five years ago? Were you trying in vitro—"

"We're not going to talk about it, Dad."

As if I'd slapped his face. "All right, we *won't* talk about it. But I'll still have my say. Whatever it may have been, as always, you had to be first to the finish line, didn't you? So you took a short cut that wasn't on the map, got lost in the jungle, and two people died. Colin, what possible accomplishment could have seemed so important?" He shakes his head. "That insatiable drive of yours—I've never been able to understand it."

"I'm sorry you can't understand, Dad. Sorry for both of us."

Whatever he was going to say next catches in his throat. He coughs, chokes. I fill a glass of water from the pitcher at his bedside, help him down a few swallows.

He looks back my way, calmer now. "Well, he's a beautiful child, Colin. However he got here, he's my grandson, and I'm grateful to have seen him. Please take good care of him and his mother."

"I will. Promise."

◇◇◇

As Robbie and I start down the sidewalk, he says, "Your daddy's nice, Uncle Colin."

"Yes, he is. Did you like talking to him?"

"Oh, sure. And I liked the cookies too. Now, can we go get what you promised me for pretending you're my daddy?"

"You bet. Double-dip cone, right?"

"Chocolate. Both scoops."

"But don't forget, not a word to Mommy about pretending. It's our secret."

He laughs, then tugs at my hand. "I like it when I stay with you. We always have lots of fun. Mommy doesn't let me have ice cream and cookies. She says sugar is bad for kids, but *I* don't think it's bad." A cloud spreads across his face. "I wish you really *were* my daddy."

Sucker punch. I never did believe people actually die of heart-break, but in this moment, I'm not sure. I struggle for breath. Robbie looks up at me like a curious little bird on a branch. "Are you okay, Uncle Colin?"

Kid misses nothing. "Sure I'm okay. I wish I were your daddy, too. But being your uncle's pretty good, isn't it?"

His smile clears the cloud. I've seen that expression for a lot of years, reflected back at me from mirrors. Sometimes, when Robbie and I are playing, I catch Joyce looking from one of us to the other. But she never says anything, and neither do I.

"Come on," I say. "Ice-cream cones, then we're going to pick up Uncle Bernie. Don't want to keep him waiting. We're going to the fireworks, remember?"

He jumps up and down. "I love fireworks. We gonna watch them up real close?"

"No other way to do it. That's why we're going early. Get a good place to sit."

"I want Uncle Bernie to tell me stories about those bad guys he catches with his private eye." I see wheels turning in the kid's head. "Uncle Colin, does Uncle Bernie *always* catch the bad guys?"

I brush my hand over that unruly clump of hair above his right ear. "Bet on it, Kiddo. No bad guy ever gets away from your Uncle Bernie."

Author's Note

The 1970s were an exciting time in medical science. The word "engineering," whether in reference to manipulation of naturally-occurring genetic material or the natural method of reproduction, set off fierce debates in medical, social, and religious circles.

The initial response to any new idea is usually a strong negative, and Reproductive Engineering was no exception. One of the hottest wrangles in this field centered on in vitro fertilization, the insemination of an egg and subsequent early embryonic development in a laboratory vessel. Opponents argued that this would be disastrous, that there likely would be monstrously abnormal babies and children with severe emotional problems; furthermore, the institutionalization of reproduction would mean the end of family life as we know it, and before long there would be government-mandated organized breeding of supermen, and restricted reproduction by persons deemed less desirable.

Proponents claimed that in vitro fertilization would alleviate a form of human suffering, the anguish of couples unable to have children naturally, and that these babies would be people who'd otherwise have no lives at all. It was further argued that since research in humans and other animals indicated that damage to very early embryos had an all-or-nothing effect (either the embryo died at that point, or survived to be born normal), the risk of increased birth defects seemed small. As for governmental intervention in reproduction, the point was made that governments already had ample means to manipulate populations at gunpoint; the problem was not the sperm, but the gun. As for in vitro fertilization causing sweeping changes in our social structure, particularly our family lives, it was suggested that if this unlikely eventuality really did come to pass, it might not necessarily be bad.

With time, people usually come around to accept change, and thirty-three years after the birth of the first IVF baby, the dispute over in vitro fertilization appears resolved. Millions of humans have received the gift of life through union of a spermatozoon and an egg in a plastic dish, rather than a fallopian tube. Yes, there have been some abuses of the procedure, but the negative effect on society has been, at most, negligible.

As a young doctor doing a laboratory fellowship in Reproductive Genetics, I was fortunate to have a front-row seat at the race to produce the first IVF baby. From the outset, the team of Drs. Robert G. Edwards and Patrick Steptoe were in the lead, and they crossed the finish line with the birth of Louise Joy Brown, on July 25, 1978. Dr. Edwards had begun his goal-directed studies on in vitro fertilization and ovum/embryo culture in the mid-1960s at Johns Hopkins University, then went back to England and teamed up with Dr. Steptoe, a gifted pioneer in the use of the laparoscope. By the midseventies, it appeared that Edwards and Steptoe might announce success at any time, and suspense was tremendous. Still, scientists around the world kept at work. But in many countries, the USA included, direct or indirect governmental opposition hampered investigators.

The great majority of contestants were honest, honorable scientists and doctors, but in the frenzy to claim the prize, some interesting chicanery surfaced. The Law of Publish and Perish was not suspended, and I heard accusations that some scientists, in an attempt to add to their list of publications without giving aid to the enemy, had omitted small but critical considerations in their protocols, such as the constitution of culture medium. A prominent worker in the field was discredited and disgraced when word got out that he'd avoided having to pay fees for anonymous sperm donors by providing samples himself for his experiments. Another highly-regarded scientist lost all his credibility when he announced success with in vitro fertilization, but could not provide proof. An obstetrician in New York with much-questioned scientific credentials claimed to have fertilized an egg with sperm from the woman's husband, but before he could replace the embryo into the woman's uterus, his department chairman learned of his clandestine operation, and disposed of the contents of the test tube. (Yes, it *was* a test tube, not a petri dish). The upshot was a lengthy, acrimonious, highly-publicized trial. Emotions became so intense, I remember thinking someone could end up murdered.

To the best of my knowledge, though, no one did get murdered or even blackmailed in connection with the in vitro fertilization race. The specific events in *A Perilous Conception* are entirely of my imagination, as are the people who populate the pages of the book. No relationship should be inferred between these characters and any real person, living or dead.

To receive a free catalog of Poisoned Pen Press titles, please contact us in one of the following ways:

Phone: 1-800-421-3976
Facsimile: 1-480-949-1707
Email: info@poisonedpenpress.com
Website: www.poisonedpenpress.com

Poisoned Pen Press
6962 E. First Ave. Ste. 103
Scottsdale, AZ 85251